More Praise for Cry Havoc

"Mix up a kilo of Grisham and a whole lot of Clancy with today's glaring headlines and you get CRY HAVOC. John Hamilton Lewis is a master thrill-maker."
—Mary-Ann Tirone Smith

"John Hamilton Lewis gives us a disturbing world, a plethora of villains, and almost no way out. He ushers the reader carefully through the labyrinth. CRY HAVOC is nicely plotted, richly detailed, and worth every page."
—William H. Lovejoy, international author of *China Dome* and nineteen other novels

"CRY HAVOC by John Hamilton Lewis is a pulse-thumping page-turner rich in duplicity, diabolical maneuvering and political intrigue."
—Judith Kelman

"John Hamilton Lewis has a deep and profound insight into the messy reality of today. By the time we are finished with the literate, spare prose of CRY HAVOC, we know more than we may want to know about the dark forces that propel all of us, worldwide, into an uncertain future."
—Kit Sloane, The Margot O'Brien Mysteries

"Fast-paced, provocative, and very, very timely."
—Tom Coffey, author of *The Serpent Club*

"Noir, in books and films alike, is back in fashion. And CRY HAVOC tells you why."
—Ed Gorman

CRY HAVOC

John Hamilton Lewis

Printed in U. S. A.

For information address:
Durban House Publishing Company, Inc.
7502 Greenville Avenue, Suite 500
Dallas, Texas 75231
214.890.4050

Library of Congress Cataloging-in-Publication Data
John Hamilton Lewis, 1943-

Cry Havoc / by John Hamilton Lewis

Library of Congress Catalog Card Number: 2004098664

p. cm.

ISBN 1-930754-74-4

First Edition

10 9 8 7 6 5 4 3 2

Visit our Web site at
http://www.durbanhouse.com

Book design by Jennifer Adkins

This book is dedicated to my father,

John Hamilton Lewis, Sr.

ACKNOWLEDGEMENTS

There are many people who helped make CRY HAVOC become a reality. I especially want to thank my partner in life, Karen. Without her support, sensitivity, and wealth of ideas, this book would not have been possible. Special thanks to my beautiful daughters, Tracy, Emily, and Lauryn, for showing me the error of my ways.

Personal thanks to Richard Sand, Robert Middlemiss, Kit Sloane, Chris Holmes, Ben Small, Annie Sperling, Jennifer Adkins, and Kay Garrett for their valuable input and professionalism.

Idealism flees in the face of reality.

—Friedrich Nietzche

Prologue

Taipei, 1988

"My compliments to your chef. Absolutely delicious!"

Ping-yi Cong watched from across the table as Brent Bosworth chewed his last piece of sushi.

"What's the name of this fish again?" Bosworth asked.

"Fugu." Cong refilled their saki cups. "It's what you Americans might refer to as puffer fish."

Bosworth downed his saki, then wiped his mouth with a hot towel. "Whatever, it's damn good."

"In Asia, it's considered quite a delicacy. I acquired a taste for it when I was stationed in Tokyo, during my days in the Foreign Service. My chef is one of the few licensed fugu chefs outside of Japan. I sent him there to be trained. It took more than two years." Cong gestured at the steaming porcelain saki bottle. "The saki we've been drinking is mixed with fugu testi. Such a potion is said to give men great stamina with the ladies."

"Speaking of which?" Bosworth's gaze moved to the female musician playing the traditional Chinese sixteen-stringed zither at the back of the room. "I've been away from civilization for too long."

"In due time." Cong poured more saki. "My chef is preparing a final dish, *Shirakoyaki.*"

Bosworth's cup rose and fell. "As they say in Texas, *bring it on.*"

"*Shirakoyaki* is a specialty made from grilled fugu roe, and takes a little time to prepare," Cong said. "Chinese etiquette normally dictates that business not be discussed at the dinner table. However, while we wait, I'm most anxious to hear about your findings."

"The geological work has been completed." Bosworth slid a bound leather folder across the table. "The original data's inside."

"Are there other copies?"

Bosworth shook his head. "As agreed, they've been destroyed."

"Good."

"The results are far more favorable than anticipated." Bosworth lowered his voice. "Geological samples indicate a huge repository of sulfur-free oil. Perhaps the last major find of its kind on earth."

Taiwan's Minister of Development stared at the geologist. "What are the reserve estimates?"

"Two hundred billion barrels. Maybe more."

"And natural gas?"

Bosworth belched softly. "In excess of two hundred trillion cubic feet."

"I see." Cong touched a knuckle against the tip of his nose. *Reserves rivaling those of Saudi Arabia,* he thought. *Incredible.* The American geologist had just confirmed what he'd suspected for years. Such a find would bring untold wealth and power to his island nation. But then the inevitable question surfaced in his mind. How to avoid war with China if Taiwan attempted to develop the field?

"Seismic data indicates that the north shore of the Eldad Reef would be the most promising site to begin initial exploration—"

Cong held up a hand, cutting the geologist off. "Ah, I see the *Shirakoyaki* has arrived."

Light danced in Bosworth's eyes as two girls wearing red *cheong-soms,* slit high on the sides, entered and knelt beside the table. Music from the zither filled the air as they served the food.

Cong sipped his beer. "Try the *Shirakoyaki,* Mr. Bosworth. I'm sure you'll find the taste most agreeable."

Using chopsticks, Bosworth deftly popped a piece into his mouth and chewed. "Excellent, Cong. You've definitely made a fugu lover out of me."

Cong watched the geologist devour more of the grilled roe. "Whenever I dine on fugu, I'm reminded of an old Japanese folk song," he said. *"Fugu wa kuitashii, inochi wa oshishii."*

"Sorry, I only caught the fugu part." Bosworth loosened his tie and drank half a glass of beer. "Saki and beer is a helluva combination. So what's the little folk song mean?"

"I want to eat fugu, but I don't want to die."

Bosworth unfolded his now-cold hand towel and wiped his face. "No doubt, it's the kind of food that'll send you to heaven."

"Fugu fish carry a nerve toxin five hundred times deadlier than cyanide. That is why chefs specializing in its preparation have to be licensed." Cong toyed with his chopsticks. "Even so, more than two hundred people die each year from poisoning."

"It's getting hot in here." Bosworth pulled his jacket off. "Could you turn up the air conditioning?"

"When a neuron or nerve cell sends a message, tiny pores or channels in the neuron's membrane open to let sodium ions enter the cell. Fugu toxin blocks these tiny pores, which in turn prevents any signaling in the nervous system." Cong sat impassively. "The result is rapid paralysis."

Bosworth stared across the table. "Paralysis?"

"Yes, Mr. Bosworth. At the moment, you are experiencing the beginning stages. You might die quickly or suffer a long, excruciatingly painful death." Cong shrugged. "The toxin affects people differently."

"You've poisoned me?" Bosworth tried to stand, but his legs would not respond. "Why, in God's name, Cong? Our arrangement—we had—"

"An unfortunate but necessary precaution. It would have been imprudent on my part to trust you with the knowledge of what lies beneath the Spratly Islands. Greed tends to wag men's tongues, and you would have sooner or later compromised our secret." Cong picked up a silver bell and jingled it several times.

The musician bowed her head and stopped playing the zither.

Moments later, a man entered the dining salon and stood next to Cong.

"Now, if you will excuse me, Mr. Bosworth, I'll leave you in the capable hands of my pilot, Mr. Lee." Standing, Cong gestured at the pilot. "He will see to your final arrangements over the South China Sea."

Immobilized, Brent Bosworth watched Cong walk out, holding the leather folder. His last coherent thought was wondering why his arms wouldn't move.

We have just enough religion to make us hate, but not enough to make us love one another.

—Jonathan Swift

One

"HARPIE."

Gerhard Esch stared at the e-mail.

"HARPIE."

A single word sent from the other side of the world, instructing him to initiate the largest financial transaction of his life. He sipped his espresso, then typed in a password that brought up a program enabling him to incrementally purchase ten billion dollars' worth of assorted world currencies, bullion, and oil futures contracts in major global markets. Esch felt his chest expand. To avoid detection by interested market watchers, he made his transactions through numbered accounts at foreign banks not overly concerned with where their money came from.

The president of Trident Holdings entered the necessary codes and clicked the "Send" button. As he sipped espresso, he watched the machine confirm the transactions had been executed.

Esch turned his chair and fixed his gaze on the window behind his desk. Beyond the floor-to-ceiling plate glass of his 76th story Manhattan penthouse were spectacular views of the Hudson River on the west, the East River, and all of Central Park. Pigeons wheeled overhead as barges plowed gray waters. He glanced at the four television sets, each carrying a different news channel, lighting up the wall next to his desk. Typical talk show bullshit, he thought. The market wasn't due to open for another hour and a half. He picked up his secure line and dialed.

"Yes."

"Monetary transfers have been completed," Esch said.

"Are the transactions secure?"

"Yes. Our business is being conducted anonymously through overseas banks. Positions are staggered and should be fully established within two weeks."

"Excellent. How much leverage will we have?"

"Since there will be minimal hedging, approximately thirty to one."

"Contact me through the normal channel when you have finalized details."

The line went dead. Gerhard cradled the receiver, his eyes on the phone for a long moment. Excitement mixed with fear of the unknown sent a shiver down his back. What if the model he had so carefully constructed contained a flaw? Impossible. Wasn't it a historical fact that money always flowed to commodities of value, like gold, when panic struck currency markets? Gerhard remembered the countless commodity and stock charts he'd studied with his father, Dieter Esch, a prominent Frankfurt banker.

"See, my son, there is a cause-and-effect relationship for everything that happens. Prices rise and fall. People take long and short positions. The trick to making money lies in identifying the relationship and acting upon it."

Gerhard leaned back in his chair. How fortunate his life had been. His father had schooled him well about *cause and effect,* and making money. But it was his mother, Hanna, to whom he owed his strength. After making the terrifying journey from Northern Turkey to avoid starvation, fighting thieves, murderers, and mafia criminals along the way, she had been the only member of her family to reach Germany alive. Gerhard's father met the beautiful

Kurdish refugee at the headquarters of a Middle Eastern restaurant chain, where she'd worked her way up to the position of director of purchasing. Six months later, they married. When Gerhard reached the age of five, Hannah began teaching him about Islam.

Prince Abdul bin Suleiman Nasser's vista was limited only by infinity. Unlike in the foothills and valley below, temperatures were cool at his mountain home high in the Sarawat. After morning prayers, he spent quiet time on his balcony contemplating the vastness of Allah's creation. He took great comfort in knowing the holy cities of Mecca, to the north, and Medina, to the south, lay just beyond the horizon.

As absolute master of his realm, he held sway over life and death for those inside his world, and for countless others residing on the outside. For him, it was the ultimate power—one he had exercised on numerous occasions. A single word to an associate and a life would cease to be. The sort of power that turned rational men mad. Being a student of the world, he'd seen it happen many times before. Weren't the pages of history littered with idealistic men turned despot? But, in this respect, he considered himself different. As a thoughtful man, he knew how to avoid the mistakes of others. Death, he realized, while often necessary, was a serious matter that should not to be taken lightly. After all, he told himself, possession of power wasn't a sin; the transgression lay in becoming consumed by it.

Abdul was one of fourteen brothers and sisters. His father, Haseem, a wealthy Yemeni businessman, had made his fortune as a construction contractor for the Saudi royal family. Abdul was the firstborn of two sons and a daughter from Haseem's third wife, a Saudi princess.

Like thousands of other members of the Saudi royal family,

Abdul had been born to wealth. But unlike his siblings and distant cousins who squandered their inheritances on Swiss villas, yachts and other playthings, he had followed his father's advice and expanded his part of the business. After graduating from Oxford and receiving advanced degrees from Wharton's International School of Business, Abdul spent the next quarter-century transforming his company, Alhannah, into a potent economic force. Now worth more than forty billion dollars, Alhannah's flag, with the distinctive profile of his prized black Arabian stallion, flew over banks, hotels, construction firms, trading companies, and hi-tech corporations around the world.

Abdul had learned much from his father. And, like his father, he had become a devout follower of Saudi Arabia's Puritanical version of Islam, Wahhabism. His cherished memories of the quiet walks they had shared in the desert still burned in his mind. Beneath the infinite Arabian sky, the young prince had learned about the Bedouin traditions of his father's youth, and his rise from poverty.

"Bedouins have always been the true Arabs, my son. When the Prophet first raised His sword, we came out of the desert to fill His armies. Bedouins were the driving force behind Islam. At that time, we lived beneath the stars and took what we wanted. We recognized no borders, and paid homage to no king." Haseem placed a hand on his young son's shoulder and stared into his eyes. "Today, most of our people have been corrupted by the West. They are filled with want and greed. Heed these words, Abdul. Use the West and learn how to make money, but do not be beguiled by their godless rhetoric. While consuming our oil, they bless the Zionist invader's claim to Palestine. Now their infidel armies sweep into the lands of Arabia like pestilence."

Prince Nasser remembered the glint of light in his father's eyes when he pointed toward Israel. "By the blood of the Prophet which runs through our veins, if I could change my tractors into tanks, I would turn them against the Jews and liberate the holy city of Jerusalem."

Such a moment had truly been a sign from God.

Seating himself at a table on the shaded balcony, Nasser called for tea and fruits. He wore a conservative gray *bisht* over a stark-white *dishdasha,* and the traditional checkered Saudi head cover. Tall and slim for an Arab, the prince had a dark complexion, high cheekbones, and long, curved, hawk-like nose, the stereotype of which caused him bemusement. Streaks of white ran through his black hair and manicured beard, but his most distinguishing feature was his eyes. They were the depthless, black pools of a predator.

Nasser stared out at his prized garden, filled with assorted date palms, fig trees and bougainvillea. Desert shrubs and flowers of ochre, blue, yellow, and red blended harmoniously around a manmade pond, providing quiet, languid symmetry.

My oasis!

A servant arrived with a silver bowl of fruit. Drops of water pearled on recently picked dates and purple figs. Nasser's special blend of tea imported from his plantation in Sri Lanka steamed inside a polished stone cup.

"Is there anything else you require, Highness?"

Nasser waved the servant away. He slipped his sandals off, the Italian marble cool beneath his feet. Lifting his cup, he inhaled the fragrant brew before tasting. Within two weeks, he would control three hundred billion dollars in currency, oil and precious metal contracts. *A princely sum.* The prince allowed himself a rare smile. Enough to wreak havoc on the Western world for years to come. His hand moved to the leather-bound Koran on the table. He opened the book and silently read.

For it is written that a son of Arabia would awaken a fearsome Eagle. The wrath of the Eagle would be felt throughout the lands of Allah and lo, while some of the people trembled in despair still more rejoiced; for the wrath of the Eagle cleansed the lands of Allah; and there was peace.

Touching and reading from the Holy Book gave Nasser strength, kept him focused.

Fans clicked overhead, the air redolent of freshly brewed tea and fruit sweating from newly severed stems. Sitting very still, Prince Abdul bin Suleiman Nasser closed his eyes and contemplated his plan.

An impressive sight.

Sheik Mahmoud Moussawi watched Nasser's fortress-like home come into view from behind darkened bulletproof windows. *Gibraltar* was the first word to enter the sheik's mind. The country estate covered more than five hundred acres in the mountainous region south of Jeddah, Saudi Arabia's second-largest city. The house gave the appearance of an impregnable castle that had been carved out of the mountainside by a medieval king. In the distance, flags of Saudi Arabia and Nasser's corporation, Alhannah, flew from the ramparts.

The Mercedes stretch limousine's engine purred nicely as the plains gave way to the foothills of the Sarawat Mountains paralleling the Red Sea. Moussawi sank back into the soft leather folds and stared at Prince Nasser's country estate.

Is this the kind of man I've been dealing with? A wry smile touched the sheik's dark lips. *A man who fancies himself a medieval king?*

Money to finance operations for Allah's Army had been Moussawi's first connection to Nasser. That was three years earlier. His decision to form an alliance with the prince had not been political. It had been made out of necessity. Funds from his Sh'ia benefactors in Iran had slowed to a trickle in the aftermath of 9-11. Then the tap was turned off after American and British armies invaded Iraq and Afghanistan. Now the cowardly mullahs were pissing all over themselves for fear of going the way of Saddam.

The sheik scratched his beard. Had he put his head into the lion's mouth by aligning himself with Nasser, this medieval king? He didn't know the answer. The only thing he knew for sure was the political landscape in the Middle East had changed like shifting desert sands.

How strange the ways of Allah, Moussawi thought. *A Sunni prince and a Sh'ia cleric joined in holy alliance.*

Moussawi watched the Saudi landscape speed by. The barren land reminded him of the wretched conditions in southern Lebanon, Gaza, and the Left Bank. Yesterday, like today, Palestinian life was a grim affair. He remembered, as a child, picking his way barefoot over the rubble and open sewers in the streets of his small village. Captured aromas of coffee, incense, freshly baked pita bread and cardamom were the only fond memories that remained. The ever-present animal dung and cordite were the smells he remembered most.

The eternal scents of Islam.

Moussawi massaged his foot, badly damaged when he was a boy by a piece of Israeli shrapnel. Because there had been no medical facilities, he had spent his adult life walking with the aid of a cane. The pain was always with him, lurking, waiting. Now, temporarily arrested by the drug, the pain came mostly during the night, along with sounds of exploding shells and screaming villagers.

The sheik stared at the desert. Rocks protruded from the arid soil like baked bones of prehistoric reptiles. The lands of the faithful were harsh and unyielding, beating men down. Praise be to Allah for Islam to ease the life struggles of true believers. Yet, despite being surrounded by enemies, Israel had achieved greatness in less than fifty years, while the vast majority of the Islamic world remained trapped in an unending cycle of poverty. *Why?* Why had Allah, in His infinite wisdom, cast a blind eye toward the faithful? Now, Arab leaders wanted peace with the Zionist invaders. Imagine. Settling for an independent Palestinian state on the arid outcrops of land of the West Bank and Gaza.

Zionist supremacy validated before the world.

Unthinkable!

Moussawi had spent his life studying the Koran and dreaming of becoming an important religious leader. Now, at age fifty-four, his dream had become manifest, his cane and disfigured foot symbols to the faithful. He was the unquestioned spiritual leader of Allah's Army. But, as a monotheistic religion, Islam made no justification for the separation of church and state. Consequently, the sheik increasingly found he had to think, plan, and act like a politician. As head of the Middle East's most important group fighting for the liberation of Palestine, he vehemently opposed turning over sacred Palestinian lands to the Zionist enemy. The problem was that Allah's Army had been steadily losing financial and political support. Traditionally hard-line Arab states were increasingly reluctant to be linked to groups perceived by the West as terrorist organizations. Now, the Lebanese government, with Syria's blessing, threatened to expel Allah's Army if holy martyrs continued to cross into Israel and attack civilians from their headquarters in Tyre.

Beyond the darkened windows of the speeding limousine, Prince Nasser's house grew larger against the cobalt Arabian sky. No question, Moussawi thought, he was in a delicate position. All because America and the European Union demanded that Arabs make peace with Jews.

Peace!

The word buzzed in Moussawi's head like an angry bee. Next month, American and EU delegations would be accompanying Israeli Foreign Minister Benjamin Levy to Egypt to lay groundwork for implementation of the Wallace Plan. What would become of Allah's Army if the Arab League adopted this satanic plan? Moussawi closed his eyes. The mere stroke of a pen could wipe them out.

How ephemeral power was, Moussawi thought from the luxury of his limousine. *Wiped out by the mere stroke of a pen.*

The prince was still on the balcony when his bodyguard, Yousef, arrived. "Sheik Mahmoud Moussawi is waiting, Highness."

"Show him in, Yousef." Nasser put his slippers on and stood.

Moussawi, shorter and heavier than the prince, stepped forward, steadying himself on his cane. The two men embraced, exchanging obligatory kisses on their cheeks.

"My dear Sheik Moussawi, I trust your journey was a pleasant one?"

"Most pleasant, praise be to Allah, and your kind assistance." Moussawi looked around nervously. "It is almost noon and—"

Nasser held up a hand. "Remember, I have a small mosque on the premises. We would be honored by your presence for Friday prayers."

After completing the *rakat*—the cycle of prayer—Nasser took Moussawi to his dining salon. Keeping with Bedouin tradition, oversized pillows and silk rugs from Iran and Turkey covered the floor. Servers arrived with freshly baked pita bread, followed by plates of stuffed grape leaves, hummus and tahini, surrounded by sliced tomatoes, cucumbers, olives, onions, and pickles. Smells of spice and meat grilling on skewers wafted pleasantly as the two men ate. After appetizers, water bowls for hand rinsing were provided before the main course of lamb and basmati rice topped with slivered almonds. Fruit bowls, coffee, and thinly layered honey and pistachio pastries completed the meal.

Moussawi licked traces of honey and crushed pistachios from his fingers. "Allah be praised, an excellent fare."

"Lamb from the Jiddah merchants has no equal," the prince said. Then he signaled for a *narghile*.

A servant set the water pipe between the two men and lit the dark Turkish tobacco.

For a time, they smoked and spoke of inconsequential matters, before Nasser moved the conversation from light to serious. "Many loyal *jihadis* have been arrested and handed over to the infidels."

Sheik Moussawi shook his head. "Sadly, the lands of Mohammad, peace be upon Him, no longer offer refuge for His holy warriors."

"Islam will never be safe until the nonbelievers have been purged."

Moussawi caught the coldness in Nasser's gaze. As a child, he had seen that look. He remembered the hooded bird riding his father's gauntleted arm, and his excitement when the falcon's hood was removed. It had been his first glimpse into the eyes of a predator.

"The West grows bolder. Their influence expands, while our ability to fight diminishes," Moussawi said. His pudgy fingers dipped into the fruit bowl. "Israel continues slaughtering innocent Palestinians, and the once-loyal patrons of Allah's Army close their eyes. All they know are words and rhetoric."

"Our leaders are in the pockets of Western infidels for economic reasons," Nasser said. "They are afraid of being exorcised from the New World Order." The prince placed a fig in his mouth and chewed. "Still, Allah, in His infinite wisdom, may have provided us a way to reverse the current situation."

Moussawi leaned forward.

"Calls for *jihad* by our mullahs and holy warriors have been reduced to trivial conversation. Unless Islam is united, it will be impossible to defeat the Zionist militarily." Nasser steepled his fingers and tapped his lip. "In order to win, we must first lose."

"Lose?"

"War, business, politics are merely games, my dear Moussawi. And games, properly planned, have predictable outcomes." Nasser studied the Sheik. "The Israeli Prime Minister Wasserman is looking for an excuse to unleash the Zionist army. His life's goal is to drive the Palestinians back to Jordan and Lebanon. I suggest we give him an excuse to do just that."

"What?" Moussawi's eyes widened. "Drive the Palestinians from their homeland. Allah's Army will never allow that to happen."

"Lambs fighting lions. There can be only one outcome to such a game."

"By the Prophet, peace be upon Him, I do not understand where you are going." Moussawi grasped his cane as if to steady his thinking. "Who will stand against the Zionist if not Allah's Army? Why have we been establishing sleeper cells throughout the West if not to strike the infidels? Look what we accomplished in Spain. With a train bomb and a few casualties, we overthrew the government."

"In the overall scheme of things, the Madrid attack accomplished little more than to harden world opinion against us." Nasser gestured indifferently. "Allow me to return to the subject at hand, my dear Moussawi. None of the Arab states want millions of Palestinians flooding back across their borders. If such a thing were to happen, regimes would be toppled."

"More reason for Allah's Army to remain strong."

"To remain strong, you must first know your enemy," Nasser said. "Delegations from the United States, Europe, and Israel are going to Egypt next month to lay the groundwork for a comprehensive Middle East peace plan."

"A peace plan designed by Satan." The sheik smoothed a thumb along his cane. "Has a date been set?"

"The paperwork must make its rounds through diplomatic

channels and go through the various rewrites. That should take about four months."

"By the sword of the Prophet, I wish there was a way to foil these blasphemous efforts."

"Look long enough for a way, and you will find it," Nasser said. "The question is do you want a real *jihad* that will defeat the Jews once and for all, or continue to play silly games with no end in sight?"

The sheik's lips pressed into a thin line. "Seeing Zionism uprooted from Palestine is what I've devoted my life to."

"Then, my dear Moussawi, listen to what I have to say. The 9-11 attacks cost the United States more than a trillion dollars. Such losses cannot be sustained by any nation." Nasser smiled, but his eyes remained cold. "In order to defeat the West we must cripple their economies. Then and only then can Palestine be liberated."

"Cripple their economies?" Moussawi arched an eyebrow. "How can we hope to accomplish such a thing? The West, with their technology and armies, has unlimited resources. Even after disagreements over invading Iraq, their intelligence agencies continue to share information. Security is tighter. Look how easily Iraq and Afghanistan fell, Saddam pulled from a rat hole, trembling like a coward, Qaddafi giving up his weapons program. The list goes on."

"Before Allah, all things are possible," Nasser said. "Infidel strength is rooted in the confidence of their economies. A confidence already eroded by dirty accounting practices used by their major corporations. Investors lose their life savings while corporate executives cash in stock options. Destroy the remaining vestiges of confidence and the West will fall. We already have more than six thousand *jihadis* operating in sleeper cells spread across the United States, Europe, and parts of Asia. With them it could be done."

Moussawi nodded. "Fortunately, our *jihadis* are loyal. Each is dedicated to martyrdom and blends well into the population."

"Therein lies our strength," Nasser said. "We must establish them into one thousand independent units, with no more than five men per unit, including the team leader."

"That's a total of five thousand men," Moussawi said. "What about communication?"

"Laptop computers equipped with advanced encryption programs will be provided to each team leader. Messages sent from a central command post will be routed in such ways that they cannot be intercepted." Nasser gave the sheik a penetrating gaze. "I have a plan to defeat the Zionists and cause great mischief for the infidels. Only the two of us and Allah will know the details."

"A plan?" Moussawi's eyes took on an unnatural light. "By the Prophet, peace be upon Him, I cannot wait to hear the details."

The prince smiled, then touched the side of his hawk-like nose. "I suggest we discuss the details later this afternoon after you have rested. However, before we retire, here is something you will find interesting." Nasser removed a document from his robe and spread it on the low table. "Allah, in His infinite wisdom, is providing well for us. If these long-term weather reports are accurate, the United States, Japan, and Europe are in for a bone-chilling winter."

Moussawi picked up a date and rolled it between his fingers. "Insha'Allah, the winter of their discontent."

Two

Four months after the meeting between Sheik Moussawi and Prince Nasser, Elvira Roberts' rocking chair creaked as she watched new snow gather along the windowsill. A bitter cold had crept inside her small Brooklyn apartment. It was working its way into her bones. Why hadn't the landlord purchased the heating oil? She'd asked him about it when the weather first began getting cold.

"Another week," he'd say. Always another week.

That had been more than a month ago, and still there was no heat. Wincing from her swollen joints, she pulled the shawl higher around her shoulders. Now over eighty-years-old, her ebony face was shrunken and lined from years of hardship and labor. As a younger woman, she had been robust and healthy, cleaning as many as five houses in a day. "One for each of my children," she would jokingly say. Back then her husband and friends referred to her as "Elvira the oak." So long ago, she thought. Now her skeletal frame was bowed by arthritis. Elvira picked up the white doily in her lap, a gift from her late husband, Joe, and rubbed it against her cheek.

Wind whistled through the cracks as snow swirled. It began

sticking to the windowpane. Elvira tried moving her toes, but found they had no feeling.

Why hadn't the landlord brought that heating oil?

"Don't just sit there, girl. Move around. It gets the circulation going."

Her late husband, Joe, used to tell her that when her joints first began to swell. Elvira moved the doily to her cracked lips. She thought about standing, but the effort seemed too great.

If only Joe could be here.

She would fix breakfast. Afterwards, they would drink coffee and talk as dawn broke over the tenement. Remembering such mornings, Elvira stared at the gathering snow and thought about her life.

Over the years, she'd lost her husband and children through disease, drugs, and crime. Now everyone she had ever loved was gone. Elvira shivered, as much from loss as from cold. She'd never expected much. So why had she been left alone in this dirty one room apartment? Hadn't she been a good Christian? Over the years, she had prayed for her family to have decent housing and minimal necessities. Yes, she'd prayed for those things, but God's ears had been closed. Elvira no longer prayed. Instead, she passed the time in her rocking chair, staring out the window.

The snow thickened as the cold continued to invade the old woman's body. Her eyelids were heavy, but at least she felt more comfortable.

Now would be a nice time to sleep.

The rocking chair creaked as darkness pearled around her. Clutching her doily, Elvira Roberts closed her eyes, wondering when the landlord would fill the heating oil tanks.

Near Jeddah, Prince Nasser clicked off the television. For once the weather experts had it right. Most of Europe, Asia, the

United States, and Canada were experiencing unseasonably cold weather. Homeless people were beginning to die of exposure. The West would soon come begging for more oil, a lot more oil.

Nasser's flesh tingled as he saw Allah's plan unfolding. *Insha'Allah,* Mecca and Medina would soon be under his control. Feeling greatly satisfied, the prince went to his desk and called for his bodyguard, Yousef.

"You rang, Highness?"

"Get the car ready. There is a cultural festival outside Jeddah. I feel in the mood to purchase a new camel."

Dust, flies, and the smells of urine, sweat, and dung filled the air at the site of the camel beauty contest. Nasser sat in a shaded chair, fanned by attendants, as breeders paraded their prize camels before a handful of judges.

"That one has the right look, Highness," Yousef whispered.

Nasser glanced at his bodyguard, catching the excitement in his eyes. "No one knows camels like the Yam tribesmen. Tell me what you see, Yousef."

"He rises above the other beasts like a conquering prince, Highness. See the curve of his neck—long and thin. His eyes are big, so as to see everything." Yousef leaned closer to Nasser's ear. "Look at the droop of his lower lip, and the fleshy high hump. He is certainly a royal mount, Highness, and will sire a fine brood."

Nasser nodded. "See to it, Yousef, but do not pay too much. Then I wish to visit Jeddah."

The prince leaned back in his seat and watched his bodyguard walk toward the camel merchant. Unlike most of his Yam tribesman, Nasser's bodyguard had light skin and straight brown hair. Qualities he'd picked up from his mother, an Italian photographer, who had fallen in love with the towering dunes that marked the western perimeter of the Rub al Khali, known as the Empty Quarter where the Yam lived. She had fallen in love with the Yam's chieftain, Achmed Nisseri, Yousef's father, and embraced Islam. Moments before his wife died giving birth to their son, she asked her husband to educate Yousef in the West. To honor his wife's dying wish, Achmed went to Nasser's father at a *majlis,* a gathering where citizens can directly appeal to their leaders for help, advice, and sometimes emergency cash, to ask about the education of his son. A petition Nasser's father had granted.

Nasser saw the camel merchant gesticulating wildly as Yousef opened the bargaining. He wondered how bold the merchant would be if he knew about Yousef's prowess with a knife. *Yes,* the prince thought, his father had been wise to educate Achmed Nisseri's son.

An hour later, Nasser watched the swollen sun sink into oblivion as his stretch Mercedes limousine sped toward Jeddah. "I shall call him Ali Khan."

"A fine name, my prince," Yousef said. "God willing, we will take him to the Empty Quarter. It will be interesting to see how Ali Khan crosses the Sands."

The neon lights of Jeddah lit the darkness like the sun. Skyscrapers, shopping malls, and snarled traffic surrounded Nasser's limousine. Along chic Tahliyah Street, the prince observed lines of teenage boys wearing baggy, low-slung pants and baseball caps turned rakishly backward. They idled beside chauffeur-driven cars full of teenage girls with veiled faces and bodies covered head to toe in black *abaya.*

"Look at them." Nasser leaned forward. "See how our youths trade their robes for the dress of American street gangs. The *mutawaeen* should arrest them."

"Given the proper authority, our state religious police would make short work of them," Yousef said. He glanced in the rearview mirror at Nasser staring at the street scenes. "In the Sands, where I was born, cell phones will never replace tribal traditions. When the Yam and other Bedouin tribes heard the call of the Prophet, peace be upon Him, they rode out of the desert with Him to victory."

"We Bedouins are the only true Arabs," Nasser said. "Since the beginning of time, we have crossed the Empty Quarter and kept the Faith."

Yousef honked at the unmoving traffic. "The Sands, and serving you, are enough for any man, my prince."

"What are they doing now?" Nasser asked. "Paper balls are flying between the teenage riffraff."

"I believe they call it numbering, Highness."

"Numbering?"

"Yes. They are exchanging cell phone numbers."

"The *mutawaeen* should stop such practices."

"We are turning away from our Islamic laws," Yousef said.

"Allah sees the wickedness of his people." Nasser leaned back into the leather folds. "A cleansing of Islam is at hand."

"A cleansing, Highness?"

"Very soon." Nasser closed his eyes. "Now, I wish to return home."

Grant Corbet walked to the window and stared out. The CIA's Deputy Director of Operations was tall and fit, with sandy brown hair and well-defined features. The kind of man women imagined sitting on a buckskin horse on a mountain, staring at distant horizons. His eyes were cool-gray and intelligent, but tinged with a sad resignation. After years in the field, Corbet had seen death's many grotesque forms. Now, at forty-nine, he directed the agency's covert activities from behind a desk.

Ordinarily, the rolling green grounds behind Grant's office at the CIA's Langley headquarters were a pleasing sight. But today skies were gray, a light snow falling. Winter had come to the nation's capital in the middle of September.

Grant shook his head, returned to his desk and clicked on CNN. A reporter stood beside the weatherman. Behind them a map flashed, viewing the earth from above the Arctic ice cap.

"All right, Jim. The forecast is calling for more cold air. There have already been a number of power blackouts across the northern United States. This is a time when people should be wearing windbreakers, not dressing like Eskimos.

"Variable weather like this begins in this area, when polar and tropical jet streams fight for supremacy, and the polar stream wins." The weatherman's pointer touched a section of the map. "Another factor is the North Atlantic Oscillation. The NAO is the dominant mode of winter climate variability in the North Atlantic region." The pointer moved on. "At times, this pattern oscillates from positive to negative. Right now we are entering a negative phase. This kind of rapid climatic change means parts of the world will probably suffer extreme climatic conditions, while other areas experience little out of the ordinary."

"That brings us to Antarctica," the anchor said. "We have another set of problems there."

An image of Antarctica replaced the Arctic ice cap.

The weatherman's pointer moved. "Temperatures have been rising around the South Pole over the past five decades. That means Southern Mexico and all of Central and South America could experience warming trends."

"Just the opposite of what we're experiencing here."

"That's correct," the weatherman said. "Take a look at the overlay of the Larson B ice shelf. You can see how it has been disintegrating at an unprecedented rate over the past month. Only last week, a Rhode Island-size piece of ice broke away."

"Can this warming trend be attributed to the buildup of greenhouse gas emissions?"

The weatherman frowned. "Looks like it. Experts are having a hard time finding another culprit."

"Let's get back to our problems at home," the anchor said. "What are some of the possible ramifications from this NAO negative oscillation?"

"Power shortages and crop damage, to name two," the weatherman said. "If current conditions remain the same, we might well be in for the same kind of extreme winters experienced in the early sixties."

"We're out of time, Jim. Thanks for giving us a better understanding about today's remarkable weather shift." The anchor looked into the camera. "For all the latest information, log onto our website at www.cnnweather.com. After this station break, we will be switching you back to Mary Yu in New York."

A knock at the door turned Grant's head. His counterpart, Deputy Director of Intelligence, Jack Sweeny, came in.

"Hey, Jack. What's up?"

Before sitting, the lanky Texan set two Styrofoam cups of black coffee and a bag of assorted Krispy Kremes on the desk. "Doesn't get much better than this."

Grant chuckled and picked up a raspberry-filled doughnut. "Not if you don't mind dying from clogged arteries."

"Today's the big day." Sweeny added cream and sugar to his coffee. "Think they'll get the Wallace Plan moving?"

"I spoke to Ira Bettleman, and he thinks it looks promising," Grant said. "It all depends on Chairman Tartir sticking to the agreement."

"Good afternoon, I'm Mary Yu from CNN Headquarters, New York. We have a breaking story."

The two men turned to the television set.

"CNN has just learned of yet another death attributed to the unseasonably cold weather sweeping the country. We will now take you to our CNN correspondent in Brooklyn."

The image on the screen changed to a reporter standing in front of a tenement apartment house.

"Mary, the body of Elvira Roberts was discovered by a neighbor just over an hour ago. A team of paramedics arrived earlier and are in her apartment." Snow dusted the reporter's head. "A neighbor found Mrs. Roberts in her rocking chair with a shawl around her shoulders. There has been no heating oil in the apartment complex since the unusually cold weather began. Repeated requests by residents for the landlord to provide heating oil have been ignored. Ah, here come the paramedics."

The camera moved to the front door of the apartment house. Two medics were wheeling a gurney through the narrow opening. A gust of wind raised the sheet on one side. Snow swirled around a withered black hand clutching a doily.

"Christ," Grant whispered.

"We better start bracing ourselves for more of the same," Sweeny said. "Japan's rice production has been crippled. Food shortages have reached critical levels in China. They could be facing the worst famine in decades."

"The leadership's in denial," Grant said. "A matter of face."

"Not a lot of room for face when people are starving." Sweeny bit into a doughnut. "Our meteorologists are predicting that Europe, North America, and Northern Asia from Central China up could be facing the worst winter in over a hundred years."

"Fuel prices are already going through the roof. That could wreak havoc on the world economy." Grant sipped his coffee. "Working on possible scenarios?"

"Several, but none of them good." Sweeny folded his hands. "As it stands, the U.S. can only provide about seventy percent of the energy required for protracted winter conditions."

"And?"

Sweeny grimaced. "The country could become paralyzed if

the southern regions get hit hard."

In Alexandria, Egypt, Colonel Adham Kamel finished the flight inspection and patted the side of his AH 64 Apache Helicopter. The Hellfire missiles gleamed ominously beneath the sun. *A fine machine,* he thought. The metal was warm to his touch. Adham smiled at the irony. If nothing else, Americans knew how to make weapons of war.

Palm fronds rustled in sea breezes around the El-Salamlek Palace Hotel's cliff-top helipad where Adham stood. Fortunately, the cold weather plaguing Europe and North America had not visited Egypt. His eyes moved to the powdery beaches lining Montazah Bay that opened to the Mediterranean. Seagulls circled over bikini-clad women sipping drinks, sunning themselves. Yachts belonging to the privileged cut frothy wakes through blue water.

Adham turned away and closed his eyes to the image. The whispering palms took him back to his childhood and life around the oasis.

El Khârga, the village of Adham's birth, was a poor place far from the grand palaces and mosques of Alexandria and Cairo. Images of the blind and withered cleric sitting cross-legged on dirty carpets were still indelibly imprinted on his mind.

Adham remembered going with his father to Sheik Momoud's tattered canvas tent when the faithful gathered to hear the truth.

It is the duty of every Muslim to stand with the Palestinian people against Israel and America.

"Our mullah speaks the words of God, my son. If I had two good legs I would join the fight against the Zionist." His father told Adham such things when they sat beneath the stars traveling from the deep desert by caravan to Cairo.

Adham listened, finding comfort in his father's words and

strong arms.

After selling their goods and buying provisions, his father joined other tribesmen to drink tea and smoke hashish. Warmed by fires of camel dung, Adham sat spellbound as the men exchanged tales of the desert and heroic deeds of the prophet, Mohammad.

But the days of his childhood were gone, Adham thought. Everything about the life he had known was gone—everything except his memories. Even a formal education in England and a military career could not steal those away. The words of his father and Sheik Mamoud still rang in his ears.

It is the duty of every Muslim to stand with the Palestinian people against Israel and America.

Adham lit a cigarette and fixed his gaze on the horizon, studying it with a pilot's eyes. Sea and sky joined at the apex of infinity. He could not tell where one ended and the other began.

"God has chosen you for this mission," his contact in Allah's Army had told him.

Yes. He was only a grain of desert sand in Allah's universe, but what a powerful grain. Adham flicked his cigarette over the cliff. For some time he stood quite still, the hot blood of his Bedouin heritage coursing through his veins.

Adham retrieved his prayer rug from inside the AH 64 Apache cockpit. Then he removed a black-and-white photo of his wife and two sons.

Praise be to Allah they will be well provided for.

Colonel Adham Kamel put the photo back inside his shirt pocket, then went inside the hotel's small mosque to speak with his God.

Approaching Alexandria's El Nozha Air Force Base, the Israeli jet bearing the Star of David on its tail banked in preparation for landing. The city founded by the great Macedonian conqueror in 331 BC glistened like a pearl beneath cloudless skies and summer sun.

"Won't be long now," Thornton McIver said. The U.S. Undersecretary of State for Middle East Affairs put several folders in his briefcase and snapped it shut. "Chairman Tartir has agreed in principle to the Wallace Plan. No turning back now. His public statements have locked him in."

"I don't know," Benjamin Levy, Israel's Foreign Minister, said, his mouth drooping in skepticism. "What Tartir says and what Tartir does are more often than not two very different things. He's famous for coming up with new demands at the eleventh hour."

"Yes, but this time Egypt and Jordan are putting some muscle behind their rhetoric. I predict we'll have a peace agreement signed by year's end."

Levy chuckled. "I hope you're right, my friend. Perhaps this meeting will mark the beginning of a lasting peace. I'm getting too old to keep fighting those in my government who want to push the Palestinians back into Jordan and Lebanon."

"There're those on both sides who oppose peace," André Madelin, the EU representative, said. "Unfortunately for them, the vast majority of the world is sick of conflict."

Levy glanced out the window. "I would like to think you are right, André. But I fear conflict is the essence of man's nature."

"The Israeli, American and EU representatives will be arriving in approximately ten minutes, Excellency."

Egyptian president Hassan Fadel glanced at his aide. "The honor guard has been assembled?"

The aide replaced the telephone. "Yes, Excellency. All is in order."

Fadel nodded and sank back into the limousine's plush leather. For a moment, Egypt's president lost himself in thought as the buildings of Alexandria passed beyond view. There would be generous American and EU aid packages in the offing if he could moderate a serious peace agreement between the Palestinians and Israelis. Of course, he had tried a number of times before and failed. But this time was different, wasn't it? This time had a sweet smell of triumph to it. The trick would be for him and Jordanian Crown Prince Abdel Agha to make sure that Chairman Abdullah Tartir, a man famous for his last-minute maneuverings, accepted Senator Wallace's peace proposal in present form. Then a true peace agreement could be implemented. The fundamentalist movement sweeping the Middle East would no longer have the Israeli-Palestinian conflict as a rallying point to spread hatred.

Yes, Fadel thought.

Next to Fadel, Prince Agha hummed pleasantly as the motorcade pulled onto the tarmac at El Nozha Air Force Base.

The Israeli jet glinted in the sunlight as the pilot followed the traffic pattern. Soon it would vector from base leg to final approach.

Colonel Kamel's AH 64 Apache Helicopter lifted off a moment later and locked onto its intercept course. Adham gave a final look at the sun worshipers and luxury yachts. The control stick was a final friend as his Apache skimmed over Montazah Bay's sparkling waters.

President Fadel, Prince Agha and Chairman Tartir walked past the honor guard and waited on the tarmac. Security personnel representing various contingencies trailed behind, filing off to either side of the red carpet. A military band, polished instruments winking in the sun, warmed up on the podium erected beside the entrance to the terminal. Here the visiting dignitaries would make brief statements to the press.

Prince Agha shaded his eyes, squinting toward the approaching aircraft. A dark speck lifted behind the Israeli jet. He glanced at Fadal. "Part of your security arrangements?"

Fadal stared at the Jordanian crown prince. "What do you mean?"

Agha's eyes focused on the approaching El Al jet. "The helicopter escort."

"Where?"

"Allah-u Akbar!"

Colonel Adham Kamel released the missile and stared transfixed as the Hellfire raced towards its target seventy-five yards away.

A moment later, the light of a second sun flashed in the sky as the jet's fuselage disintegrated. A second explosion sounded as Adham's Apache helicopter was consumed by a fiery golden ball of jet fuel.

Three

Director of Central Intelligence Zacharias Holden had a telephone tucked under his chin when Grant Corbet and Jack Sweeny walked into his office. A digital map of the Middle East was illuminated on a screen behind his desk. On top of the credenza were three model ships that Zach had constructed during his days in the Navy. Their full sails billowed against phantom winds.

The DCI spoke softly over the secure line while massaging the bowl of his favorite pipe. A habit, Grant knew, that helped his friend and mentor think.

Holden's appointment as Director of Central Intelligence by President Stewart had been one of those Washington rarities based on merit rather than politics. In the aftermath of 9-11, Zach had acted quickly to streamline the agency to the preeminent status it had enjoyed during the Cold War glory days. One of his first official acts had been nominating Grant to his former post as DDO. After Grant's success in stopping the international terrorist, Basha, there had been no opposition on the Intelligence Committee. Shortly afterwards, Jack Sweeny had gotten the nod as DDI.

"Grant Corbet and Jack Sweeny are here now. Yes, Frances,

I'll let you know the moment we wrap up."

The DCI replaced the telephone and nodded at the phone. "My conversation with Secretary of State Merriman ended with her all but declaring war against the PLO. The President, Senate and members of Congress are furious. For once, the EU is outraged." Holden filled his pipe, fired the tobacco and exhaled a cloud of smoke. His eyes moved from Sweeny to Grant. "Assessment?"

"I spoke to Ira Bettleman," Grant said. "He indicated that Prime Minister Wasserman wants to move against the Palestinian authority. He's got the backing of Likud and Labor to mount an all-out strike. The only thing holding him back is getting a green light from State and the EU. I should know more later today."

Zach frowned. "What have we got on the Egyptian pilot?"

"Intel out of Egypt and Israel is pretty thin," Sweeny said. "Our people are checking out the pilot of the Apache. With the help of Egyptian intelligence, we found a twenty-five-thousand-dollar wire transfer sent to the pilot's personal bank account two days before the jet was downed. We're working back to see where the wire originated. Other than that, Tartir emphatically denies involvement in the downing of the plane. He's promised full cooperation with the international community to find the responsible party."

"Anyone taking credit?" Holden asked.

"Not so far," Sweeny said.

Holden raised an eyebrow. "That leaves Tartir in the hot seat."

"The other groups know what would happen if they claimed responsibility," Grant said. "They also know Tartir is out of wiggle room. The Israelis aren't going to hold back, and from the look of it, no one is going to try and persuade them otherwise."

"You know the Middle East better than anyone, Grant." Holden drew on his pipe. "Why would Tartir put himself in such an untenable position?"

"He wouldn't. I think once we've dug deep enough, we'll find the pilot wasn't working alone." Grant tapped his fingers together. "Three of the world's most respected diplomats and their entourages were deliberately targeted in front of Tartir, the Egyptian president and the Jordanian crown prince. Tartir's brash, but not stupid. Especially when you consider that Levy was the Palestinians' best friend in the Israeli government. Whoever pulled this off had to have a helluva lot of on-the-ground intel and field support."

Holden nodded. "I agree, but this time innocence isn't going to help. Tartir's the one responsible for controlling terror. His repeated failure to rein it in is going to cost the Palestinian people dearly."

Grant and Sweeny stared at the DCI.

"Get your paperwork in order between now and Friday. We've been invited to Camp David for the weekend." Holden's world-weary eyes found his three ships as they sailed on frozen blue waters. "Thor's hammer is about to fall, and Tartir's standing on the anvil."

In Jeddah, three days later, Prince Nasser clicked on CNN's World Report. He felt good about being back at his country estate. His trip to Riyadh, while hectic, had gone as expected. The Middle East had erupted, prospects for peace incinerated with an exploding Israeli jet. Now members of the Royal Family were caught in what Americans called a Catch 22. Be ostracized by the West and stick to the traditional line that Israel's illegal occupation of Palestine was the underlying cause of hostilities? Or side with the West, condemn the downing of the Israeli jet as an act of terror, and risk insurrection at home by fundamentalists?

Damned if you do. Damned if you don't.

Nasser poured a cup of mint tea and sipped. Like the ticking of a wind-up clock, Chairman Abdullah Tartir's time would soon run out. And the prince had been funding arms shipments for the chairman's Martyr's Brigade for years through a complex banking network.

Imagine a million-dollar payment to the Egyptian pilot's family traced to a Swiss bank, and linked to Tartir.

"Tick, tock." Nasser chuckled and clicked on CNN.

"Hello. I'm Rachel Sobel at CNN Central, Tel Aviv. The tinder-box known as the Middle East ignited again following the suicide missile attack on an Israeli jet by Egyptian Air Force Colonel Adham Kamel. Colonel Kamel has been identified as a member of Egyptian President Hassan Fadel's security team." A picture of Kamel flashed on the screen. "Now three of the world's most respected diplomats and their staff are dead, and the region is bracing for war as governments around the world express their outrage. For an update, we take you to CNN's correspondent in Jerusalem."

Nasser's eyes crinkled at the fear etched on the reporter's face. In the background, tanks and armored military support vehicles rumbled through the street. Cars burned along Jaffa Street, and shop windows were broken. Dust clouds billowed around angry Israeli mobs running alongside soldiers waving flags and shouting, "Free Israel from Palestinian murderers."

The scene switched to another reporter. "Rachel, not less than an hour ago, a high-ranking Israeli official told me that the final blow to an already-faltering peace process had been delivered in Alexandria. Here in the holy city of Jerusalem the situation continues to deteriorate. The all-too-familiar sounds of sirens are continuous. The air is thick, smelling of gasoline and burning rubber. It hangs like a deadly fog over this divided city. Last night, after an emergency session with his cabinet, Prime Minister Ezer Wasserman ordered the Israeli army to seal the West Bank and Gaza. Calls for restraint by Chairman Tartir, who remains in Egypt, have been ignored. With Israel mobilizing for war, leaders of Hamas, Islamic Jihad, Hezballah, and Allah's Army have vowed to fight to the last man if Palestinian territories are attacked." The camera focused briefly on the moving armored column. "Things promise to get worse before getting better, Rachel. Disposing of the dead is becoming a serious part of the struggle between Israelis and Palestinians. Morgues throughout the city are overflowing. Bodies are stacked two to a gurney. Others are being laid in hallways. With the incredibly tight security, Palestinian families are being prevented from claiming family members. This is especially inflammatory for Muslims, who believe burial should take place as soon as possible. Bodies are traditionally wrapped in white shrouds and placed in graves with the head pointing toward Mecca."

Nasser clicked off the set. He sipped tea, the mint taste fresh on his tongue, and reviewed events. Predictably, the Israeli army, with the blessing of the United States and European Union, had sealed the West Bank and Gaza. Tens of thousands of Palestinians surged against the Israelis, only to be cut down. By day's end, hundreds were dead and a dusk-to-dawn curfew imposed.

More death would follow.

The more militant oil-producing states like Iraq, Libya, and Iran were calling for an oil embargo against the West. As confidant to the king and crown prince, Nasser had planted a few seeds of his own while in Riyadh.

"Oil is our most powerful weapon, Highness. But I counsel restraint in using it. Saudi Arabia should be seen as a moderating influence at next week's Arab summit. Agree to an embargo against the West as a last resort, and only if our Palestinian brothers are forcibly exiled to Jordan and Lebanon."

"Your advice is sound, Abdul bin Suleiman Nasser," the king had said. "You have a feel for dealing with infidels, especially the meddlesome Americans. I would like you to accompany the crown prince to the Arab summit."

"Yes, Highness. As you wish."

Nasser closed his eyes and whispered, "Cry havoc and let slip the dogs of war." The words filled his head like prayer or prophesy.

The Israeli response had moved faster and with more force than even he had expected. True believers were now witnessing Zionist armies driving Palestinians out of their ancestral homeland. The oil-producing states had no alternative but to impose an oil embargo, which would force a military response by the West. Muslims around the world in turn would galvanize under a single voice. *A true jihad,* Nasser thought. Old Arab regimes that catered to the West would be swept away like grains of sand. And out of the chaos, a Prince of Islam would emerge to rule the sacred lands of Mohammad.

Nasser peered at the bottom of his teacup. His reflection stared back amidst the gently swirling leaves.

Grant Corbet watched Maryland's Catoctin Mountains pass beneath the VH-60 Blackhawk helicopter. Layers of fresh, early fall snow blanketing the land did little to lift his sense of gloom.

What the hell's going on? he wondered. *It's like the whole damned planet's gone off its axis.*

The thought activated the same cold fingers that had tickled the hairs on the nape of his neck while he'd hunted Basha. Nightmares still plagued him over how close he'd come to losing his beloved daughter, Jenny, to that international terrorist.

Thank God that's all past. Jenny's happily married and the mother of a fine son. And me? The doting grandpa.

After Basha had been neutralized, serious peace negotiations between Israel and the Palestinians resumed. A world weary of terror had watched both sides move toward adopting the peace proposal former president William Hollings negotiated during his final months in office.

Then the big meltdown, Grant thought.

Palestinian President Tartir refused to sign the peace proposal late in the negotiations. Charges and countercharges flew, followed by a new *intifada.* Suicide bombings increased, and Israel's army responded. Blood and tears flowed. President Stewart's two-year-old administration initiated new negotiations. Senator Frank Wallace and Zach Holden were dispatched to the Middle East to firm up support for the senator's peace proposal. Moderate Arab states embraced the Wallace Plan and pressured Tartir to accept it on face. Secretary of State Frances Merriman and Undersecretary Thornton McIver persuaded Israel to do the same. World news focused on the long-sought peace coming to the Middle East.

Then the Israeli jet carrying peace delegations from the United States, Europe and Israel was shot down by an Egyptian helicopter pilot. American and Egyptian intelligence agencies followed the money trail and uncovered a million-dollar trust established in a Swiss bank by President Tartir's Martyrs' Brigade in the pilot's wife's name. All too convenient, Grant thought. Even so, another peace plan had been blown to hell.

Grant's gut knotted. The Middle East was disintegrating and alliances becoming sharply defined in an increasingly divided world. Years of fieldwork in Asia and the Middle East told him the implications this time could be catastrophic.

"Touchdown in five," the pilot said.

Across the aisle, Grant saw Zach Holden massaging the bowl of his unlit pipe while he pretended to read the *Wall Street Journal.* Next to the DCI, Jack Sweeny stared out the cabin window. Throughout the twenty-five-minute flight from Andrews Air Force Base to Camp David, the three men had retreated into their own peculiar silence.

Grant looked outside, his gaze focused on a county truck salting an overpass. His mood darkened as thoughts of Jenny, swirling snow, and an exploding Israeli jet whirled in his mind.

Lori Ramirez, the President's press secretary, waited with a Marine driver when Grant's helicopter touched down. The chopper's blades whipped up snow as the three men huddled and disembarked.

"Welcome to Camp David," Ramirez said. The press secretary's lips were pressed into a practiced smile. "You'll have a little time to freshen up before meeting with the President."

Zach handed his bag to the driver. "What's the agenda?"

Ramirez shrugged. "There'll be an informal lunch at Laurel and a meeting with security advisors in an hour. After that, it's anyone's guess."

Grant took in the pastoral beauty of Camp David as he rode to his cabin. The cottages, nestled and snow-roofed amid thick growths of oak, poplar, ash, hickory and maple, were all named after trees. Skies were gray, and ice clung to bare branches. The crisp air smelled of snow and wet bark. Squirrels foraged for acorns beside the winding paths used for walking and jogging.

The jeep stopped in front of a cabin, smoke coming from the stone chimney.

"You've been assigned to Birch." Ramirez looked at Grant. "You must have friends in high places. Menachem Begin stayed here once."

Birch, a rustic but comfortable cabin, smelled of warm cedar. It had two bedrooms and two baths with vaulted ceilings. The well-lighted working area had been equipped with a secure telephone line. A fire crackled in the stone fireplace, logs piled neatly on the hearth.

After unpacking, Grant opened a bottle of mineral water and

clicked on CNN. An anxious reporter, wearing a flak jacket, faced the camera. "Israeli defense forces have now completely surrounded the city of Jenin with tanks, armored support vehicles and bulldozers. Just hours ago, Israeli soldiers, using teargas and rubber bullets, dispersed thousands of rock-throwing Palestinians."

The screen switched to mobs of Palestinian refugees hurling rocks and Molotov cocktails at the advancing Israelis. Rage burned on wild-eyed, brown faces, but there was fear as well.

"Refugees are being told to gather their belongings and report to the military white zone located on the outskirts of the camp." In the background, the pop-pop-pop of automatic weapons sounded. A ghastly haze hung over the camp. Apache helicopters were silhouetted against the dying afternoon sun, and Israeli F-16 jets streaked overhead. "I'm being told that we have to leave this area," the reporter said. "We've just learned the destruction of terrorist facilities in Jenin will begin in approximately three hours."

Grant's features remained impassive as he watched the carnage. He knew the drumbeat of the roiling Middle East. There would be winners and losers this time, but ancient hatreds would remain. In less than an hour, he might be called on to tell that to his President.

"Christ."

He popped two Tums, then dialed Major General Ira Bettleman's direct line. The Mossad chief picked up on the second ring.

"I understand you're at Camp David."

Grant caught the edge in his friend's voice. "Word travels fast."

"We still have a few sources. How's Jenny? I understand you've become a doting grandfather in your old age."

"Jenny's well, thanks," Grant said. "She and Leighton bought a new home. Harlin's got his own room and is growing like a weed. I'd spoil him rotten if I could get down to Houston more often."

"Grandchildren tend to have that effect on us," Bettleman said. "Jenny's happiness is the one worthwhile thing that came out of the Basha affair. She gets a good husband, and you get a healthy grandson."

"I suppose that's one way of rationalizing it." Grant looked out the window. Snow glistened on tree limbs, the sun a silver smudge behind gray clouds.

"What's the weather like?" Bettleman asked, breaking the uncomfortable silence.

"September, and I've got logs on the fire. Damned scary."

"That's one problem we're not facing. Something about jet streams." Bettleman's voice turned serious. "Have you been watching the news?"

"Yes. What's your take, Ira?"

"No holding back," Bettleman said. "We're cleaning out the rabid dogs and physically removing anyone remotely connected with terror groups. Tartir's finished. He's got nowhere to go. Especially since the CIA linked his Martyrs' Brigade to the million-dollar payment made to Adham Kamel's family."

"That stinks, Ira. Someone dumped the information in our laps."

"You think because the story smells, it becomes personal?"

Grant sighed. "You honestly think Tartir's directly involved?"

Silence spun down the line. "No, but he's part of the money trail. Besides, at this point, it doesn't matter what I think. Events have moved beyond that. How to handle the refugees has become my immediate concern."

"If they're forced out, the conflict will spread," Grant said. "Muslims are uniting in a way I haven't seen before. There are rumblings about an oil embargo."

Bettleman grunted. "Just don't go forgetting your friends after our operations are over. Your President and the EU have given their blessings."

"We don't forget our friends," Grant said.

A distant sigh emanated from the Holy Land, ending the call. "Tell that to the Afghanis."

An hour later, Grant sipped iced tea with Jack Sweeny and FBI Director Sean O'Dell in the Laurel conference room, waiting for the President of the United States to arrive. Other officials talked quietly in small groups.

Secret Service agents were strategically stationed around the room, their identities obvious from the earpieces and alert eyes. Everyone stood, the room becoming silent when the Chief Executive walked in, followed by an attractive woman, her black hair pulled back in a bun.

Sweeny nudged Grant. "The agent following the President is Lindsey Caspare. She's the service's best pistol shot. Holds all the records."

Grant nodded, absently checking his short fingernails, his thoughts focused on the first time he'd spoken with the then newly-elected President.

"I finally get to shake the hand of the man who stopped Basha." Abigail Stewart's grip had been firm, her eyes steady. "You are to be commended, Mr. Corbet. You've served your country well."

O'Dell brought Grant back to the present. "The President was quite an equestrian in her teens," he whispered. "That's how she got the code name JUMPER. She was captain of the American Olympic team, and a favorite to medal."

Grant glanced at O'Dell. "I didn't know she was an Olympian."

"She wasn't. At the trials, her horse fell. Abby broke her back. She hasn't ridden since."

"Ouch." Grant grimaced. "You wouldn't know by looking at her."

"The President's an example of what a good surgeon can do. She made a complete recovery, except for a little stiffness when it's cold."

"You pick up all these tidbits from her background check?"

"Yep, the Bureau's got files on just about everyone." O'Dell grinned at Grant and Sweeny. "Even spooks."

Grant watched the President stop to exchange a word with an aide. Her face was pale, but calm. No question, she possessed a kind of easy elegance that made her an international icon. Tall and slim, wearing little makeup, her chestnut hair contoured the curve of her neck. She dressed casually in a forest green and tan sweater over dark slacks. "Quite a lady," he said. "Very insightful."

"Quite a lady, and quite a linguist." Sweeny munched on a doughnut. "Fluent in five languages. Definitely knows how to separate substance from politics."

"She lost her husband in a small plane crash just after being elected to her first term in Congress, didn't she?" Grant said. "Odd, she never remarried."

"Politics became her life. Only took her ten years to get the nomination." O'Dell chuckled. "She turned this fucking town upside down when she snuffed Hollings reelection bid."

Grant nodded. "Beat the living hell out of him. Now she's an international icon. The public loves her."

"Because she doesn't lie." Sweeny wiped away doughnut crumbs. "Insiders who thought she'd be a pushover had a rude awakening."

O'Dell downed the rest of his tea. "Plenty of bigwigs have crapped in their drawers when she flashed those violet eyes."

"Amen to that." Grant said. "Better get going. Looks like the fun's about to begin."

The President seated herself at the center of the immense table. Conversation muted as she nodded to other guests taking their places. On the President's right sat Secretary of Defense Collin Jeffers, a retired four star general who'd commanded coalition forces during Desert Storm. Secretary of State Frances Merriman sat on the President's left. The SecState's face appeared composed, but Grant caught the hardness in her eyes over the death of Thornton McIver.

National Security Advisor, Axel Bembry, a former ambassador to Saudi Arabia, was next to the Secretary of State. Next in the pecking order came Zach Holden, Sean O'Dell, and the Attorney General. Grant and Jack Sweeny took their seats at the far end of the table.

"Everyone's seated, so let's bring this meeting to order," President Stewart said.

The room became silent, heads turned toward the President.

Abigail Stewart's gaze passed from one person to the next, landing briefly on Grant. "An act of war has been initiated against Israel, the European Union and the United States of America by Abdullah Tartir's Palestinian Authority. My ambassador and friend, Thornton McIver, was murdered, along with a number of other fine men and women. The PA acted like a hostile nation and is being treated as such." Flecks of violet hardened in Abigail Stewart's eyes. "Prime Minister Wasserman is confident Israeli forces will control the Left Bank and Gaza by mid-week. The aftermath, and how we plan to deal with future problems, is what concerns me." The President looked at the DCI. "Your assessment, Zach?"

"Refugees will be the first area of concern. Indications are that more than a million Palestinians will be displaced." Zach glanced at his notes. "The subsequent exodus is shaping up to be a logistical nightmare, Madam President."

"Humanitarian efforts are being coordinated through the EU and Russia," Secretary of Defense Jeffers said. "The Saudi

Foreign Minister Prince Ibrahim al Zyyad and his staff are scheduled to arrive in Washington next week for talks on the refugee problem. Meanwhile, initial shipments of food, medical supplies, and clothing were airlifted from Ankara yesterday."

The President looked at her Secretary of State. "What about the UN?"

"A non-factor." Frances Merriman sipped her water. "Endless committee meetings and debates, which like most issues in front of the United Nations never get resolved."

"France, Germany, and Russia wanted to make it a UN matter, given their large Muslim populations," Jeffers said. "But all they do is talk, bluster, and demonstrate. In the end they do nothing."

Merriman set her glass down. "That's why they're handling the refugee and aid programs."

"Problem is, none of the Arab countries want the Palestinians," Zach said. "Sadly, the refugees that get relocated won't be taking a trip to the Promised Land. They'll find life a helluva lot better in the Left Bank and Gaza than in the camps in Lebanon." He turned to his DDO. "Grant, what's Ira Bettleman's view?"

"Syria, Lebanon, and Jordan have refused to take refugees," Grant said. "Ira's afraid the United States and European Union will distance themselves from the conflict once the more gruesome aspects of Israel's military operations are aired."

"Ridiculous," Axel Bembry said. The NSA had the soft, round features of the self-indulged, his shoulders rounded. "A multinational force committed to defending Israel's borders is being assembled."

"A million or more Palestinians are about to be displaced." Grant held Bembry's gaze. "Major General Bettleman's not convinced Tartir's responsible for the Israeli jet going down. How good will our commitment be if that turns out to be true and the Arab states impose an oil embargo?"

"Questioning national security commitments is not within

your purview, Mr. Corbet." Bembry rolled his pen slowly between his fingers. "Have you forgotten that Egyptian and CIA intelligence agents traced a million-dollar trust earmarked for the pilot's family back to Tartir's Martyrs' Brigade?"

"I haven't forgotten, sir."

"Mr. Corbet?" the President said. "What's your opinion about President Tartir's role regarding the Israeli jet attack?"

Grant stared into the violet eyes of Abigail Stewart. *Hard as cut jewels,* he thought. "I agree with Mr. Bettleman's assessment, Madam President. It's difficult for me to believe President Tartir's implicated."

"Then why did Tartir's Martyrs' Brigade make the million-dollar payment?" Bembry asked. "Who else could be held responsible?"

Grant's gaze stayed focused on President Stewart. "I don't know who's responsible, Madam President, but we're digging. I do know that power and greed drive wars. Tartir's been in the game a long time, and it doesn't make sense for him to self-destruct over one insane act."

The President's manicured fingernails clicked against the tabletop. "I sincerely hope you're wrong, Mr. Corbet."

Four

Grant left his cabin an hour after dinner for his evening jog. Dry snow blew over the ground, but heaters installed next to the paths kept them clear. The sky now streaked a silver-gray, looking like swirled ash as the sun sank behind oak, birch, and walnut trees. Wind gusted from the north, and the air smelled of cedar. Smoke rose from the cabin chimneys.

A half mile into his run, Grant heard approaching footsteps.

"Mind if I join you?"

Grant glanced over his shoulder. Time seemed to attenuate as if he were in a dream. "Yes, please do. I mean, of course not."

Abigail Stewart's eyes crinkled. "Keep going, Mr. Corbet. Don't slow down because of me."

The President had a fluid stride, her breath wisps of vapor on the wind. The attractive Secret Service agent, who accompanied the Chief Executive wherever she went, held steady ten paces behind.

They ran the next two and a half miles in silence. The moon had ascended like a platinum ball behind the cloud cover when they stopped in front of Aspen, the presidential compound, twenty minutes later.

Grant waited, conscious of Agent Caspare slightly behind him. He could be dead in half a second.

The President picked up several pebbles and tossed one into the pond outside Aspen. Rippling circles spread across the dark surface. "You don't whitewash your feelings, Mr. Corbet. I admire that quality."

"It comes from being in the field too long." Grant felt his blood course from the run. "Back then, I was egotistical enough to think I could make a difference."

"Oh, you've made a difference, Mr. Corbet. I've studied your file." The President glanced up and saw moonlight catch his eyes. She tossed another pebble into the pond. "Since Franklin Roosevelt, Camp David has offered Presidents the kind of solitude and tranquility they need in order to see the world clearly. The problem is, I'm seeing some form of ill-defined madness."

Grant watched the mountains behind the trees. They were silhouetted in diffuse moonlight. A great horned owl flapped its wings and sailed into the night in search of food. "The Middle East is a netherworld," he said finally. "Islam blames the Jews for their ills."

"Israel exacerbates the situation by expanding settlements in the West Bank and Gaza," the President said.

"True, but the core problems are rooted in Arab internecine rivalries and religious interpretation." Grant felt Abigail Stewart's eyes on him. "Hatred and ignorance are difficult enemies to defeat, Madam President."

"Perhaps we'll have the opportunity to discuss that sometime." President Stewart looked past Grant, the wind feathering her hair. "I've never been more afraid for our country. Goodnight, Mr. Corbet."

"Goodnight, Madam President."

Agent Caspare moved, placing herself between Grant and the President's retreating figure.

Grant watched the silhouette of the woman Americans called

Abby walk toward the presidential compound. Her scent lingered in cold moonlight.

Axel Bembry flicked his cigarette into the snow. Through the small copse of trees in front of his cabin, he caught sight of Grant Corbet walking away from the presidential compound.

Had Corbet been having a *tête-à-tête* with the President? Was she bypassing him and seeking Corbet's counsel about the Middle East?

Bembry's gaze followed Grant until his shadow disappeared in the darkness.

Sheik Mahmoud Moussawi's dream never varied.

He saw himself as a young boy limping through the carnage, his foot a bloody mass. Panicked villagers raced madly through the dirt streets as flames leaped skyward to the sounds of exploding shells. Bodies of children littered the streets like discarded garbage. Swarms of flies descended on the wounded and dead, the air reeking of cordite. And there were the screams. Sounds no person should ever hear.

A cry of agony welled in the boy's gut.

"Nooooo!"

His eyes flew open. Cold sweat bathed his body as the hook settled in. The hunger never slept. Every night it invaded his dreams, demanding to be fed. Moussawi stared at the ceiling. If only he wasn't cursed with the pain. He had prayed to Allah for help, but all he'd ever received for his injured foot was morphine stolen from Jews. After that, heroin smuggled in from Turkey.

Allah be merciful.

The sheik's breath came fast. A sour sweat came from his

armpits. He reached for the bell on the nightstand and rang for his servant, Jamil.

Moments later, a teenage boy entered wearing a brilliant-white silk morning robe. He had large dark eyes, shaded by long lashes. His full, sensual lips curled into a pout. "You called, Excellency?"

"I must have my medication, Jamil. The chills are upon me."

"Of course, Excellency, I have already prepared your dose."

Jamil picked up the syringe, the heroin winking amber in the morning sun slanting through the shades. He thumped the vein in the crook of the sheik's arm, then inserted the needle.

Moussawi's eyes glowed from unseen light as the drug coursed through his system. A slight shudder, and his body began to relax. The world came back into focus.

Jamil rolled in a serving cart set with orange juice, coffee, hot pita bread and fruits. A single fly buzzed around the fruit bowl. Copies of two Beirut newspapers, *Al Anwar* and *AlKifah Alarabi,* were folded on the side. "Breakfast, Excellency."

"Thank you, Jamil." Moussawi accepted a glass of juice. He paused to smile at the boy before picking up a paper.

News about the summit and Palestinian refugees dominated the headlines. Hundreds of thousands of Palestinian refugees were pouring into Lebanon and Jordan. Pressure was mounting on the oil-producing countries to impose an embargo against the West. Leading clerics called for *jihad* against Israel, America, Europe, Japan, China and Russia. Throughout the Arab world, mobs destroyed all things Western. Businesses were looted, merchandise manufactured in the West burned in the streets. Leaders were powerless to impose order, lest they be perceived as enemies of Islam. Moderate voices like Egyptian President Hassan Fadel and Jordanian Crown Prince Abdel Agha had been drowned out by the favored roar of Islam.

Moussawi's excitement rose. He took up his cane, went to the window, and looked out. Sea breezes from the Mediterranean rustled the curtains. Distant sounds of traffic floated up to his suite high atop the Beirut Hilton as the city prepared for a new day. Beyond the steel and concrete an emerald green sea stretched into a world of infinite possibility.

Yes, a new day, Moussawi thought.

Just as Prince Nasser had predicted, their plan was working. And, Allah be praised, what a beautiful plan it was. They were entering a mercantile war zone. Leaders from the twenty-two Arab countries had gathered in Beirut. While they talked and conspired endlessly, he and Nasser shaped the future.

Moussawi turned from the window. "Another glass of juice would be nice, Jamil."

"Yes, Excellency."

After accepting the juice, Moussawi patted the boy's hand. "You serve me well, Jamil. Now go and prepare us a bath. I have to be at the summit in two hours."

Inside the presidential compound at Camp David, sparks danced amongst the fire's embers, casting the presidential bedroom in an orange glow. Abigail Stewart watched the shifting shadows. Sleep would not come. The nation was experiencing the most aberrant weather conditions in more than a century. Frigid air continued to sweep down from Canada. Crop failures and food shortages had been forecast. People were cold, some dying. Now the oil-producing Arab states threatened an oil embargo. The only good news was that she could now get congressional fast-track approval on her alternative energy program. Highly paid lobbyists, funded by big oil companies, had been able to block government incentives to develop solar, wind, hydroelectric, and hydrogen energy sources. How ironic that the world might soon be free from dependency on fossil fuels because of an oil crisis. It would be a nice triumph to help transform that kind of dream into reality.

The President got out of bed, slipped on her robe, and went to the kitchen. Some hot chocolate might take away the edge. She mixed milk and powdered chocolate together and placed the cup in the microwave. When the timer sounded, she wrapped the cup in a napkin, walked into the den, and switched on CNN.

"It's a surreal scene here at Jenin," the correspondent said into the camera. "The Israeli army has leveled most of the town. Tens of thousands of displaced refugees are marching toward an unknown fate at the Lebanese border."

The camera zoomed in on a broken line of men and women carrying wrapped bundles, many infants hung from their mothers' necks in shawl slings. Carts rattled and donkeys brayed as the line of refugees trudged toward the horizon.

"People that remain in Jenin have an almost catatonic look on their faces," the correspondent said. "They mindlessly step over bodies littering the streets, clinging to what little provisions they can find."

"Thank you, Arturo," the CNN anchor said. "The scene is truly shocking. We will now switch to our affiliate in Beirut, where a representative for the Arab League is about to make an announcement."

The camera focused on the Saudi Foreign Minister, Prince Ibrahim al Zyyad. Standing by his side was the Palestinian president, Abdullah Tartir. Security personnel kept reporters and cameramen at a distance.

Zyyad stared into the camera. "Despite condemnation from the Arab League for the tragic deaths of Undersecretary of State Thornton McIver, Israeli Foreign Minister Benjamin Levy, and EU Ambassador André Madelin, Israeli forces continue to wage a war of aggression and terror against the Palestinian people. Despite offers of cooperation from the Arab League and President Tartir, Israeli forces are systematically murdering and forcing Palestinians out of their homes. Zionists committed these crimes with the support of the United States, the European

Union, Japan, Russia, China and other pro-Western countries. These actions represent more than a war against the Palestinians. They represent a war against all of Islam." The Foreign Minister's jaw tightened. "Today the Arab League unanimously decided to delay retaliatory measures in order to make a final effort for peace. Next week, I leave for Washington, DC, to hold meetings with representatives from the United States, Russia, Japan, China, and the European Union. I pray that Allah, in His infinite wisdom, will guide us down the path to a fair and just peace."

Abigail Stewart finished the last of her hot chocolate, then clicked off the set and walked outside onto the deck. In the moonlight, the cold air held her breath like a silver cloud. Trees cast gnarled shadows within shadows, and stars glittered icily over the white-crusted landscape. Images of a teenage girl riding in the Olympic trials conjured in her mind unexpectedly.

The girl's eyes were wide, filled with light. She felt invincible, immortal, as her horse, Bermuda, sailed over the final jump. Then Bermuda's front hooves hit the ground. A sickening snap, and girl and animal tumbled into darkness…

Abby wrapped her arms around her chest and walked back inside.

Grant picked up his telephone just past four a.m. "Corbet."

"Mr. Corbet, I apologize for waking you at such an hour," President Stewart said.

"Madam President." Grant sat up.

"A delegation from the Arab League will be arriving in Washington next week to discuss ways to avoid an oil embargo and possible war in the Middle East."

"How can I be of help, Madam President?"

"I'm asking you to be a direct participant in those talks."

"Will I be working directly with Mr. Bembry?"

"No," the President said. "I've decided to bypass normal protocol and would like you to report directly to me."

Grant felt his gut knot. "I'm honored by your confidence."

"I'll see that you're fully briefed. Goodnight, Mr. Corbet."

The knot in Grant's gut tightened as he hung up the phone. He stood and walked the cabin, fists clenching and unclenching. Surely the President knew that by asking him to report directly to her, she had put him on a collision course with Axel Bembry.

In Taipei, Ping-yi-Cong clicked off the television, poured two brandies, and handed one to his security advisor, Huang zi-Jen. "Your opinion."

"By standing next to Abdullah Tartir, the Saudi foreign minister sent a message to the West."

"Which is?"

"An oil embargo will be imposed if the upcoming talks in Washington fail to produce results."

Cong swirled his brandy. "The Arab world, and, to a greater extent, all of Islam, has been unwittingly snared in a trap from which there is no escape. Their regimes are precariously balanced. Extinction beckons on either side."

"There is no doubt they face danger from within and without," Huang said. "But what choice do they have except to stand with Tartir? Riots have broken out all over the Middle East. More than a hundred thousand people in Cairo marched on the presidential palace."

"Therein lies a second message." Cong sipped his brandy. "Islamic leaders who side with the West will be swept from power."

"True, but the West has undoubtedly planned for such an eventuality. Their military will be called in before allowing the oil to be cut off."

"A tiger attacking a hare," Cong said. "Yet all might not be as it seems."

Huang looked at the President of Taiwan across his brandy glass. "We have been together many years, my president. I sense hidden meaning to this conversation."

Cong nodded, eyes fixed on his security chief. "I fear many forces are at work here. In due time, the clouds will part and reveal the true color of the sky. Now leave me. I want to study the dossier on Grant Corbet you prepared for me."

Alone in his office, Cong opened the folder. The years had been kind to the DDO. He looked very much like the CIA field agent Cong had dealt with when he was Minister of Development twenty-five years earlier. Light lines on the forehead, a sprinkling of white hair around the temples, but the same strong face. Clear gray eyes, always a mystery to an Asian, stared out of the photo at Cong.

"You have aged well, Grant Corbet."

Cong touched his right ear. The plastic surgeon had performed an excellent reconstruction. A chill traced its way down the president's back. Had it not been for Corbet, he would be dead right now. The young CIA field officer had risked his own life to save him from an assassin sent from the mainland more than two decades ago. The bullet meant for Cong's brain had instead ripped off his ear when Corbet knocked him down.

How curious the ways of heaven, he thought. *The nameless assassin made the journey to meet his ancestors, while I survived to become the president of Taiwan. Joss.*

Cong finished reading the dossier, then walked to the window. His gaze moved across Taipei's skyline, taking in the new construction. Cars, buses, motor scooters, and trucks streamed along the crowded streets. The sight pleased him greatly. Despite being ostracized by most nations, Taiwan had emerged as one of the world's leading economies. But there were powerful forces who wanted the island reunited with mainland China.

Unbelievable!

"So how to use this conflict with the Arabs to benefit my beautiful island," Cong asked himself. He looked at his *wei-qi* board. The Arabs had not announced an oil embargo, merely threatened one. And most of the world needed additional energy because of the weather. A cat and mouse game. Taiwan's president closed his eyes. A dangerous game, indeed, or as the old Chinese saying went: "As dangerous as spurting sand out of the mouth at a shadow."

Cong studied his *wei-qi* board and placed a stone on a lined juncture. No question, he had a powerful card to play in the international game that could possibly prevent reunification with China. Still, there would be great danger if he acted in haste. He would either save or destroy his beloved country.

Am I listening to the siren's song?

Cong remembered Brent Bosworth's mouthed words around the delicate Shirakoyaki fish delicacy that would kill him, as clearly now as when they were spoken almost twenty years ago.

Geological samples indicate a huge repository of sulfur-free oil. Perhaps the last major find of its kind on earth.

Familiar guilt wrapped around Cong's insides. Killing the American geologist had been an unfortunate but necessary act to protect the secret of what lay beneath the Spratly Islands.

Two hundred billion barrels. Maybe more. Natural gas estimates in the hundreds of trillions of cubic feet.

Cong watched the glass-and-steel structures of Taipei glisten in the fading light. At age fifty-six, his Machiavellian climb through the party's ranks had paid off. He had achieved his life goal of becoming president. And, as Taiwan's head of state, he was not about to turn his country over to China. Grounded in that thought, Cong made his decision. If the Washington talks failed, he would take a gamble and contact Grant Corbet.

Five

President Abigail Stewart stared at the White House lawn through bulletproof windows. The sun rose in an incredibly blue sky, bringing brief respite from the cold weather plaguing the nation. Trees swayed in the breeze, their bare branches filled with yellow light. Beyond the fence, traffic streamed along busy streets, while tourists aimed mini-cams and cameras at the most famous residence in the world. Hidden from view were the invisible men and women of the Secret Service, the FBI, and Homeland Security. Thousands of them charged with keeping the nation's capital under the highest alert.

The President's eyes followed a cardinal, a flash of scarlet, as it lighted on the birdfeeder she had personally installed in one of the rose gardens. "What do you think the delegation from the Arab League will be bringing, Frances?"

"Madam President, I'd like to tell you a cohesive plan to avoid economic disaster," Secretary of State Frances Merriman said. "But it could be a roadmap to war if they play the oil card."

Abby watched the cardinal tentatively look around before pecking at the seed log. A second peck, then airborne. She remembered how the assassination of Austrian Archduke Franz

Ferdinand in Sarajevo had ignited World War I. Could history be repeating itself with the downing of the Israeli jet carrying three of the world's most distinguished diplomats? Another act of madness, and once again the world found itself staring into the abyss. Only this time, if war came, the battle would be for the world's oil reserves, not territory.

A mercantile war of greed and power on my watch!

The President felt a chill creep down her back as she turned and took a seat behind her desk. Abby's gaze focused on her Secretary of State. "What if we're being manipulated in some macabre way? What if Tartir's nothing more than a patsy, that the assassinations of McIver, Levy, and Madelin were orchestrated by a splinter group opposed to the peace process?"

"It's the waiting," Frances Merriman said. "Waiting is always the worst part. There are too many *what ifs*."

President Stewart looked at the desk photo of Bermuda, her first horse and the most loved. She sat astride it as a three-year-old, innocent to the ugly ways of the world. "War scares the hell out of me, Frances. I shudder to think we and our allies acted precipitously."

The Secretary of State's voice softened. "These are difficult times, Abby, but it's important to stay the course. Don't waver, or put too much stock in what people like Grant Corbet have to say."

"I've asked him to be a direct participant in the meetings with the Arab League," the President said.

Frances Merriman raised an eyebrow. "That little protocol breach won't sit well with Axel."

"The hell with protocol, I want the best people around me." President Stewart's pen touched a file on her desk. "Zach Holden believes Corbet understands the Middle East better than anyone."

"I'm sure the Deputy Director of Operations is quite competent, Abby, but let's look at what we know." The Secretary of State leaned her chin against interlocked fingers. "It's unlikely Tartir's a patsy. He, more than anyone else, has repeatedly proven to be against the peace process. Since Oslo, every time an agreement acceptable in principle to both sides reached the table for signature, Tartir derailed it. More damning is the money trail. The million dollars paid to the Egyptian pilot's family leads straight to Tartir."

"Sounds logical, Frances, but logic is seldom the driving force behind violent acts. It's self-interest."

"What are you saying, Abby?" The Secretary of State watched Abigail Stewart's violet eyes darken.

"I'm in agreement with what Grant Corbet said at Camp David. Assassinating three high-profile diplomats wasn't in President Tartir's best interest."

"Have the cells been activated?" Nasser asked.

"All is in order. The last of the laptop computers were delivered to Japan early last week."

"Have the *jihadi* been properly instructed?"

"They look and act like ordinary citizens. Each has been trained to blend in." Moussawi rubbed his hands together. "To further ensure security, only cell leaders know how to contact other members."

"Excellent." Prince Nasser poured mint tea. "The troublesome Americans and their allies will soon learn how illusory their safety is."

"*Insha'Allah.*" Moussawi accepted a cup. "They deserve to pay a great price for the sadness they have wrought upon the faithful."

"Fear not, my dear Moussawi. The infidels will suffer great harm at the hands of our *jihadi*. Soon every Muslim will comply with God's orders to kill infidels."

"Still, I worry about our messages being intercepted," Moussawi said. "One mistake and the infidels will descend on us like locusts."

"Your concerns are unwarranted." Nasser folded his hands. "Each cell has been assigned a different code for communication purposes. No two codes are the same. Our computers are equipped with the latest encryption programs." The prince sniffed his tea, his nostrils flaring at the mint aroma, then sipped. "Dedicated fiber-optic lines will transmit outgoing messages to private phone links at my software companies in the United States, Europe, Hong Kong and Japan. Coded messages will then be connected to a secure line, where they can be transmitted without fear of interception. Incoming messages are handled in the same manner, only in reverse."

"You have planned well, my prince," Moussawi said. "When do you plan to send our brave *jihadi* their assignment?"

"After next week's talks have been concluded, I will know more." Nasser leaned back against a pillow and stared out at the desert. "I am accompanying Crown Prince Faisal and Foreign Minister Zyyad to Washington. My understanding is that a reception has been planned at the White House."

Moussawi scowled. "Perhaps you will have the opportunity to meet America's great new leader."

"Never take your opponent lightly," Nasser said. "There is strength behind Abigail Stewart's desert-flower eyes."

"A woman leading the Great Satan." Moussawi finished his tea. "Surely, a jest of Allah."

"Learn from history, my dear Moussawi. Remember Britain's Iron Lady, and what she did to the Argentines when they invaded the Falkland Islands." Nasser refilled their cups. "Actually, I'm looking forward to meeting America's Abby. It will be interesting to get a feel of what kind of woman she is."

The lead Secret Service agent checked the President's

morning appointments when he saw Axel Bembry turn into the hallway. He quietly studied the NSA's approach, his gaze moving from the gray suit pockets to the suede folder he carried. Always paid to be careful, the agent thought, even though anyone close to the presidential office had to pass through seen and unseen metal detectors.

"Is the President in?" Bembry asked.

"JUMPER will be down shortly, sir."

The President arrived several minutes later, followed by her personal bodyguard, Lindsey Caspare.

"Come in, Axel," the President said.

Behind closed doors, Abigail Stewart took a seat behind her desk. "Coffee?"

The NSA laid his folder on the desk. "Please."

"What's your read on an oil embargo?"

Bembry stirred a packet of Equal into his coffee. "I've received assurances from those close to Crown Prince Faisal that an embargo is a last option."

The President glanced out the window. Morning fog covered the White House lawn, and lightning shimmered in dark clouds. The bird feeder was deserted. A few large drops of icy rain pelted against the glass. "War will come if they impose an embargo."

The NSA chuckled. "I seriously doubt that will happen. They have nothing to gain and everything to lose."

"I've asked Grant Corbet to sit in on the Arab League meetings."

Bembry's cup stopped its delicate arc. "Corbet?"

"That's right. He's friendly with the Israelis, and familiar with Middle East politics. He's got the kind of knowledge we'll need when we sit down to talk."

"With all due respect, Madam President, I think you should reconsider. We need unity in these meetings, and Corbet's not known as a team player." The NSA set his cup down. "Frankly, on several occasions, he's gone over the top."

"The only people I'm aware of coming down on Mr. Corbet are you and your predecessor, Bert Lybrand." Abigail Stewart stared across the desk. "If memory serves, Lybrand's the one who got fired."

Bembry went cold. "Madam President—".

"Not now, Axel." The President held up a hand. "There's too much at stake to be arguing about turf. Corbet will be reporting directly to me. I expect your full cooperation."

In Tel Aviv, Major General Ira Bettleman looked up when his deputy, Jacob Eisenberg, walked in. The Mossad director was a powerfully built man with white hair, a broken nose, and dark, unreadable eyes. "Well?"

Jacob took a seat across from his boss and opened a folder stamped *Top Secret* in red. The file codename was ZOR, the Hebrew word for Tyre. He removed several photos and slid them across the desk. "Our operative in Tyre got these shots of Sheik Moussawi getting off a Cessna Citation II yesterday. The young man beside him is his boychick, Jamil."

Bettleman grunted. "Who does the jet belong to?"

"We're checking the plane's registration numbers. It's a custom job. The interior resembles something out of *Arabian Nights.*"

"Any leads on who ordered the plane?"

"Two years ago, Opal Aviation out of Brisbane placed the order, then sold it to a man using the name Abdul Hamadi. He paid cash."

The Mossad chief leaned back in his chair, eyes on the ceiling. "It will be interesting to learn who Sheik Moussawi's wealthy friend or patron is."

"Our operative got a look at the flight plan." Jacob lit a cigarette and exhaled. "The plane took off from Jeddah."

"That's a start," Bettleman said. "Where are we on the MASD

project? I'd like to get one or two inside Moussawi's headquarters. The sheik has been a little too quiet these past months for my liking."

"Dr. Levine told me the Miniature Aerial Surveillance Devices have performed well under laboratory conditions," Jacob said. "He wants another month before he'll sign off on field testing."

"See if you can nudge the good doctor along." The Mossad chief went to the bar and poured two coffees. "I agree with Grant Corbet. This Tartir mess smells. Something is dirty, but so far hasn't raised its ugly head."

"There's always a rotten corpse to be found in the Middle East," Jacob said. "Only this time the rest of the world is supporting us."

"Lip service," Bettleman said. He blew on the rim of his cup and sipped. "They don't have a half billion madmen surrounding them."

In Riyadh, Prince Nasser watched the servant pour brandy for Saudi Crown Prince Faisal and his foreign minister, Prince Ibrahim al Zyyad. It amused him to see how easily the tenets of Islam were ignored by members of the royal family. Instead of piously following the word of the Prophet, most royals turned into whoremongers, gamblers and drunkards when visiting Western playgrounds outside the Kingdom. For them, the minaret's call to prayer had been reduced to little more than a means of staying in power.

Well, Nasser thought, all things under Allah's universe were subject to change. The apostates would soon be drinking their brandies in hell.

"The West will try to break our coalition in Washington," Faisal said. "The Arab League delegates publicly stand as one behind our resolution. It's the private meetings that bother me.

How they will act behind closed doors, only Allah knows."

"They will have a hard time making mischief." Zyyad sipped his brandy as sunlight caught its dancing gold fires. "The heads of all oil-producing states, including Indonesia and Nigeria, have signed the resolution calling for an oil embargo if the Palestinian genocide is not stopped."

"Our Muslim brothers have made promises before." Nasser folded his hands. "Their vows have a way of vanishing in a desert wind when gold is offered."

"Riots are becoming increasingly unruly throughout the region," Faisal said. "Mullahs are further inflaming the people with their calls for *jihad*. A sudden shift in the wind, and the Royal House could fall. We face dangers from our own people on one side, an infidel invasion from the other."

Faisal and Zyyad exchanged a glance. Nasser sipped his tea, warmed by the fear he saw sparkling in their eyes. "Allah may have provided a path through this Western treachery."

The crown prince's and foreign minister's heads turned.

"We have no alternative but to impose an embargo if the Palestinian problem is not favorably resolved," Nasser said. "If we fail to act together on this matter, regimes throughout the region will fall."

"Just because there is a declaration threatening an embargo does not mean we can enforce one." Crown Prince Faisal drained his brandy. "If the West declares war, we risk annihilation."

"War is not an idle threat," Zyyad said. "I have it from the highest authority there will be a massive military response if an embargo is imposed. Armies around the world are on high alert."

"The West will try and limit our options," Nasser said. "They will want us to delay imposing an embargo, and increase production to ease their energy shortfall created by the unseasonably cold weather."

"We could never agree to such conditions," Faisal said. "Such a strategy would topple the Royal House. The people would see us rewarding the Palestinian oppressors and rise up."

Zyyad refilled his and Faisal's brandy snifters. "You mentioned a possible path provided by Allah, Prince Nasser. Tell us about it."

"The infidels do not care about Islam, or the Arab people. They care about oil." Nasser lit a Turkish cigarette. "I suggest letting our enemies know in the strongest terms that the Prophet's sacred lands will be transformed into an inferno if they attempt to make an invasion."

Faisal set his brandy glass snifter down. "Destroy the oil fields?"

"I recommend demolition experts be immediately dispatched throughout the region to prepare the sites," Nasser said. "Then, if the infidels come, let them feel the fire of the Prophet's sword."

"What if the other states refuse to go along?"

"Highness, I fear the oil-producing states are left with little choice. Cooperate with infidels and face insurrection at home, initiate an oil embargo and face a war we cannot win."

Zyyad pulled on his goatee. "Perhaps Prince Nasser sees a golden thread in Allah's path."

Nasser cleared his throat. "Highness, the West is soft, and dependent on the energy we supply. Their Zionist allegiances will shift if they are convinced the oil fields would be destroyed."

"How can we convince them of our resolve?" Faisal asked.

"I suggest we give them a demonstration." Nasser's eyes crinkled. "It's the kind of demonstration that will show our people's resolve, while convincing the infidels of the futility of an armed attack. What I have in mind is a kind of spectacular damage control."

"You wanted to see me?" Grant asked.

Axel Bembry picked up his gold pen, twirled it slowly through his fingers then aimed it at the DDO. "A delegation from the Arab League will be arriving in three days to try and save their collective asses."

Grant took a seat and sipped coffee from a Styrofoam cup. He watched the NSA lean back in his chair, the point of the pen moving toward the ceiling. On the corner of Bembry's desk sat the *red phone,* his direct line to the President. Expensive artwork and a gallery of framed photographs documenting meetings with foreign dignitaries, senators, and prime ministers hung from paneled walls. Grant kept his face neutral, but the trappings of pomp drew his disdain. A glorified jackass.

"Side talks will be held with key oil-producing states," Bembry said. "We want to stave off a possible embargo. I'm confident the Saudis will privately support our actions. I've maintained close ties with Crown Prince Faisal, Foreign Minister Zyyad, and other members of the royal family." A wisp of a smile touched Bembry's lips. "The other oil producing states should fall in line once the Saudis are on board." Soft fingers turned the gold pen. "My concern, along with that of the President, is the position the more hard-line regimes will take."

"The Muslim world is in an uproar," Grant said. "I wouldn't count on much support from the Saudis or any other Islamic state."

"Sticking to your idea of appeasement, eh, Corbet? Still believe Tartir's an innocent victim?" Bembry flipped open a file. "I don't know if you recall, but our paths have crossed before."

Grant set his cup down. "I remember."

"You blew an operation during my term as ambassador to Saudi Arabia. It says here you screwed up another operation in Nabulus. You shot and killed a Palestinian leader on an unauthorized raid with the Mossad." The NSA stared at Grant, his eyes holding an undefined light. "You made a martyr out of Ali Naji."

"Read further and you'll see that Naji had kidnapped one of our agents," Grant said. "I went in with the Israelis to get him out."

"But you failed." Bembry tossed a photo across the table. "Take a look. I count eight bullet-riddled bodies. One of them belongs to the agent you attempted to rescue."

"What are you implying, Bembry?"

"Merely making a suggestion," Bembry said. "President Stewart's administration is committed to a strategy that our allies, for once, are in total agreement with." The NSA put down his pen and folded his hands. "Face it, Corbet. You've fucked up more than once. I'd suggest keeping your lone wolf mentality about Tartir's innocence and what Muslims will or won't do to yourself. It doesn't fit."

"Don't talk to me about fucking up." Red-faced, Grant stood and leaned over the desk. "Thirty American soldiers died because a shipment of explosives weren't intercepted in Riyadh. Want to know why? You took it upon yourself to whisper into Zyyad's ear, one of the men you've maintained a close relationship with. His goons got wind of it and changed the delivery location."

Bembry glared at Grant. "We needed to keep the Saudis apprised."

"Bullshit! If you'd kept your nose out of company business, those thirty American soldiers would be walking around today."

"You've gone too far, Corbet." Bembry's face flamed. "I'll see you—"

The NSA's words died in the air as Grant walked out.

Gerhard Esch arrived at his Trident Holdings office early the next morning. The traders and staff would not arrive for another hour. At the bar, he prepared a double espresso, then went to his desk. He turned to the window and stared at the barges, dark shapes in the mist covering the Hudson River. The moon, a silver glow behind the clouds, slowly disappeared as the gray dawn broke hard and cold. Distant horns sounded as the city began to come to life.

Putting down his espresso, Esch clicked on his computer. He checked the latest currency and precious metal prices from Tokyo. Excellent! The dollar, euro, and yen continued to spiral down. Precious metal and oil futures continued to move sharply upward. HARPIE was performing just like his model had predicted. Five months had passed since he'd purchased ten billion dollars in futures contracts for Nasser. Counting gains leveraged at thirty to one, the prince now controlled more than four hundred billion dollars in currency and bullion contracts.

By following Prince Nasser's lead, Esch now controlled over one billion dollars of similar contracts in his personal account. He smiled thinly as his gaze moved around the plush surroundings of his New York City penthouse suite. Not bad for the son of a German banker and Arab restaurant executive.

Esch finished his espresso, typed in a password, and brought up a hidden icon. He entered the necessary code words to access HARPIE's trading program and began rolling Prince Nasser's contracts.

"It's the hottest ticket in town." Zach Holden slid the envelope across his desk to Grant. "Reception will be held in the Blue Room at the White House. An international gathering of bigwigs! All the stops will be pulled out."

Grant opened the envelope and stared at the invitation, personally signed by the President of the United States. He slipped it inside his coat pocket and went to the coffee bar.

"You look tense," Zach said. "Anything you want to talk about?"

"Bembry and I had words." Grant sat across from his boss. "I'm sure I haven't heard the end of it."

"I wouldn't waste a lot of thought on him. Bembry's feeling threatened because the President wants you in on the Arab League meetings. You probably screwed him up on getting another picture for his wall." Zach filled his pipe, applied fire, and exhaled. "His reaction was predictable. The NSA's a political animal, a Washington insider with little substance. He waves his ambassadorship to Saudi Arabia as credentials. He'd be the first to take credit when a situation goes right, and the first to point fingers when it goes wrong."

Grant sipped coffee without tasting it. "He dug up the Ali Naji dirt, and accused me of blowing an op in Saudi Arabia when he was ambassador."

"Words to enhance his position," Zach said. "Those skeletons aren't going to rise up and bite you. Bembry blew your cover in Saudi Arabia, and thirty American soldiers died."

"He's hiding behind the Saudis' right to know."

"Listen to me, Grant. I've worked with three presidents and a half-dozen NSA's. Some were good, some bad." Zach relit his pipe. "The lady in the White House doesn't sacrifice principle for political expediency. Bembry's out of his depth, and she knows it. That's why you're sitting in."

Six

Grant mixed a martini, then walked to the window in front of his condominium. The full moon looked like a sand dollar in a sky glittering with stars. In the distance, he saw the lights from the White House. An image of President Abigail Stewart formed in his mind. He could see every curve of her face, every fleck of violet in her eyes. Tomorrow afternoon, he would privately brief her about the Middle East.

"Abby."

What was America's first female President thinking inside the world's most famous residence? Energy shortages, crop failures, war in the Middle East, terrorist attacks at home, budget deficits were just a few of the problems weighing on her shoulders.

Grant sipped his martini, a now-familiar ache forming in his stomach. *Such lovely shoulders she had. Strong enough to bear the burdens of us all.*

Washington lights glittered over his gossamer reflection. Grant finished his martini, then went into the study and logged onto the Internet.

"You've got mail."

Grant set his drink down and clicked on Jenny's screen name.

Hi Daddy:

The new furniture for Harlin's room arrived and looks great. Now I can only hope he won't destroy it. LOL When are you going to make a pilgrimage to Houston and see your grandson? He'll be grown before you know it. Some handsome man I know gave him his gray eyes. I've attached a few recent pictures. I miss you.

Love,

Jenny

xoxo

Grant stared at nothing. Twenty years in the killing fields of the Far and Middle East had cost him dearly. Losing a wife and a chance to watch Jenny grow up had been a steep price to pay. And what did he have to show for it? Nothing! Nada! Oh, he'd won a few victories, but in the end nothing had changed. The battleground known as the Middle East would forever remain an endless river of grief.

Grant clicked on Jenny's attachment and looked at the smiling face of his grandson.

The next morning, Grant flew with Vulcan Systems vice president Andrew Stranahan in a company helicopter to Vulcan's UAV (unmanned aerial vehicle) testing facilities near Reston, Virginia.

"You think Vulcan has the goods this time around with the Thunderbolt?" Grant asked.

"TBOLT tests have been impressive," Stranahan said. "With a noise level of only fifteen to twenty decibels, we can slip into all sorts of interesting places."

Grant slipped off his seat belt. "Amazing, my daughter's cat purrs louder than that."

Vulcan's CEO, Zil Poloski, waited outside the landing ramp beside a company limousine.

"Welcome to Vulcan, Grant," Poloski said. "I think you'll

appreciate our latest gadget."

Grant buttoned his overcoat. "I've heard good things from Andy."

"Preliminary results have been quite extraordinary," Poloski said.

Grant idly watched a skein of geese fly overhead, dark shadows against a gray sky. "Let's take a look at what you've got, Zil," he said.

The three men settled around a conference table. Behind the glass wall they could see the technicians at their workstations.

"We'll be able to watch the test from here," Stranahan said. He opened his briefcase and passed a folder to Grant marked TBOLT Project, Top Secret in red. "You'll want to review the final specs before we begin."

Grant whistled. "Battery powered. No wonder it's so quiet."

"Quiet, fast and lethal," Stranahan said.

"A nightmare for the bad guys, now that we can target the bin Ladens of the world," Poloski said. "If you're ready, I suggest we begin the test."

One of the technicians clicked on the plasma monitors in the overhead projection room. A moment later TBOLT was airborne.

"Looks like a miniature B-2." Grant's gaze moved to the digital readouts. "Zero to one hundred fifty mph in six seconds, fifteen-inch wingspan. Impressive."

The lead technician flipped a switch, and the drone's forward camera focused on a forest located on the southern sector of Vulcan's testing grounds.

"TBOLT is almost impossible to detect until it's too late," Stranahan said. "You'll see what I mean in a minute."

The drone slowed, then hovered. Remote rear and side cameras were activated, bringing up a three-hundred-sixty-degree image on the monitors. A side camera zoomed in on a mannequin one hundred fifty yards east. Telescoping crosshairs locked onto the target. A moment later, the mannequin's head disintegrated.

"Christ," Grant said. "A near-silent hit."

"Thirty-two caliber, triple charged, titanium hard, ceramic bullet. Range one hundred seventy-five yards without a drop." Stranahan chuckled. "No place to hide."

TBOLT moved into the forest, gliding silently through the trees. Sensors picked up a remote-controlled Nissan on a dirt road moving at forty miles per hour. The drone swooped down and silently attached itself to the roof just as the car moved into a clearing. A hundred mannequins, dressed like Muslim fighters, were arranged in a semi-circle. The Nissan pulled into the center of the mannequins and exploded into a giant fireball. When the smoke cleared, the one hundred mannequins had been obliterated.

Grant leaned back in his chair. "Whoa."

Prince Abdul bin Suleiman Nasser looked through the wall of glass in the sunroom of his estate in the heart of Virginia horse country. Snow covered the usually green rolling hills. Yet, despite the cold weather, the land appeared soft with its scenic winding roads, forests and quaint towns. So unlike the craggy mountains of rock and endless stretches of desert that made up the Arabian Peninsula. The prince thought about the many nights he had sat alone in the desert. The vault of heaven would open with a million stars illuminating Allah's creation. Those nights had tempered his soul and taught him the true meaning of faith. Nothing but wind, sand, and the braying of his camel separated him from his God.

Nasser's eyes moved to his stables, where a trainer exercised one of his many Arabian stallions. Such magnificent animals! He remembered the words of the Prophet. *Horse you have no equal. You fly without wings, and conquer without swords.* Nasser closed his eyes and saw Mohammed leading his army across the desert atop his legendary steed, el-Buraq, destroying the enemies of Islam. Sunlight glinted off scimitars as the holy warriors of God swung honed blades over their heads. Dust billowed beneath their horses' thundering hooves, and the indomitable green banners of Islam blew in the wind.

Then the horse had been a proud weapon of war, not an indulgence for the rich. Anger twisted Nasser's gut. The passage of time and technology had destroyed a proud way of life. Soon that would change. The prince closed his eyes. With Allah's blessing, he would resurrect that which once was.

"Highness, Lawrence Escope has arrived."

Nasser turned to his bodyguard, Yousef. "Show him in. We will take lunch here in the sunroom."

Lawrence Escope had been the consummate Washington insider for a number of years. Now, the former Nevada senator used his many contacts as a lobbyist for Nasser's holding company, Alhannah. He set his briefcase down and shook hands with Nasser. "Highness, it's been too long since you've been stateside."

"Have a seat, Lawrence. Lunch will be served shortly." The prince began preparing his water pipe, a gift from his father. He studied the decorative brass joints, noting they needed polishing. "Public opinion is running against Arabs."

Escope looked out the window at the stables below. "Public opinion has its own particular ebb and flow. What's important now is maintaining your friendships in Washington."

"And if there is an oil embargo?"

"An embargo could have serious consequences, Highness,"

Escope said. "I strongly advise against such action."

"I have little say in Arab League decisions." Nasser drew on the pipe. "My concerns are about possible punitive actions against Alhannah Holdings in the event of war."

"Money is the great equalizer in Washington. I suggest we begin greasing a few palms."

Nasser's black eyes turned on the lobbyist. "I pay you well to promote Arab/American cooperation. It is your responsibility to see that Alhannah is protected."

Escope felt chilled by Nasser's gaze. "I'll set up a meeting with Axel Bembry after tomorrow's reception. He's close to the President's ear. More importantly, he's got political ambitions of his own."

The prince rotated the pipe stem between his thumb and forefinger. "Whatever we arrange in the way of contributions must not be linked to me, or Alhannah."

"I understand, Highness." Escope turned a palm up. "There are ways. Leave everything to me."

"Well?" Zach Holden turned away from his computer when Grant walked in.

"God help us if the wrong people ever get their hands on TBOLT." Grant handed his boss a copy of the specifications. "I watched it silently hover, then take out a target one hundred fifty yards away. Next it glided through a thick forest, attached itself to a moving vehicle, and obliterated a hundred look-alike *Mujahudeen* mannequins."

Zach filled his pipe and struck a match, his gaze never leaving the sheet. "For a device with just a fifteen inch wingspan, it's a lethal little bastard."

"TBOLT can stay airborne forty-eight hours and reach speeds up to two hundred twenty-five miles per hour," Grant said. "It can be launched independently, from a plane, missile or long-range UAV."

"That makes it operational anywhere in the world." Zach exhaled a stream of smoke. "It only weighs fifteen pounds. What happens if there's a malfunction and a bad guy picks it up?"

"TBOLT's one plaything best left alone." Grant chuckled. "Vulcan developed a highly charged plastic bonded explosive designed to detonate in the event of malfunction. If the mechanism fails, there's a second failsafe. Anyone attempting to tamper with the internal parts will trigger the explosive."

"I'm not so sure I like what TBOLT and its highly charged PBX stands for," Zach said. "I can only imagine how invasive this new technology will become. I still cling to the notion that men in the field are an intelligence agency's best assets."

"The rules of the game have changed," Grant said. "Nine-eleven ushered in a new era. Any fanatic with a gun, basic chemistry knowledge, or a willingness to die can become a player."

Zach leaned back and drew on his pipe. "Maybe it's time for me to get the hell out of this business."

"You've been at it too long to quit now, boss." Grant smiled at his mentor. "I better get going."

"Meeting with the President?"

"Yep. I'm nervous as hell."

"Don't let those eyes get to you." Zach went back to reading the report on TBOLT. "See you tonight."

Lindsey Caspare was stationed in front of the President's office when Grant arrived. "Good afternoon, Mr. Corbet. JUMPER is expecting you."

Behind the closed door, Grant came to attention.

The President, seated behind her desk, closed a folder and looked up.

"Good morning, Madam President."

"Good morning, Mr. Corbet." Abigail Stewart stood and gestured to the seating area. A tray of coffee, fruit salad, and croissant sandwiches sat on the table.

The President picked up a croissant filled with ham and cheese. "Help yourself. The White House pastry chef has quite a reputation."

Their eyes briefly met. A tremor ran through Grant's hand as he poured two cups of coffee.

"Nervous?" The President smiled.

"Scared to death," Grant said. "I'm a little out of my element being alone with the President of the United States."

Abigail Stewart's laugh came as easily as the smile. Then her face turned serious. She placed her hand over his. "I'm afraid too, Grant. The kind of fear I'm living with is well beyond my imagination."

Grant stared across the table. The warm touch of her hand lingered. "I don't envy your position, Madam President."

"Let's dispense with the Mr. Corbet and Madam President, shall we? You're my personal advisor. In private, I'd prefer you to call me Abby. We'll get a lot more accomplished keeping our meetings informal."

Grant set his cup down. "I'd like that, Abby."

"Good, I'm glad that's out of the way," the President said. "All the players are in town. Tonight's reception is designed to ease tensions. The real work begins tomorrow around the negotiating table."

"Where would you like to begin?"

"You've worked the field in Asia, and more recently, the Middle East. Tell me about the Arabs. I want to know what kind of people we're dealing with. What are your expectations?"

Grant's gaze moved from his hands to the violet eyes. "We're dealing with a strange duality. Arabs love our freedoms, but despise our morals and defense of Israel. They hate the corruption and cruelty of their leaders, but will defend men like Abdullah Tartir to the death."

"Defend dictators who won't give them the freedoms they covet?" The President shook her head. "You'd think they'd want something better for their children."

"Basically, they're angry people who feel humiliated," Grant said. "Arab societies are in a dismal state. To foster religious correctness, knowledge is stifled by entrenched social, institutional, economic, and political impediments. This is further complicated by authoritarian modes of child rearing that suppress curiosity and initiative. Most women are illiterate, and the media is biased. Consequently, the majority of Muslims have been left out on scientific progress and political reform. What little educational system they have left is stagnant. As for my expectations, I don't have any."

"Pity how far they've fallen." The President picked up her ham and cheese. "Arabs and Islam enjoyed a golden age during Europe's Dark Ages."

"Then there was an obsession with philosophy and science," Grant said. He watched Abby chew thoughtfully, then dab her mouth with a napkin. "Arabs invented the paper mill that launched the publishing industry. Contrast that with today. In one year, Spain translates more books than the total of all Arab nations combined for the past fifty years."

"You think they'll impose an oil embargo and risk war with the West?"

"It's certainly a possibility. Most Arabs have short fuses. Nothing will ignite them faster than armies of infidels attacking Islam's sacred soil." Grant hesitated. "My bet is the fields will be destroyed if Arab lands are invaded."

"That's a bit of a leap, isn't it?" the President said. "Such an act would mean economic ruin."

"Except for a few cruel leaders, Arabs have no love for the modern world. Most yearn for yesteryear, a time when Bedouin tribes lived beneath the stars and roamed the desert taking what they wanted." Grant crossed his legs. "In the Western sense, Arabs understand little about love, but they know a great deal about hate. They're a patient lot with long memories. Hatred of Jews and infidels is passed from one generation to the next through schools and stories."

"Their schools are abominations that poison young minds." The President selected some fruit salad. "What about the stories?"

"They're a way of life in the Arab world. Some people call it 'getting sand under their feet.' Endless repetition of these tales is how common people learn about great Arab civilizations of the past." Grant smiled grimly. "Storytellers generally exaggerate actual events to fit Arab ideals of bravery. The stories fuel fierce nationalism, and a desire to return to the past."

The President spooned her fruit salad. "Whatever happened to truth and reason?"

"In the Middle East, those virtues have been supplanted by rage," Grant said. "Jews have become surrogates for Arab hatred of one another. By building the modern state of Israel out of a desert, the Israelis exposed Arabs as savage, tribal people, ruled by a religion that condemns human achievement. The Arabs were humiliated. For them, it is the ultimate punishment because it strips away their delusions of grandeur."

The President stared at Grant. "You really think there's a possibility they will destroy the oil fields rather than avoid war with the West?"

"Given current conditions, that's how I see it unfolding," Grant said.

"There're people in my cabinet who would disagree with your assessment."

"I hope they're right." Grant watched a shadow pass over the President's face. "Like I said, Abby, we're dealing with a mad society. They're multiplying, in terrible poverty, at an alarming rate. Young Muslims increasingly see the United States and Israel as one and the same enemy. Millions of ignorant, angry men armed with guns and plastique, their heads filled with perverted religious zeal, is a recipe for global disaster."

Abigail Stewart's eyes focused on nothing. "Looks like the challenge for the United States will be finding a way to modify the recipe with more palatable ingredients."

Grant nodded.

"You haven't eaten anything, Grant."

"Too nervous, I suppose."

President Stewart wordlessly poured him more coffee.

Seven

President Abigail Stewart looked into the full-length mirror in her dressing room. She turned from side to side. Her reflection stared back, not unkindly. She wore a long, black dinner gown and beaded top. Her jewelry consisted of South Sea pearl earrings, a single strand of ten-millimeter Mikimoto pearls, and an emerald-cut diamond dinner ring.

Despite her calm façade, Abby felt the weight of building pressure. The most important night of her presidency, and she could not shake a growing dread over the way world events were unfolding. More troubling, she had lost confidence in a number of her security advisors concerning international policy. No question, most members of her inner circle were well-intentioned. The problem, she realized, was they had been trained to deal one-on-one with state leaders. But all the diplomatic training in the world could not have prepared them to deal with the mad society Grant Corbet had described earlier that afternoon. Her thoughts momentarily stayed on him, reflecting on his easy acceptance of his fears, while she knew from his file of his unwavering courage.

After their earlier talk, the clarity of purpose with which she and other world leaders viewed the downing of the Israeli jet had blurred. Throughout her political career, she had always sought cause and effect patterns when making important decisions. What if Abdullah Tartir wasn't responsible for the assassination of three of the world's most respected diplomats? Grant Corbet didn't believe the Palestinian president to be that foolhardy.

"If not Tartir, who?" Abby looked at her reflection, the contoured gown, pearls, and ring, but there was no answer offered. She watched her eyes darken, and wondered if Grant's distinctive gray eyes mirrored his thoughts as well. Distinctive eyes were both a blessing and a burden.

Beyond the window, snow and ice patches glowed whitely beneath the moon on the White House lawn. A chill ran down Abby's spine. She wrapped her arms around her chest, her thoughts turning to Grant Corbet. More and more he was gaining her trust. He would be at tonight's reception.

Axel Bembry watched Grant walk into the Blue Room. Familiar anger pricked his skin. He pulled at his white tie and wing collar.

"What's the matter?" Lawrence Escope's gaze followed Bembry's. "You look ready to fight."

"Corbet's been stepping on my turf," Bembry said. "The President has this bizarre notion he's an expert on the Middle East."

"Wasn't he station chief in Israel before becoming Deputy Director of Operations? That should give him some credibility."

"He blew two operations." Bembry's eyes followed Grant through the crowd. "One of them during the time I served as ambassador to Saudi Arabia."

Escope sipped his martini. "We've been friends for years, Axel, so what I'm about to tell you is strictly between us."

Bembry glanced at the lobbyist without replying.

"The Arab League is prepared to announce an oil embargo if the Israelis are not called off and substantial reparations paid to the Palestinians."

"I thought you had assurances that Saudi Arabia wouldn't support such a move."

"The situation in the Middle East has changed," Escope said. "Leaders are worried about being overthrown if they are perceived as siding with the West."

Bembry turned to Escope, his voice low. "For Christ sake, don't they know there will be war if they initiate an embargo?"

"A lot can happen between now and the end of the negotiations." Escope patted Bembry's arm. "We have a friend in Prince Nasser. He's close to Crown Prince Faisal and generous with his political contributions."

Bembry nodded. "Where do the prince's interests lie?"

"Prince Nasser has substantial investments throughout the U.S., Canada, Europe, and Asia. He's concerned his holding company, Alhannah, will become embroiled in a political struggle that he opposes."

"I recall he made a sizable donation to New York City after 9-11." Bembry's gaze drifted to the Saudi delegation at the far end of the room. "Let's see how the negotiations go. Depending on how things play out, I might be interested in learning a little more about this Prince Nasser."

"Ladies and gentlemen, the President of the United States."

All heads turned, the buzz of hushed conversation turned to silence. Waiters carrying champagne and hors-d'oeuvres moved against the walls. Then the doors to the Blue Room opened, and President Abigail Stewart walked in.

Grant's expression did not change as he watched the President, but his heart rate picked up a beat at the sight of her.

She moved confidently, smiling and nodding, stopping to shake a hand here or there. Her image, blurred by backlights, made her appear as if she had been sprinkled with silver dust. She continued down the aisle, and then she was next to Grant.

Abby put a hand on his shoulder and leaned over. "You look pretty dashing for a spook, Grant Corbet."

As Grant watched the President walk away, he saw Axel Bembry glaring at him from the far side of the room.

Prince Nasser, resplendent in a shimmering white *bisht* over a white *dishdasha,* caught the exchange. His head cover, also shimmering white, was topped with an old-style Saudi *agal* made of gold. He turned to Lawrence Escope. "Who's the man the President just spoke with?"

"Grant Corbet, CIA Deputy Director of Operations. He's one of the President's advisors on Middle East affairs during the negotiations. Some people say he's a loose cannon, Highness. He used to be station chief in Tel Aviv."

"Ah." Nasser's gaze followed Grant. "I've heard of him. He's the man who tracked Basha."

Escope glanced at Axel Bembry, who was speaking to Secretary of State Frances Merriman and the Chinese foreign minister. Moments earlier, he'd seen the flash of fury that passed over the NSA's face when the President stopped to speak with Grant. "I'll start working the crowd, Highness," Escope said. "I want to make sure Alhannah's donations are producing the right friends for us."

Nasser touched Escope's arm. "And the meeting with Axel Bembry?"

"Taken care of," Escope said. "I'll be seeing him within the week."

"Fine. Now I suggest you go and see who our friends are."

The prince watched Escope drift into the crowd before shifting his gaze to Grant Corbet. The DDO was talking to FBI Director Sean O'Dell. *A loose cannon, maybe, but nonetheless formidable.* Nasser filed the thought away before going to join Crown Prince Faisal and Foreign Minister Zyyad.

Nasser accepted a glass of mineral water from a passing waiter, idly listening to Zyyad chat with the Arab League's ambassador. He saw President Abigail Stewart and Secretary of State Frances Merriman stop and exchange a few words with Grant Corbet and Sean O'Dell.

Interesting.

A presidential smile for Corbet as she walked away.

The prince sipped his mineral water. All around him the world's power brokers mixed, mingled, smiled, and toasted each other. The air, redolent with scents of expensive perfume and aftershave, was filled with sounds of hushed conversation and the clink of expensive crystal.

Washington in all its splendor, Nasser thought. Friends and enemies gathered together to see how they could enrich themselves at the expense of another.

Negotiations began the next morning. While heads of state from Arab countries were scheduled for private meetings with the President at the White House, the diplomatic delegation, headed by Secretary of State Frances Merriman, arrived at the Saudi Embassy at nine a.m. After formalities were observed, the delegation was ushered inside.

"Welcome to our embassy," the Saudi attaché said. "Please come this way, I'm sure you will find our facilities adequate."

Grant walked with the delegation behind Frances Merriman into the immense conference room. Waiters had set up a refreshment island of coffee, tea, water, and various juices.

"Shall we begin?" the Secretary of State said.

"Of course. Saudi Foreign Minister Prince Ibrahim al Zyyad gestured to the long conference table.

The Western delegation took their places behind nameplates on one side of the table, representatives of the Arab League on the other.

Frances Merriman looked across at the Saudi foreign minister. "The Coalition is gravely concerned about developments in the Middle East."

Grant focused on his notes, knowing from past experience that *gravely concerned* introduced the possibility of military action into the dialogue.

"The world economy will be jeopardized if the oil-producing states follow through with their threats of an oil embargo. Such an act would result in serious consequences."

Zyyad tapped a forefinger against his lips. "We do not wish to see relations with our Western friends damaged. As we have repeatedly stated, the crisis in which we find ourselves can be resolved by restoring dignity to the Palestinian people."

"Turn the leadership of the Palestinian Authority over to a war crimes tribunal," British Foreign Minister Harold Dickens said. "After that condition has been met, talks can begin about establishing a Palestinian homeland."

"The downing of the Israeli jet took place over Alexandria," Zyyad replied. "The Egyptian government has the matter under investigation."

"This is not an Egyptian matter." Frances Merriman sipped her water. "The leadership of the Palestinian Authority committed an act of war against the civilized world by deliberately shooting down an Israeli jet carrying peace delegations from the United States, the European Union, and Israel."

"The act was committed in Egypt. Proving the guilt or innocence of President Tartir is clearly an Egyptian matter."

Grant listened to the SecState and ministers from the British, French, German, and Russian delegations banter with Arab League representatives for the next two hours with neither side changing position. Then it was time for a break.

At the coffee bar, Grant had a sinking feeling about the outcome of the talks. Both sides were trapped and could not for political reasons alter their positions. He accepted a cup of thick Arabian coffee from a liveried waiter. The young man's eyes, a little too quick, marked him for Grant as a security agent.

"Ah, Mr. Corbet, I'm glad to see you are participating in the negotiations."

Grant turned and stared into the black marble eyes of Prince Nasser. For a moment, the two men appraised one another.

"Thank you," Grant said.

"Allow me to introduce myself," the prince said. "I am Prince Abdul bin Suleiman Nasser."

"I recognize you from media photos," Grant said. "You made a generous donation to the city of New York after 9-11."

Nasser waved a casual hand. "The least I could do. I have many business interests in the United States and consider your country a second home. Personally, I felt violated by the attacks on the Twin Towers and Pentagon."

"Most of the world has been violated by recent events." Grant stole a glance at Axel Bembry speaking with Prince Zyyad. "It's a pity that the actions of a few affect the lives of many."

"It has always been so," Nasser said. "Fanatics and despots have no geographical boundaries. Many have left their mark in my region of the world. They wait like hyenas, always ready to slip in during the night and feed off the helpless."

Grant looked at Nasser. "Your negotiators aren't giving us much to work with. Intractable positions will lead to a break in relations."

"What did you think our position would be?" Nasser stroked his goatee. "Millions of people have taken to the streets. Governments will be toppled if the Arab League is seen as a puppet of the West."

"An oil embargo will lead to war," Grant said. "The same regimes will be replaced as a result."

"Ah." The prince touched the side of his nose. "You in the West fail to recognize that the key to the Middle East is religion, not oil. Restore Palestinian dignity, and there will be talk of more pleasant matters." Nasser looked beyond Grant. "People in the streets are not listening to your threats of war. They believe Allah will protect them."

Grant watched the corners of Nasser's mouth curl into a semblance of a smile, but his eyes said something else. "Perhaps the negotiations will turn out that such a theory won't have to be tested," he said.

Nasser bowed slightly. *"Insha'Allah."*

Eight

"What have you got?"

Jacob Eisenberg sat across from his boss, Ira Bettleman, and opened a folder. "The Cessna Citation II Moussawi flew to Tyre belongs to Oasis Hotel Corporation."

"What does Moussawi have to do with a hotel corporation?" Bettleman lit a cigarette and passed the pack.

"Oasis operates more than thirty luxury resorts scattered throughout the world," Jacob said. "After a lot of digging through a labyrinth financial network, we learned it's a wholly owned subsidiary of Alhannah."

"Abdul bin Suleiman Nasser." The Israeli spymaster whistled. "A multi-billionaire, Sunni, Saudi prince, and a Sh'ia cleric who leads Allah's Army—"

"Certainly makes for strange bedfellows, eh?" Jacob turned a page of the report, squinting through his cigarette smoke. "Even though we're still a month or so away from getting the go-ahead to test the Miniature Aerial Surveillance Devices, I've drafted a plan to snatch Moussawi."

"That's a kick in the ass." Bettleman leaned back, exhaled and watched the smoke curl toward the ceiling. "I hate like hell having to wait, but it would be counterproductive to rush the good doctor. Meanwhile, how do you plan getting the MASD's inside Moussawi's Tyre compound?"

"Moussawi's boychick, Jamil, goes to the market every other day. When the time is right, we'll have several men in place." Jacob stubbed out his cigarette. "There will be heavy security around Jamil, but our guys shouldn't have much trouble planting one or two on him."

"Nasser's financial network sounds more than a little complex," Bettleman said. "Some financial guru must be managing things for him. See if we can't get a lead on the money man."

"Will do." Jacob picked up his folder and left.

Lawrence Escope chose an upscale Mediterranean Washington, DC, restaurant for his meeting with National Security Advisor Axel Bembry. Good food and wine, complemented by dimly-lit booths, made for easy conversation.

"I hear they make a mean halibut," Escope said.

Bembry downed his martini. While eating the olive, he signaled the waiter for a refill.

"Something wrong, Axel? You haven't said two words since we got here."

"It's Corbet," Bembry said. "He's moving in on my turf."

"You mentioned that at the reception." Escope sipped his own martini. "Have you spoken to the President about it?"

"She made the sonofabitch her personal advisor." The NSA swallowed half of his fresh martini. "I might as well fucking resign."

"Nonsense," Escope said. "You can get a lot of political mileage out of the current crisis. Prince Nasser can be counted on as a friend."

"I got word she had a private meeting with him." Bembry stared into his fresh drink glass, his right eye twitching. "Did you see the way she acted around him at the reception?"

"The way she acted around him? I don't follow."

"Abigail Stewart, the President of the U.S. of fucking A, for Christ's sake. She looked like she was going to dissolve into a pool of estrogen every time she got near Corbet."

Escope leaned forward. "You think the attraction goes beyond professional respect?"

"I know the look." Bembry scowled. "I'd bet she's fantasizing jumping his bones right now."

"Maybe you're reading too much into this, Axel." Escope set his glass down. "Last I heard they were both single adults."

"I don't give a fuck what they are." Bembry clenched his fist. "The talks are down the toilet. Coalition forces will move if there's an embargo. Big things are about to happen, and Corbet's cut me out of the goddamned loop."

"An embargo is exactly what will happen unless the West modifies its stance and gives priority to the Palestinian problem."

"For Christ's sake, that's not going to happen, Lawrence." Bembry motioned for the waiter before draining the last of his drink. "Have you forgotten the Israeli jet being blown out of the sky carrying delegations from the United States, Israel and the European Union on their way to make peace with the Palestinians?"

"True, but the jet was shot down in Egypt," Escope said. "They want to handle the investigation. If Tartir's guilty, then he'll face Arab justice."

"Investigation—Arab justice." Bembry laughed. "Empty rhetoric. So cut the bullshit, Lawrence. Tartir's having a grand old time in the Cairo Sheraton penthouse. In the real world, he's out of wiggle room. The million dollar trust traced back to the Egyptian pilot's family has been linked to his Martyrs' Brigade."

"Look, we're not going to solve the Middle East problems

over dinner," Escope said. "But we can help one another."

"Ah, at last, we come to the heart of the matter." Bembry raised his fresh drink. "What's on your mind?"

"What sanctions will the coalition impose in the event of an oil embargo?"

"The obvious," Bembry said. "Assets frozen, diplomatic relations and communications cut, air transportation halted, deportations. The Muslim world will be isolated."

Escope tapped his fingers together. "Prince Nasser has long been a supporter of the United States. His holding company, Alhannah, has world-wide interests unrelated to oil. It would be a shame to see his companies become embroiled in events beyond his control."

"That's how it goes sometimes," Bembry said. "Now tell me what's really on your mind."

Escope lowered his voice. "I know you've entertained political ambitions beyond the NSA's office, Axel. My client, Prince Nasser, one of the world's wealthiest men, can be extremely generous. He could help you achieve those ends, with no strings attached. Who knows, you might be in a position to make a run for the White House. The prince believes our country needs a leader like you who has an intimate understanding of the Middle East."

"No strings attached?"

Escope caught the glint in Bembry's eyes. "No strings."

The NSA took a breath. "I don't suppose it would hurt to get Nasser a temporary pass if an embargo is announced."

"And I'll put a man on Corbet," Escope said. "If there's anything going on between him and the President, we should be the first to know."

"Excellent," Bembry said. He rubbed his hands together. "Now what were you saying about the halibut?"

The following evening, Grant looked beyond the balcony of his Washington, DC, condominium in the direction of the White House. "Focus," he kept telling himself. Focus on anything other than what he was feeling about the President of the United States.

He went to the sofa and clicked on the Arab news network, Al Jazeera. The breaking story was in Arabic, with English subtext. Saudi Foreign Minister Prince Ibrahim al Zyyad's face filled the screen as he prepared to speak to the camera.

Here it comes, Grant thought. He sat on the couch and picked up a glass of white wine.

"Regrettably, recent talks in Washington, DC, failed to produce the positive results the Arab League had hoped for. Israeli carnage in the West Bank and Gaza continues as more than a million Palestinians have been forced to flee their homeland." The television image shifted to streams of refugees crossing into Lebanon. Babies, their faces streaked with dust, screamed in their mother's arms. Old men and women too tired to continue were shown falling by the wayside.

"Led by the United States, the West has rejected Arab League proposals aimed at restoring dignity to our Palestinian brethren," Zyyad said. "Again, they have cast their lot with the Zionist invaders. But rest assured, my brothers, the faithful have not stood idly by in the face of these atrocities. Muslims around the world have united to combat Zionist and infidel trickery."

Grant sipped his wine and focused on the Saudi foreign minister's black eyes: a quick glance down, and for an instant he thought he detected a flash of fear behind the cold, unwavering stare.

"The Arab League and ministers from other Muslim nations have unanimously agreed to cut off the lifeblood of the West. Beginning immediately, oil shipments to the West are cancelled until the Palestinian issues are resolved equitably." Zyyad held up a finger. "There are those in Western countries who threaten war against the sacred lands of Islam if an embargo is imposed. I say to these warmongers that there should be no mistake about our resolve to defend the Faith and our territories. If infidel invaders come uninvited, they will arrive in hell."

Grant leaned forward as the television image shifted to an oil rig in the desert. Moments later, a gigantic fireball blossomed, followed by the sounds of multiple explosions.

"Shit." Grant sat frozen, his gaze fixed on the billowing smoke and flame filling the screen. The television image switched to an Al Jazeera anchor. He clicked off the set, went to his office, and placed a call to his station chief, Terry Falco, in Tel Aviv for a briefing.

An hour later, Grant refilled his wine glass, then clicked the television set back on. "Now we take you to our representative in Cairo," the Al Jazeera anchor said.

Street scenes of thousands of people rejoicing materialized.

Grant jumped at the sound of his secure telephone. "Corbet."

"How's the weather?" said Ira Bettleman's gravelly voice.

"Cold and getting colder," Grant said.

"Did you catch the Al Jazeera show?"

"Beautifully scripted and choreographed," Grant said. "Looks like the Middle East regimes saved their collectives asses by assuring the people their governments wouldn't cave to world pressure."

Bettleman grunted. "I'm sure there're plenty of soiled pants in a number of Western capitals."

"Those were no ordinary explosions," Grant said. "They obliterated the well."

"I just got a preliminary report," Bettleman said. "The charges were set deep to destroy the well's infrastructure."

"Terry Falco reads it the same way. He doesn't think there's any way to repair the damage." Grant pressed the chilled wine glass against his forehead. "Christ, how did the situation get so far out of control?"

A sigh from Israel. "There are no easy answers, my friend."

Nine

Prince Nasser sipped the strong, bitter coffee as he watched a CNN report on Militant Islam. Angry mobs throughout the Middle East were shown shaking their fists, whipping themselves, and screaming "death to infidels" in dusty streets. Omnipresent mullahs watched the spectacles through baleful eyes.

The prince, while embracing the faith, especially Wahhabism, the extreme version of Islam practiced in Saudi Arabia, never stopped being amazed at the way common street people thought. Born in ignorance and poverty, with no chance to succeed, they were led about like donkeys. They lived in mud huts and watched their children grow up uneducated. They saw the enormous wealth of the royal families, who considered them street animals, yet willingly became martyrs for causes that had nothing to do with their own lives. Nasser smiled thinly. Rabble believed anything. Tell them they were part of a *jihad* against the enemies of Islam, and they were happy. Such was the power of religion.

"Insha' Allah."

Nasser allowed himself a moment of satisfaction. The pieces of his plan were coming together nicely. As written in the Koran, he saw himself as the son of Arabia who awakened the fierce eagle that cleansed the land. Then, out of the rubble, he would rise to become the true Prince of Islam.

Mecca and Medina under my control.

Of course, there would be those opposed to his leadership, but he had planned for them. Nasser smiled. After what lay in store for the infidels, HARPIE would net close to a trillion dollars. That would buy quite an army.

Yes, the prince thought, soon the nonbelievers would tremble before the true faith.

In New York, Gerhard Esch set his Starbucks espresso down, then clicked on his computer. His HARPIE model could not have performed better. Since the Al Jazeera airing of Saudi Foreign Minister Zyyad's speech, currency markets had gone into free fall, while precious metals and oil futures had soared. No question, blowing up the oil well for the world to see was a masterful touch. If things continued according to plan, Prince Nasser would emerge as the world's first trillionaire.

Esch chuckled, clicked a program, and brought up his own account. He studied the charts and graphs for a long moment. Close to one and a half billion in leveraged contracts. Things were moving along nicely. He drained his espresso and dropped the cup in the wastebasket. Esch put his hands behind his head and stared at the barges moving slowly over the Hudson River's dark water on their way to unload cargo. Nasser might become the first trillionaire, he thought, but being the world's only remaining multi-billionaire wasn't a bad second.

In Taipei, President Ping-yi Cong rubbed the smooth surface of the white stone between his thumb and forefinger before placing it on his *wei-qi* board. He stared at the lined junctures and saw a definite pattern taking shape.

Sun Tzu's *Art of War* said, "Know your enemy." Cong's gaze slowly passed over the board. So, between Islam and the West, who was the enemy? Muslim leaders, afraid of being overthrown, had been forced to unite with their people against the hated infidels. And, because three internationally respected diplomats were blown out of the sky on their way to forge a peace agreement, the West remained uncompromising in their position toward Palestinian leader Abdullah Tartir.

Cong poured a brandy and sipped. Incredible that Tartir had committed an act of war against the West. In fact, Cong thought, so incredible as to not be believed. Not that it mattered. Palestinians, run out of the Left Bank and Gaza, continued to flood into neighboring Arab states. The opposing sides were now caught in what Americans called a *Catch-22*. A situation he had hoped to see develop in the great scheme of things for more than fifteen years. Taiwan's president enjoyed the brandy's warmth as it spread through his belly. Beyond the open curtains, the lights of Taipei winked at him through a neon haze of exhaust fumes and factory smoke. He would have to deal with improving air quality soon. But first, he would gamble Taiwan's future.

Cong went to his desk and placed a call to Grant Corbet.

"Assessment?" Zach Holden asked.

"They rigged the oil fields in advance, anticipating the talks would bottom out. I suspect the pipelines are lined with explosives as well." Grant sat across from his boss. "Last night's light show served a dual purpose: a warning about launching an invasion, while reassuring the home folk that the governments stand with Islam. Now it's a matter of who blinks first."

Zach filled his pipe and struck a match. "Hard to imagine

seventy percent of the world's oil supply blown up."

"Jacob Eisenberg has picked up on something," Grant said.

The CIA director arched an eyebrow. "Eisenberg's a good man. What's he got?"

Grant passed a photo across the desk. "Shortly after the Arab summit in Beirut, one of Jacob's operatives got a shot of Sheik Mahmoud Moussawi getting off a private jet in Tyre."

Zach drew on his pipe. "And?"

"Mossad traced the jet's registration back to the Oasis Hotel Corporation. After a little digging, they discovered that Oasis is a wholly owned subsidiary of Prince Abdul bin Suleiman Nasser's holding company, Alhannah."

"Interesting. Nasser's gone out of his way to create a good public image with us over the years. What do you suppose his link to Moussawi and Allah's Army is all about?"

"Money's the only connection I can think of," Grant said. "I met Nasser at the Saudi embassy during the talks. Something about him didn't sit right. Nothing specific, just gut instinct."

"Your gut has always served you well. Maybe Jacob has stumbled onto something. If a nasty relationship exists between Nasser and Moussawi, it would have to be money. The prince has got plenty of that commodity. Plus the fact, it's no secret that Allah's Army, along with several other groups, have been going through a drought since Iran pulled back and began focusing their efforts on stirring up the Shiites in Southern Iraq."

"Ira agrees. He's convinced there's a link between the two."

Zach pushed a button, and a map of the Middle East appeared on the screen behind his desk. "You think Nasser and Moussawi are behind the Israeli jet going down?"

"It's possible," Grant said. "Nasser's got money, Moussawi the men."

"If a verifiable link could be established, that would exonerate Tartir and a lot of blood would be saved."

"I've got our people working with Mossad to uncover

Nasser's financial network. Preliminary reports reveal a tangled web."

"Not surprising, but keep digging."

"On another topic, I got a call from Ping-yi Cong," Grant said. "He wants a meeting with me in Taipei. Said he might have a way out of the Middle East situation for us."

Zach touched a knuckle to his lips. "Cong's slippery as an eel, but you saved his life once. You think he's got something credible?"

"I doubt he'd call me with something bogus. I booked a ticket on tonight's flight from New York. With luck, I'll be back the following day."

"You'll be in for one helluva jetlag," Zach said. "Let's hope Cong's not wasting our time."

"The Arab press is calling the Palestinian relief effort a Zionist conspiracy to exterminate Palestinians." President Stewart shook her head. "They're alleging that the thousands of tons of food and medicine shipped into Lebanon and Jordan was deliberately poisoned."

"Arabs never miss an opportunity to miss an opportunity," Secretary of State Frances Merriman said. "The camps to house the sick and wounded are rife with corruption. Tons of food and medicine have been stolen by various militias, repackaged in Arabic, then sold to the Palestinians on the black market. The poor devils are being exploited by their own people."

"What about the supplies that haven't been stolen? Are they getting out to the people?"

"Pandemonium reigns," the SecState said. "There's massive infighting over who will distribute aid packages. The Jordanian and Lebanese governments want to supply refugees in their own way, the Arab way, without help from international relief organizations. Hundreds of people, waving freshly printed business cards, show up daily calling themselves the legitimate government authority."

"The entire situation is appalling. Pigsties are being called refugee camps. The Left Bank and Gaza have been reduced to a wasteland. Tens of thousands of refugees are pouring into Lebanon and Jordan. No running water, no electricity—" President Stewart's eyes clouded. "We're sinking into a quagmire, Frances. People at home are freezing, energy prices soaring, crop failures, airline industry on the verge of bankruptcy, the stock market in shambles—the list goes on. We've got an oil embargo and the possibility of a major war staring us in the face."

"Life has no certainties, Abby, only a series of possibilities." Merriman looked at the President, not liking what she saw. Telltale circles under the eyes, pale complexion, crimped lips—signs of wear from holding the most powerful job in the world. "Who could have possibly foreseen how these events would unfold?"

Abigail Stewart looked beyond her Secretary of State. "I don't believe in portents, but something's not right. It's almost as if the forces of evil have aligned against the civilized world."

"I pray you're wrong, Madam President."

Abigail Stewart's gaze caught the old photo of herself as a child riding Bermuda as soon as the Secretary of State had left. Where had all the years gone, and why were her thoughts drifting to the past again?

Outside her office, gray clouds scudded across the sky. *Gray,* she thought, *the color of Grant's eyes.* Clear eyes that glowed with affection one moment, and reflected a vague detachment the next. Eyes capable of showing anger. She had seen them grow cold during his exchange with Axel Bembry at Camp David.

Grant would be on his way to Taiwan tonight to speak with

President Ping-yi Cong. A way out of the Middle East situation is what Cong had said. Could that possibly be true, or was it only another possibility in a long series of dead ends?

Ten

"Grant Corbet." Ping-yi Cong stood and bowed slightly. Taiwan's president walked around his desk, wearing a white silk Mandarin shirt. The office lighting was subdued, with overhead spotlights focused on a collection of Ming vases. "It has been many years, old friend. I trust your flight was a pleasant one."

"Traveling has lost its allure." Grant accepted the offered hand. "You look well, Mr. President."

"Please, let us dispense with formalities." Cong pointed to his reconstructed ear. "If you had not stopped that assassin, we would not be having this meeting."

"I'd like to have our discussion this evening," Grant said. "I'm booked on the morning flight."

"Of course, but first we must take time to dine together. My chef has prepared a special dish in your honor, *Shirakoyaki*."

Grant looked across the desk.

"*Shirakoyaki* is made from fugu, what you Americans call puffer fish. In Asia, it is considered a great delicacy."

"I've eaten it in Japan," Grant said. "I understand chefs must be specially trained."

Cong nodded. "The toxin is quite deadly. But not to worry,

my chef has achieved the highest ranking from the Japanese Culinary Institute."

The ivory chopsticks, inlaid with delicate jade dragons, were cool against Grant's fingers as he inserted a piece of fugu into his mouth. Soft Chinese music played in the background as the two men ate in silence.

When the meal was completed, Grant accepted a hot towel from a hostess and wiped his hands. "An extraordinary meal. I'll have to include Taiwan in my travel plans more often," he said.

"It was good of you to come on such short notice, Grant. You will always enjoy most honored guest status in Taiwan." Cong waited for the table to be cleared, then filled a pair of white porcelain cups with green tea. He held up one of the cups before passing it to Grant. "These were made in Hangzhou more than two thousand years ago."

Candlelight from ebony pagoda holders shined through the eggshell-thin porcelain as Grant studied the intricately designed crane on the cup's side. "They're beautiful."

"The crane symbolizes longevity," Cong said.

Grant made no reply and waited for Cong to taste the tea first.

Cong inhaled the brew and sipped. "Tea before conversation helps put things into proper perspective, eh?" He placed a file folder on the table. "It's no secret I'm opposed to reunification with the Mainland."

Grant lifted his cup and nodded.

"Old Friend, a stone has been cast into a pond. How far the ripples will reach, who can say?" Cong's gaze moved beyond Grant. "The only thing for certain is that the complexion of the world will change."

"Times are dangerous, Old Friend."

"The future of my country could well be determined by what is said here tonight." Cong fingered the crane on the side of his teacup. "Have you heard of the Spratly Islands?"

"An uninhabited archipelago in the South China Sea, with possible gas and oil deposits," Grant said. "The islands are claimed by China, Taiwan, Vietnam, Malaysia, Brunei, Indonesia, and the Philippines. Economic activity limited to commercial fishing, and strategically located near several primary shipping lanes."

"The territorial dispute over the Spratly Islands cannot be settled diplomatically or peacefully between the claimants." Cong refilled their cups. "Since there is no recognized claim, rightful ownership could be determined through the International Court of Justice in The Hague."

Grant focused on the bottom of his teacup. "I'm no legal expert, but it sounds logical."

"This file contains seismic data. I also have geological samples of a covert survey I conducted back in 1988 that are ready to ship for your analysis." Cong slid the folder across the table. "More than two hundred billion barrels of sulfur-free oil are beneath the Spratlys. Natural gas estimates exceed two hundred trillion feet. Probably the last find of its kind on earth."

Grant whistled. "Those reserves rival Saudi Arabia."

"I'm willing to assign Taiwan's claim on the Spratly Islands over to the United States," Cong said. "Given the current crisis, the International Court would certainly render a favorable ruling concerning ownership. The West could avoid war in the Middle East because they would no longer be dependent on their oil."

"That's a generous offer," Grant said. "What's the quid pro quo?"

"Protection, friendship, recognition—assurances that Taiwan will remain independent. And, of course, a share in the oil and gas reserves." Cong's intelligent eyes glistened in the candlelight. "I advise sending teams to the Spratlys for further tests. However, the situation could become unpleasant if China got advanced warning about a huge oil find."

"They'll find out soon enough, one way or the other," Grant said. "But then again, foreign policy's not my field. All I can promise is to get your proposal to the right people."

"That's all I ask, Old Friend." Cong stood. "I have a very fine Napoleon brandy just waiting to be opened. Why don't we go into the sitting room and discuss the possibilities?"

Heavy snow was falling when Grant's flight touched down at Ronald Reagan National Airport. His driver took his overnight bag at the gate and led him through customs to the waiting limousine.

"How was your flight?" the driver asked.

"Long and choppy," Grant said. "I see the weather's turned from bad to worse since I've been gone."

"Snow's supposed to be with us for the next several days." Not getting a response, the driver glanced into the rearview mirror and saw that Grant had nodded off. So much for the glamour of traveling, he thought.

Forty-five minutes later, Grant's driver had passed through three checkpoints and parked inside the sprawling CIA headquarters in Langley, Virginia.

Zach Holden looked up from examining one of his model ships. Tweezers repaired the loose rigging. "Two hundred billion barrels?"

"The seismic data and geological samples are being analyzed now." Grant pushed a folder marked "TOP SECRET" in red across the desk. "Details are in the brief."

"And?"

"My feeling is the results will be validated. Cong's ultimate goal is to keep Taiwan independent of China. The stakes are enormous, so he wouldn't toy with something like this."

"No harm having a team check out the geological samples." Zach tapped his pipe.

Grant watched him begin filling the bowl with tobacco. "Aren't you smoking more than usual?"

"Probably." Practiced fingers tamped down the tobacco. "Sign of the times, I suppose. Helps me think."

"Why not try another one?"

"What—another pipe?"

Grant smiled. "Forget I mentioned it."

"This pipe is my best friend." Zach's eyes carried a hint of amusement before turning serious. "So, who else knows about this?"

"Cong assured me we are the only ones to see the documentation," Grant said. "He told me he's kept the information secret for almost twenty years, even from members of his own party."

"I'm sure he wouldn't want word of an oil find like this getting back to the Mainland." Zach struck a match and drew on his pipe. "Our immediate concern would be getting dragged into a war with China. What's your take?"

"Based on what we know, I'd say the risk would be worth the effort. We're experiencing abnormal weather conditions, power shortages, rising prices, crop failures, and cold-related deaths." Grant's hand came up in a cutting gesture. "If coalition forces invade the Middle East, and the oil fields are destroyed, we'll have global chaos."

"What would be different by going to war with China?" Zach looked at Grant through a cloud of smoke. "They've got the capability to destroy most of Asia."

"It would be a gamble, but I doubt China would risk war with the coalition, especially if the International Court rendered a favorable ruling legitimizing our claim to the Spratly Islands. China knows they'd be defeated in the end. Their economy would be crushed, and Taiwan would remain independent."

"A lot of snags along the way," Zach said. "There's the matter of face. It's conceivable China would throw it all away before being humiliated."

Grant nodded.

"When are you going to speak with the President?"

"I've sent over a copy of the brief I gave you. She might want to run it by several of her advisors without having me around."

"I don't envy your job. Our lady over at 1600 Pennsylvania Avenue is under increasing pressure now that public attitude has become as foul as the weather." Zach carefully returned his model ship to its place of honor. "More than two hundred thousand people marched in Los Angeles, Chicago, New York, and DC yesterday, demanding we send troops and take the oil. Larger demonstrations are planned. Senators, congressman, governors, and business leaders are becoming more militant by the hour."

"I keep looking at recent events, beginning with the downing of the Israeli jetliner, as a coordinated operation."

Zach carefully wiped a piece of dust off the sail. "Problem is there's no pattern, just a helluva lot of dead ends."

Grant picked up his direct line on the second ring. "Corbet."

"I finished reading your brief," Abigail Stewart said. "It's a bold objective, but you're suggesting we reverse our longstanding China policy."

"A lot of pieces would have to fall in place for it to work." Grant tightened his grip on the receiver. "I met with Zach this morning. He thinks we might be trading one war for another."

"He's right, but if the data's accurate, it might provide a way out of the current crisis." A moment of silence filled the line.

"Or, we could be jumping from the frying pan into the flame."

"I'd hate to be the one making the decision," Grant said. "There's a lot of ifs either way."

"It appears the world will be much different no matter which way we go," President Stewart said. "If you're free for dinner, drop by around seven, and we'll discuss it."

"I'll be there."

"Grant?"

"Yes."

"I'm glad you're back."

Eleven

Abigail Stewart tilted her head and gazed into the mirror. She applied a touch of perfume. Chestnut hair fanned over her tan mohair sweater. Her face was unlined, except for tiny crow's feet around her eyes. *Liz Taylor eyes.* She'd overheard the comment more than once. Her late husband, Richard, had often said hers were prettier.

More than twelve years had passed since Abby had lost her husband in a small airplane crash. After the tragedy, politics became her life, and she went on to become the first female President of the United States. More than a job, the power of the presidency became her surrogate lover. But the crushing responsibilities had exacted a toll. A world on the precipice of war, an oil embargo, riots over gasoline, the worst cold snap in a hundred years—an endless list of problems. Maybe that was why she'd begun to think about life after politics. Images of Grant Corbet increasingly drifted along the corridors of her mind. No doubt, an attraction existed between them. She remembered their conversation at Camp David after their run, moonlight shining in his serious gray eyes. There had been no practiced political lines, no suave talk aimed to impress her with his knowledge. She felt a

palpable chemistry between them that night. Now, at private briefings, their hands often touched and lingered a moment longer
than necessary. Occasionally, when she caught a glimpse of the
way he looked at her, he'd smile and glance away. What emotions
lay behind those gray eyes? Desire? Perhaps love? Love tinged
with fear? Silly things that made unspoken words all the more
sought-after.

"So, how does one make his feelings known to the first lady
President of the United States?" Abby asked her reflection. But
the image in the mirror only stared back in silence.

Abby buzzed for her bodyguard, Lindsey Caspare. A moment
later the agent appeared.

"Grant Corbet will be joining me for dinner." Abby rubbed
her hands together. "I've dismissed the chef for the evening. I
haven't cooked in a long time."

"Enjoy the evening, Madam President. You'll do just fine. I'll
see you're not disturbed." Caspare's eyes crinkled. "Mr. Corbet's
an attractive man."

"I know." Abby touched her bodyguard's arm. "Thanks,
Lindsey."

After Caspare left, Abby went into the kitchen, thought a
moment, then put a bottle of champagne into the wine box.

A simple meal, nothing elaborate, she thought.

Champagne, a poppy seed tossed salad with mandarin orange
slices, followed by oyster soup, eggs benedict, bread pudding, and
coffee. Just like New Orleans. A tinge of guilt over the prospect
of enjoying a pleasant evening with a charming man crept into
her mind. She quickly dismissed the thought. Nothing wrong with
forgetting the world's problems for one night, was there? Feeling
goose bumps cover her arms, Abby went into the living room
and put on some soft jazz.

The private investigator, a former DC detective, focused his zoom lens. He clicked off several shots of Grant nodding to his driver and climbing inside his limousine. Condensed exhaust fumes billowed from the black sedan in the frigid night air. The P.I. took a final shot of the limo's license plate number as the car pulled out into the traffic. Humming a Willie Nelson tune, he began following the limo at a safe distance.

Ten minutes later, the P.I. photographed the limo at the White House security gate. He took special care to get a shot of the license plate and to stay out of range of White House video surveillance. Carefully, he set the camera aside and punched an automatic dial number on his cell phone.

"Yes," a voice said on the second ring.

"Rooster's in the hen house."

"Stay there until he leaves, and document the time."

"Will do." Clicking off, the P.I. drove to the nearest Starbucks. A double cappuccino would be nice. It looked like he was in for a long night.

Grant followed Lindsey Caspare to the President's living quarters. He watched the agent's confident stride and wondered if Abby had spoken to her about him.

Secret Service agents stationed along the hallways stared ahead, stone-faced, as he passed. He would be spending an evening alone with the President of the United States. Or would he be spending an evening with Abby? Her scent lingering in cold moonlight, her violet eyes, her gentle voice, were ever with him.

Careful, bud, he told himself. *You're treading on dangerous ground.*

Grant watched Caspare knock on the door, noting her karate-hardened knuckles. A moment later, the door opened.

Abby.

The President's hair shimmered, her skin limned golden

yellow from the lamplight behind.

"Mr. Corbet, do come in. I'm anxious to hear about your trip."

"Thank you for showing me in, Agent Caspare." Grant turned back to the President and took the offered hand. "It's good to be back."

Abby shut the door and inclined her head to him. "I love to cook but seldom find the time. Tonight you're my guinea pig, Mr. Grant Corbet."

"Lead on," Grant said. "I'm starved."

"You must be terribly tired after your trip." Abby sipped her champagne. "I remember suffering for a week after flying back to the States with my father from Japan. Everything got turned around. Night felt like day, day like night."

Grant stared across the candlelit table. Abby's perfume wafted around him like a veil. "Japan? What were you doing there?"

"Dad was in the diplomatic corps. We moved around quite a bit before he retired."

"I understand you're something of a linguist." Grant washed down the last of his bread pudding with coffee. "You must have learned many languages while traveling the diplomatic circuit?"

"Shhh!" Abby placed a finger over her lips. "That's not common knowledge. You have no idea how much information I've picked up over the years by not letting on I understand what's being said."

"Mum's the word." Grant held up his hands. "What languages, besides English, do you speak?"

"Japanese, Mandarin, French, German—a smattering of Russian and Spanish."

"Impressive. I never could master Chinese inflections."

"It's not so hard when you've had a Chinese nanny."

After dinner, they retired to the living room sofa. Diana Krall's sultry voice, *I've got you under my skin,* drifted in the background.

"Best meal I've ever had," Grant said.

Abby touched his hand. "I'm sure you say that to all your presidents."

"Only to those who cook for me." Grant stared into her violet eyes. "Hard to believe I'm alone with the President of the United States."

Abby lifted her face to his. "I think I've wanted to be alone with you ever since we first spoke at Camp David."

Grant reached for Abby, feeling the excitement of their touch. Time seemed to attenuate as his mouth found hers. Diana Krall's voice became his last reality.

I've got you deep in the heart of me. So deep in my heart you're really a part of me. I've got you under my skin.

Abby and Grant awoke at four in the morning. Shadows played along the walls and across the ceiling as they held one another.

"A penny for whatever's going on inside that head of yours." Abby traced a line down the curve of his face.

"I'm wondering what we might be getting into."

"I was having the same thought."

"Whatever it is, I want to see it through."

Abby kissed him lightly. "Me too."

They kissed again, gently at first, then with growing passion. Arms entwining, their bodies pressed fiercely together.

After Grant left, Abby went back to bed. She reached for his pillow, inhaled his scent, and pressed it against her breasts. Their lovemaking had been a blend of passion, tenderness, and hunger. If not for the dull ache between her legs, she would have thought it a wild dream.

From his car down the street, the private detective propped his elbow on the windowsill and photographed Grant's car preparing to leave the White House. Smiling to himself, he thought how incongruous it was for him to be spying on the CIA's chief spook. He pulled away from the curb and drove immediately to Grant's condominium. Luck was with him. He found a parking spot where he could get some nice angle shots. Minutes later, the limo arrived and the P.I. aimed his camera. The shutter clicked several times as Grant got out of the car and walked to the front door, where the security guard let him in.

Later that morning, Lawrence Escope studied the photos the private detective had furnished him. Their photographic quality was excellent. No mistaking that the CIA's Deputy Director of Operations, Grant Corbet, had arrived at the White House just before seven p.m., and left shortly after four a.m. the next morning. Records at the security check points would corroborate time and date on the photos. Hot stuff for someone like Barry Shivers, the *National Monitor*'s celebrity sleaze reporter.

Escope continued to stare at the photos. He ran a finger over the prints, feeling a strange heat emanating from them. Now, how to handle Alex Bembry? War would almost certainly come to the Middle East. In the end, the Arab states would fall, but what about the aftermath? He needed the NSA to run interference for Prince Nasser's business interests. And what if, by discrediting Abigail Stewart, Bembry could be positioned to make a run for the presidency? The lobbyist's chest expanded a fraction at the thought. Well, that scenario offered all sorts of possibilities.

Escope picked up the phone and dialed the NSA's direct number.

In his mountain fortress near Jeddah, Prince Nasser didn't sleep that night. Instead, he passed the time listening to the wind howl over the plains and up through the mountain crevices.

Allah's whirlwind.

The prince imagined the thundering sounds of horses' hooves, their tails and manes streaming behind them, as the Prophet's armies streaked across the desert. Unlike present and past leaders in the Gulf who pandered to the West, he had never lost sight of his goal. The living heart of Islam beat inside Saudi Arabia. Mohammad had been born there, and the holy cities of Mecca and Medina were the spawning grounds for the world's only true religion. Yet, the Faith had been torn from within. But that would soon change. God had chosen him to settle the centuries-old struggle within Islam. There would be opposition within the Islamic world to his ascension, but he had planned for that eventuality. Those who opposed him, along with their families, would simply be killed. Thanks to the financial genius of Gerhard Esch and his HARPIE program, he controlled almost a trillion dollars in currency, bullion, and oil futures. With such vast resources, he could raise an invincible army—an army of God.

The wind increased in force as Nasser remembered visiting Jerusalem with his father as a boy. They had seen the Rock of

Abraham. "One of Islam's holiest shrines being controlled by Jews is an abomination against God, my son," his father had said.

Yes, an abomination.

Prince Abdul bin Suleiman Nasser lay still, listening to the wind. As soon as he consolidated power, he would unleash his Army of God and drive every last Israeli into the sea. Once he controlled Islam's holiest sites, he would deal with the Sh'ia heretics in Iran and elsewhere. Sadly, it might become necessary to eliminate Sheik Moussawi, and Allah's Army, as well. Nasser sighed. What else could he do? Peace in the lands of Allah could never be achieved as long as the Sh'ia refused to embrace the true meaning of Islam.

Nasser felt the blood of the Prophet coursing through his veins as he contemplated the future. Sand was falling through the hourglass of time. When it emptied, the world would never be the same. A grim smile curled his dark lips.

They have sown the wind, and they shall reap the whirlwind.

Lawrence Escope and Axel Bembry sat at a corner table inside a private club favored by government officials and businessmen. The lights of Washington, DC, burned behind them. Tight security insured an absence of weapons, microphones, and recording devices.

"How did you get these?"

"After our last meeting, I put a man on Corbet's back." Escope winked at the NSA. "I didn't believe it, Axel, but you were right about President Stewart's romantic inclinations."

Bembry whistled softly. "This could shake up her presidency more than it already is. A world on the brink of war, and Abigail Stewart sets up a White House love nest." He continued to study the photos in silence, then slipped them back inside an envelope. "Goddamned bitch. Corbet and Merriman are the only people who have her ear."

"These photos could pave the way for you to become her successor." Escope signaled for refills. "If they're handled correctly, of course."

"Handled correctly?" Bembry arched an eyebrow. "What do you have in mind, Lawrence?"

The waiter arrived with fresh martinis. Escope examined his nails as he waited for the man to leave. "Turn the photos over to a tabloid reporter I know. When he gets through with them, every news outlet in the world will be running the story. The talk shows will make mincemeat out of her. It will be Clinton revisited."

The NSA sipped his martini. "In case you've forgotten, Clinton emerged unscathed."

"Not completely unscathed," Escope said. "Wild Bill's legacy will be tarnished by his impeachment hearings. History will see to that."

"You could be reading this wrong, Lawrence. Corbet's a single adult, not some snot-nosed intern."

"It's all about perception, Axel. The world wasn't on the brink of war while Clinton dallied in the White House. National security wasn't at risk." Escope touched the side of his nose. "Besides, the public tends to forgive men easier than women for their indiscretions."

Bembry laced his fingers. "You've got my attention. Now tell me, how do I fit into this little scheme of yours?"

"While Stewart's being shredded by the press, you quietly resign and start making the talk show rounds. You act sympathetic to the President, but every now and then it slips out that Stewart didn't make the wisest decision to start playing house given the gravity of the world situation. You let it be known that the reason you resigned was because the President stopped listening to her closest advisors, putting most of her trust in Corbet." Escope raised his glass and stared at the olive. "By holding the moral high ground, you will become the party's leading spokesman, and frontrunner for next year's primaries."

"I see where you're going," Bembry said. "There's still the matter of money, and forming a campaign committee."

"Prince Nasser's a friend." Escope lowered his voice. "Twenty million should get you started nicely."

"Twenty million?" Bembry blinked at that. "You know there're campaign finance laws against individual contributions?"

"Not to worry, Axel. There're ways to maneuver. Clinton and Gore found them. So can we."

Bembry winked. "Naturally, as the former ambassador to Saudi Arabia and acting NSA, I was on the front line. I offer stability and a keen grasp of how to deal with the current crisis in the event of war. Not being overly critical of the President will play well for the women's vote." The NSA rubbed his hands together. "I like it."

"Excellent," Escope said. "Shall we order? I have a hankering for a rather fine steak tonight."

The next morning, Barry Shivers was on the early morning shuttle from New York to Washington. He caught a cab to Lawrence Escope's Pennsylvania Avenue office address. Once inside the building, the *National Monitor* reporter stepped inside an elevator, rode it to the penthouse suite, and clicked on a pocket tape recorder.

Escope walked around his desk to greet Shivers. "Welcome to Washington, Barry. Good of you to come on such short notice."

Shivers accepted the offered hand. "What do you have that's so important it can't be discussed over the phone?"

"Have a seat, Barry, and we'll discuss it." Escope gestured toward a chair. "How do you take your coffee? My secretary just brewed a pot."

Twelve

Grant, Secretary of Defense Collin Jeffers, and Zach Holden stood when the President, accompanied by Secretary of State Frances Merriman, walked into the White House office.

"Good afternoon," Abigail Stewart said. "Shall we get started? I've got a full day ahead preparing tonight's speech."

Merriman sat down. "This is one time you can bet your Energy Initiative won't get stalled on The Hill, Madam President. It would be political suicide for anyone to try and block passage."

"Hard to imagine the wake-up call required to get the necessary legislation passed." Abby glanced at Grant. "I've studied your brief. What you're suggesting is audacious, to say the least."

Nodding, Grant remained silent.

"Audacious, yes," Jeffers said. "So much so that we might just be able to pull it off."

Merriman glanced at Zach. "How comfortable are you with this?"

The DCI shrugged. "It's not an easy call, Frances. The seismic data and geological results provided by Taiwan's president have been validated. If the rest of the coalition signs on, and we get a quick, favorable ruling from the International Court about the legitimacy of our claim to the Spratlys, I'd say we should move. The big unknown will be China's reaction."

"I've had to tap our strategic reserve to cover shortages to get us through this damnable winter. Now, time's working against us." President Stewart's fingernails clicked on the table. "If the coalition moves against the Middle East, we risk the fields being destroyed. Potentially losing, or irrevocably damaging, seventy percent of the world's known oil reserves is not a gamble I want to take."

Merriman leaned forward. "Your plan to develop new alternative energy sources to free us from Middle East dependency will fly through."

"Yes, but there's no time for those sources to be developed without a continued oil supply." The President looked around the table. "Grant's plan possibly offers continuous supply."

"The question is, what's the worst case scenario?" Merriman said. "War in the Middle East, and risk destroying the fields, or risk war with China, and potentially gain the Spratly reserves?"

"A helluva choice," Zach said.

"Another risk is there's no guarantee that the estimated Spratly reserves are valid. The seismic data and geological results may prove to be a false reading." Grant glanced at Merriman. "Where would the other coalition members come down on this? Unity's imperative."

"After Zyyad's desert fireworks show the other night, I don't see any problem bringing them on board," Merriman said. "There's a lot of nail-biting in Europe and Asia. A possible sticking point might be devising a formula to equitably distribute the oil."

Jeffers refilled his water glass. "I expect a little grumbling from the French, but, in the end, we're the only one capable of standing against China."

"Very well, I think we're agreed that Mr. Corbet's proposal is the only viable option to occupying the Middle East." The

President made a note on her pad. "Collin? I want you to quietly put the Spratly military operation together. Frances? Conduct careful discussions with our coalition partners and find out how quickly we can get a ruling from the International Court of Justice. Key to all of this will be finding a way to avoid war with China."

"That's a tall order, Madam President," Jeffers said. "Despite reforms, influential elements in the Chinese military remain militant."

"War must be our last resort," Abby said. "I've met the new premier, Jen Jemin. He struck me as being much less intractable than his predecessors."

Jeffers nodded. "If war comes, I'll see we're in a position to win."

"At present, this is only a contingency plan." The President's gaze moved around the table. "There must be no leaks. No one outside this group without an absolute need to know should be brought into the loop."

Grant arrived home just after 5:30 p.m. After a quick shave and shower, he changed into slacks and a light plaid wool shirt. Then he went to the bar, mixed a dry martini, and clicked on CNN.

The anchor looked at the camera. "In a few moments, President Abigail Stewart will present her long-awaited energy policy to the American people. Sources close to the White House say that tonight's speech has a dual purpose. The President wants to clearly outline to the people her vision of what our nation's current and future energy needs will be. She also wants to press lawmakers who have opposed fast track development of alternative energy to get behind her policy; a policy President Stewart believes will ultimately eliminate our nation's dependence on foreign oil." The anchor paused. "I've just received word that the President is about to speak. Stay tuned to CNN for in-depth analysis following the speech. Now we'll take you to the Oval Office where President Abigail Stewart will address the nation."

Abby stared at Grant.

"My fellow Americans, our nation now faces its greatest crisis since World War II. Left unchecked, OPEC's oil embargo against the Western world will create global economic chaos. As your President, I want to assure you that the United States and its allies will not allow this kind of international blackmail to stand. I have directed Secretary of Defense Collin Jeffers and the Joint Chiefs to work with our coalition partners to assemble the most formidable fighting force in history. If war comes, it will be quick and decisive."

A pie chart appeared in the corner of the screen. "Today, I sent Congress a comprehensive renewable energy bill. The time for America to get serious about alternative energy is long overdue. We must stop sending oil dollars to terrorist states that recycle it into ways to kill Americans. I urge each and every one of you to let your congressmen and senators know the people of our great nation support this legislation. Yesterday, America should have freed herself from dependency on foreign oil. Today, it is imperative she do so. The future of the world's economy and environment depends on it."

A large section of the pie chart changed to red. "Currently more than eighty percent of electricity generated in the United States comes from fossil fuels, most of which are imported from the Middle East. Alternative energy sources such as solar, wind, geothermal, and biomass will reduce our dependency on foreign oil. These sustainable energy technologies, combined with prudent conservation strategies, will free America from future economic blackmail. Hundreds of thousands of jobs will be created in the U.S. economy by developing cost-effective, environmentally responsible alternative energy. Yet—" Abby raised a finger. "There are special interest groups who want us to continue to rely on conventional methods of generating electricity. Methods, I might add, that make up the single largest source of air pollution. Two thirds of our nation's sulfur dioxide emissions, a quarter of our nitrogen oxide emissions, and a third of our mercury emissions come from power plants. The people of our great land must stand together and say to the special interest groups that it's time for America to become the most important special interest group."

Grant lifted his glass to the screen. Appreciation for Abby's strength as a world leader mingled with images of their intimate moments together last night.

Barry Shivers licked a dry lip as he watched Grant's car pull away from the front of his condominium.

The private detective finished clicking off a half-dozen shots, then pulled out into the traffic. He glanced at Shivers. "Corbet left a little late tonight because of the President's speech."

"This is only the second night in a row he's gone to the White House. We need to establish a pattern. If Corbet's going to make a regular habit of slinking out in the early morning, I'll have enough to run the story."

The P.I. maneuvered around a delivery van. "I'm not a big gambler," he said, "but I'd lay odds he'll be leaving around four a.m."

Abby closed the door and laid her hand against Grant's chest. "How's my favorite spook?"

"Harried. I took Jack Sweeny out to Vulcan Industries after today's meeting to see a TBOLT demonstration." Grant shook his head. "They are going to be the bad guys' worst nightmare."

"I read the report," Abby said. "Not something we want in the wrong hands."

"You and Zach think alike." Grant kissed the tip of her nose. "By the way, that was a dynamite speech. I doubt there'll be much opposition on The Hill."

"Let's hope not. This is one issue all Americans should be united on."

Grant squeezed her hand as they walked to the living room.

Abby looked up, a slight hesitation, light as a feather. "It felt terribly awkward having to act so formal at today's meeting."

Grant smiled. "It was hard keeping my eyes off you."

Abby slipped into his arms and lifted her face to him. In the semi-darkness, she felt herself drawn to him like a courted lady to her knight. His mouth covered hers, gently at first, then with more urgency. Desire clogged Abby's throat as she pressed against him. She tried to speak, but moaned instead.

Grant kissed her neck and ears, catching the scent of her perfume, her silk robe cool beneath his hands. "God, it seems like forever since I've held you."

"When you touch me, I feel as if my heart's going to stop," Abby whispered. She stepped back, studied Grant's face several moments, then traced a line down his cheek. "My wonderful Grant Corbet. These moments with you give me the strength to face a new day."

"I don't know how you do it," Grant said. "The pressure must be unbelievable."

"I've had to learn how to compartmentalize my thoughts. Everything's in boxes, except us." Abby walked to the coffee table, picked up the remote, and clicked on soft music. She extended her hand, and they walked slowly toward the presidential bedroomMoonlight slanted through windows, dappling the room in platinum pools. From the bed, Grant watched Abby light several candles. Orange motes swam in her eyes as she moved toward him. Her chestnut hair glowed in the semi-darkness, falling around her shoulders in soft curls. Their gazes fixed on each other as she slowly untied the sash of her robe. Parting like butterfly wings, it hung momentarily before floating to the carpet.

After a duet of tenderness and passion, they held each other in the shadows.

Grant clasped her hand between his. "You're a beautiful woman, Abby."

"And you're a beautiful man." Abby moved her head to his chest. "Before you came into my life, I'd almost forgotten how it feels to trust someone completely."

"Funny." Grant's fingers moved through her hair. "You've had the same effect on me."

"You've been divorced what—ten years? Strange you never remarried."

"The right woman never came along." Grant stared at the shadows playing across the ceiling. "Until now."

"I've been widowed for about as long," Abby said.

Grant propped up on an elbow. "You loved him very much, didn't you?"

"After Richard passed away, there were times I thought I'd die from grief."

"How did you get over it?"

"The years rolled into each other, and the pain became less. You know that photo on my desk—me at three on Bermuda?"

"You named your horse Bermuda?"

"Yes. He was special. Richard always told me to keep it close by, to remind me of who I am."

"A wise man," Grant said.

"But that was another lifetime, my darling Grant." Abby hugged him, squeezing back tears. "For all those years, grief bound me to a memory. Now there's you."

While humming a country western song, Escope's private investigator clicked several shots of Grant getting out of his limo a little after four a.m. The shutter continued to open and close as the DDO exchanged a few words with the doorman before stepping inside the lobby of his condominium.

The P.I. put the camera down, pulled away from the curb, and glanced at Barry Shivers. "Same as last night."

"Gonna make a helluva story. All Mr. Corbet has to do is keep it up for another week or so." Shivers took a breath. He could already see the headlines.

Abby Plays House with Nation's Super Spook
While World Teeters on the Brink of War
by
Barry Shivers

Shivers smiled in the darkness. Things were coming together nicely. This kind of coup could open doors for him. Plus, the huge advance Escope had promised to pay once the story hit was a nice side benefit. His excitement soared as he thought about the things he expected to get from the story. Money, power, and recognition were a few. Then, there would be a book deal, followed by interviews on the nightly talk show circuit. With a little luck, and some arm twisting from Escope's contacts, he might even wind up as a columnist with the New York *Times*. Why not? They had hired a plagiarist, so why not a crackerjack reporter from the *National Monitor*? Shivers' smile broadened. That ought to shake up the sanctimonious world of journalism.

Book Two

A casual stroll through a mental asylum
shows that faith proves nothing.

——Friedrich Nietzche

Thirteen

Heated conversation and sounds from busy fingers tormenting keyboards filled the air when Barry Shivers stepped inside the *National Monitor*'s New York City newsroom. A month had passed since he'd visited Lawrence Escope in Washington and learned about Abigail Stewart's affair with Grant Corbet. The month had dragged by, but now he was ready. During that time, he'd carefully documented his story, incorporating Axel Bembry's revelation that the President had stopped listening to her closest advisors in favor of Corbet's counsel. Shivers' heart hammered. The only thing he didn't have was a photo of the nation's top spook bopping the Pres.

"Hi, Barry." A junior reporter walked up. "You're looking mighty spiffy."

"Got an appointment with Rake," Shivers said.

"Wow, must be important."

"You might say that. What say we do drinks after work?"

"Love to." She flashed him a smile and left.

Shivers whistled to himself as his gaze followed the pretty blond down the aisle. He clicked his tongue, took off his overcoat, and headed to his publisher's office.

Aaron Friedman looked up when Shivers knocked on the door. "Come in, Barry. What've you got?"

Friedman, a tall, thin man with a bent nose, had earned the nickname Rake, as in Muckraker, during his tenure in the publishing world for relentlessly sensationalizing foibles of high-profile celebrities. In his wake, countless careers and reputations had been trashed.

Shivers removed a folder from his briefcase and tossed it on the desk. "It's bitch cold outside. I could use a cup of coffee."

Friedman stared at the reporter a moment, then pressed the intercom on his desk. "Two cups of coffee, black."

The publisher's secretary appeared with two Styrofoam cups and left.

"So this is what all the secrecy's been about." Friedman picked up the folder and began to read.

Shivers silently watched.

Twenty minutes later, Friedman returned the photographs and story to the folder. He sucked his front tooth. "Pretty low, even for us, Barry."

"If you're having a morality attack, Aaron, I'll take it elsewhere."

Friedman's gaze moved to the window. A pigeon flew out of the swirling snow and perched on the ledge. "What do you want, Barry? Money, position—"

"A hundred thousand dollar bonus, and a private office for starters," Shivers said. "After that, we'll see."

Friedman stared at Shivers. "What you mean is, you'll wait and see how it plays out."

"That's how it works, Aaron." Shivers sipped his coffee. "I came up with the goods, and I intend to cash in."

"Okay, Barry, I'll bite. We'll clean out an office and let you run with this." Friedman tapped the folder. "Drop by early afternoon and sign the advance agreement. It will be the lead story in next week's edition."

"Will do." Shivers stood and turned toward the door. "See you this afternoon."

"Barry?"

"Yes?"

"I'd watch my backside if I were you." Friedman folded his hands behind his head. "This kind of story tends to have sharp teeth. It might rise up and bite you in the ass."

In Washington, Lawrence Escope arrived at Axel Bembry's office a little after ten a.m. He took a seat across from the NSA. "I got a call from Shivers. The story will break in next week's edition."

"I'll type my letter of resignation today." Bembry picked up his gold pen and rolled it between his fingers. "Not that it matters a helluva lot. I've been out of the loop ever since Corbet arrived on the scene."

"Don't worry about it, Axel. Politics is anything but static." Escope watched the tic pulse at the corner of Bembry's left eye. "Today you're down—"the lobbyist turned his palms up— "tomorrow, you're up."

"We'll see." Bembry looked around his office, his eyes focusing on the red phone, his direct line to the President. "Just make sure Nasser keeps his part of the bargain."

"Like I said, don't worry about it! To get around campaign finance laws, the money is being distributed for your benefit through appropriate donors. It will be in your account by week's end."

In Tel Aviv, Ira Bettleman opened a beer, sat down, and clicked on the Arab news channel, Al-Jazeera. The anchor's face stared back at him. "Demonstrations and riots continue to grow increasingly violent throughout the region," he said. "As the Western Coalition prepares for war, millions of people from Cairo to Amman have taken to the streets, calling for *jihad* against all foreigners. Leading clerics warn if standing governments fail to heed the call of God, they will be deposed. And now we take you to our correspondent in Amman, Jordan for an update."

"Thank you, Jamal," the correspondent said. "More than one hundred thousand faithful have clogged the streets here in Amman. The mood of the crowd grows angrier by the moment as they wait to hear from one of Jordan's leading clerics, Sheik Ali-Jalil Adnan."

The picture changed to an overhead view of the central city. A ragged wave of humanity thrust Islamic flags skyward and chanted "*Allah-u Akbar.*" The mob burned Israeli, American, and British flags in the streets, along with placards bearing pictures of the Jordanian king and his son, Crown Prince Abdel Agha.

The camera zoomed in on the grim-faced mullah, who stood behind a bank of microphones on a temporary podium. "Silence!" Sheik Adnan's voice carried over the screaming, and the mob quieted. "Infidels once again prepare to war against Islam. Allah's signs are clear in the path the faithful should follow. The sacred lands of the Prophet must be purged of all things Western. We are all martyrs of Allah. Every Muslim must follow the word of God, and strike down the foreign invader in defense of the one true faith."

Thunderous applause, followed by chants of "Death to the West" and "Death to infidels," filled the air.

The sheik lifted a hand. "Pray, and arm yourselves. The faithful will be protected by God and purity of purpose. When the invader comes, open the gates of hell and let the Sword of Allah fall."

Bettleman took a sip of beer and stared at the wild-eyed fury etched on the mob's faces, amidst dust and smoke. Sounds of Tel

Aviv's rush-hour traffic pulled him back. He clicked off the television and raised his bottle.

The intercom sounded, turning Bettleman's head. "Yes?"

"Mr. Eisenberg is here, sir."

"Send him in."

Jacob Eisenberg walked in, carrying a file folder. "You catch the latest on Al-Jazeera?"

"It's a fucked-up world." Israel's spymaster lit a cigarette. "Help yourself to a beer, Jacob, and open a fresh one for me."

Jacob went to the bar and returned with two cold bottles. "Dr. Levine gave the go-ahead for a Miniature Aerial Surveillance Device field test."

Bettleman grunted. "How long before we can put a couple MASD's inside Moussawi's residence?"

"We should know something in a day or two." Jacob took a swig. "I've got two tsetse flies on the way to our agent in Tyre."

"Tsetse flies?" Bettleman raised his eyebrows.

"The doctor tells me they're the perfect flying machine, and virtually undetectable," Jacob said. "Wait till you see a demonstration. Levine and his staff have packed a lot of nanotechnology inside a space no larger than the body of a fly."

In his country estate near Jeddah, Nasser drew on the *Narghile* and passed the stem to Moussawi. "The time is near for us to do God's work."

"Our *jihadi* stand ready." A tremor touched the sheik's hand as he inhaled a lung full of smoke. "The infidels are preparing for war. How do you think they will respond to our initiative?"

"In predictable fashion," Nasser said. "Negotiations will cease, and their invasion will begin immediately. Further actions would include shutting down air transportation in and out of the Middle East, cutting communications, and freezing our assets."

"A heavy price." Moussawi's tongue touched his lips. "Islam will be cut off from the rest of the world."

"Nothing of value comes without a heavy price." Nasser's hand waved expansively. "Oil is what the invaders want. We will deny them their lifeblood if they set one foot on our sacred soil."

"But—"

Nasser stopped him. "Think, my dear Moussawi. After our initiative, the West will have no choice but to react. Havoc will sweep the lands of Mohammad, peace be upon Him, before Islam can be purged of Western poison."

"We will have to bridge our own internal dissent," Moussawi said. "A chasm exists between Sh'ia and Sunni."

"Our joint *fatwa* will instruct a handpicked panel of clerics to reconcile these differences. In the ensuing chaos, current leaders will make private arrangements with the West, and flee with their families." Nasser drew again on the *Narghile.* "While our religious leaders talk, you and I will have an army of God to enforce the peace."

Moussawi clasped his hands. "You have planned well, my prince. When do we instruct our *jihadi?*"

"The instructions are ready to send. I have allowed two weeks for our cell leaders to coordinate with their members."

"The first day of Ramadan," Moussawi said softly.

"A fine way to begin the Holy Month." Nasser touched his fingers together. "Infidels the world over will feel Allah's wrath."

"It will be a glorious day."

Nasser nodded. "Shall we send the instructions now?"

Moussawi massaged his crippled leg. "Allah as my witness, by all means."

Nasser handed Moussawi his cane and led the way into his computer room.

"My mainframe is powerful enough to run my worldwide interests, and then some," the prince said. "The walls of this room have been insulated to block the release of electronic impulses."

Moussawi looked around. "Most impressive."

Nasser entered a series of codes, sounds of the whirring computer filling his ears. After positioning the mouse's pointer over Send, he looked at Moussawi. "Would you like to do the honors? All you have to do is click the left button."

The sheik wiped a hand on his robe. He leaned on his cane as he touched the mouse and clicked.

"The encrypted message has been sent to our one thousand *jihadi* cell leaders around the world," Nasser said.

"Our moment has come." Moussawi stepped back, his eyes on the computer screen. "Allah's sword is about to fall on the infidels."

"Only a few grains of sand remain in the hourglass." Nasser had a sudden vision of himself riding his famed stallion, Al Mukalla, white robes flowing in the wind. Feeling his body shake, the prince took a controlling breath. "In a matter of weeks, unbelievers in the United States, Canada, Europe, Russia, Japan, China, Hong Kong, and Singapore will reap the whirlwind."

Fourteen

Tyre, Southern Lebanon's largest city, hummed with activity the following day when Lefty Libowitz got off the ancient bus in front of the bustling market area. People jostled by the agent as he walked toward the Ottoman Khan Inn. He glanced across the street. Merchants and customers haggled over prices at fishmonger stalls. There were screams and curses until, at the last sane moment, goods and money exchanged hands. Gulls circled over the fisherman's port, bright, black eyes searching for entrails. Flags fluttered in the salty breeze blowing in from the Sidonian port as morning sun glinted off the nearby white, double-domed Sh'ia mosque.

Libowitz stepped inside the Ottoman Khan Inn's lively coffee house located just inside the market. To an observer, the Mossad agent was another poor Arab going to the market for coffee. He wore an old gray *djellaba* and checkered *keffiyeh*. His black hair, eyebrows, mustache, and goatee had been streaked with white.

The agent's trained eyes unobtrusively scanned the coffee house. Old men sat around tables playing backgammon and flicking worry beads. Smells of cigarette smoke, body sweat and freshly-brewed coffee mingled in the air.

A table opened near the front door, and Libowitz sat down. After ordering, he picked up an Arabic newspaper left behind by the previous customer. From time to time, he looked down the street toward the lamb merchant's stall. Jamil, Sheik Moussawi's boychick, should be arriving soon.

Libowitz had just started on his third cup of coffee when he saw several Allah's Army soldiers position themselves outside the lamb merchant's stall. The boychick would be close behind. He folded the newspaper and signaled for the check. Then he delicately palmed two MASD replicas of African tsetse flies, left some coins on the table, and went outside.

The din of the market welled around him. Streets and alleys teemed with life as merchants and customers screamed and cursed their way through ancient bargaining rituals. Smells of cardamom, sumac, cooking oil, roasting meat, coffee, and bread vied for prominence with the more pungent odors of animal dung, urine, sweat, and unclean bodies of those who lived and died here. Both sides of the dirt lanes were lined with dimly-lit, open-fronted shops where anything from heroin to munitions could be purchased for a price.

Libowitz saw Jamil's security guards approaching. He positioned himself on the side of the street and began walking toward the lamb merchant's shop. He nodded to a beggar slumped near a pile of rotting vegetables in an alleyway. Flies swarmed over the refuse and his alms bowl.

Jamil's matching *djellaba* and *keffiyeh* were brilliant white, trimmed in gold and emerald green. He walked in the middle of four guards, his face covered from the bridge of his nose downward.

The beggar stood shakily and approached the guards, his bowl extended. "Alms, alms, a few pounds for the sick and needy."

"Out of the way, beggar," one of the guards said.

"Alms—"

The guard shoved the beggar down into the street. "I said out of the way."

Grabbing the guard's leg, the beggar looked up. "Alms for the poor."

The group stopped as the guard kicked at the beggar, just missing his face as the beggar rolled clumsily away. A crowd gathered. The guard kicked again, this time knocking the beggar's alms bowl into the street.

Libowitz slipped inside the other three guards, his hand passing over the emerald lining of Jamil's *keffiyeh* as he exited.

In Tel Aviv, Ira Bettleman and Jacob Eisenberg took the elevator down to Dr. Levine's lab in the basement of Mossad headquarters.

"Welcome to my dungeon. It's not often I'm visited by those from the surface." Dr. Levine chuckled. "Our MASD's are in place. Sandwiches and cold beer are on the table in front of the screen."

"Surveillance devices that are mobile, see, hear, and look like tsetse flies?" Bettleman shook his head. "Doctor, you amaze me."

Levine adjusted the controls, and the overhead screen winked on.

"Son of a bitch," Jacob said. Sprawled out on a bed was a naked Sheik Moussawi.

"When did he get back from Jeddah?" Bettleman asked.

"Last night," Jacob said. "Our people photographed Moussawi getting off the same Cessna Citation II that's been ferrying him back and forth between Tyre and Jeddah."

Bettleman popped a beer and took a long drink. "Is that the boychick?"

"That's him," Jacob said.

They watched Jamil move beside the bed, prepare a syringe, then thump the vein near Moussawi's heel. The boychick wrinkled his nose as his face moved closer to the naked sheik.

Moussawi winced when the needle was inserted.

"I'm sorry for your discomfort, Excellency," Jamil said. "Now that your medicine is up to three doses daily, we must allow the scar tissue in the crooks of your arms time to heal."

Moussawi relaxed as the drug temporarily abated the hunger. He took a breath and rolled over. His eyes glowed from the heroin as he ran a hand under the boy's *djellaba*. "What would I do without you, Jamil?"

"It is my honor to serve you, Excellency."

The sheik's hand continued its exploration, his penis rising. "Jamil, soon there will be a special day blessed by Allah. The world will change."

Jamil stepped back, removed his *djellaba,* and let it drop to the floor. "How will the world change, Excellency?"

"You will know when it happens." Moussawi's eyes roamed the boy's body. He extended his hand. "Come to me, Jamil."

Bettleman stood as the sheik and young boy entwined on the bed. "Interesting," the spymaster said. He massaged his chin before turning to Dr. Levine. "Every word the MASD's pick up is to be sent up Priority One for analysis. Maybe our smelly heroin addict will say something in his sleep."

"Lucky our agent had the opportunity to plant a pair of our flies on the boy," Levine said. "The other is monitoring the dining and reception areas."

"Excellent. Keep me informed, Doctor." Bettleman picked up half a sandwich as he scowled at the television monitor. "Jacob, I'm not big on this kind of entertainment. Let's get back to the land of the living and discuss how the world might be changing."

"Where are we?" President Abigail Stewart's gaze moved around the table, stopping on Frances Merriman.

"Our coalition partners signed off on Grant's plan for the Spratly oil and gas reserves," the SecState said. "You could hear their collective sighs of relief. Of course, now we'll have to listen to endless squabbling over funding and manning the war effort, refugees, aid packages, loan agreements, et al. I've assured them the future distribution plan will be equitable. That should eventually satisfy them."

"Despite France, Germany, and Russia's internal Muslim problems, we're getting military cooperation across the board." Secretary of Defense Collin Jeffers tapped a file with his pen. "We can thank Foreign Minister Zyyad for all this teamwork."

"He screwed up blowing that well on primetime television." Zach Holden turned to Merriman. "How do we stand with the International Court?"

"With luck, we should get a quick and favorable ruling from the ICJ."

"What about the other claimants?" the President asked.

"Legally speaking, at the moment we are the only claimant, since none of the other countries has approached the ICJ." Merriman checked her notes. "Last month, we filed a brief asking the court to grant us 'Action to Quiet Title.' We're obliged to give notice to other countries that might have a claim. Of course, that leaves the ruling open to challenge."

"How much time does that buy us?" Zach asked.

"Two, maybe three years." Merriman shrugged. "A lot can happen between then and now."

"Drilling teams and equipment are in Okinawa waiting to move," the President said. "It won't take China long to figure out what we're up to. When do you expect to get a decision from the

ICJ, Frances?"

"Given the gravity of the situation, I expect one any day."

The President looked at Grant. "Have our satellites picked up anything out of the ordinary?"

"No, Madam President. Neither have our personnel in Taipei and Beijing. Thus far, they haven't sounded any alarms." Grant passed folders around the table. "Here are the latest satellite photos of Zhanjiang and Guangzhou, major naval bases for the PROC's South Sea Fleet. Looks like business as usual."

"That can change at any time." Abby turned to her Secretary of Defense. "What have you got, Collin?"

"While the coalition continues building its Middle East invasion force, we've quietly begun moving some pieces on the board, Madam President. The Kitty Hawk Battle Group is moving south in the Sea of Japan awaiting orders. The Royal Navy's Illustrious BG is en route to Australia, ostensibly to conduct naval exercises in the South China Sea. For backup, we have the Stennis BG standing by in the Persian Gulf." Jeffers flipped open a file. "As for the opposition, the Chinese navy recently added two Russian destroyers to their fleet. They're nasty, but we can handle anything they throw at us."

"Okay, Collin, quietly continue military deployment. Meanwhile, from the rest of you, I want options, political options. If war with China appears imminent, I want to be prepared to offer graceful and constructive alternatives."

An hour after Grant returned to Langley from his meeting with the President, Jack Sweeny walked into his office.

"Hi, Jack. What's new?"

"We've run down Nasser's financial man." The lanky Texan took a seat across from Grant and opened a folder. "Gerhard Esch, originally from Frankfurt, runs a privately held company in the Big Apple, Trident Holdings. Tony digs for him and his small staff; a penthouse overlooking Central Park, no less. As far as we can tell, Trident's sole purpose is to make money for Nasser."

Grant leaned forward. "That's something. What else have you got on Esch?"

Sweeny peeled the wrapping off a grape Jolly Rancher and popped it into his mouth. "Not much. His father, a prominent banker in Frankfurt during the sixties, seventies, and eighties, taught him the money business. Esch remained in banking until his parents had passed away. Shortly after burying his mother in the mid-nineties, he came to New York and set up Trident Holdings."

"You think Esch had a connection with Nasser before he came to New York?"

Sweeny nodded. "What else? All indications point to Nasser being his only client. Besides, it would take a ton of green to set up an outfit like Trident Holdings, something Nasser's got plenty of."

"I've been checking into Nasser's background," Grant said. "He rarely associates with non-Muslims outside of business dealings. Curious he would trust his personal investments to an unbeliever."

"Esch made the conversion. His Islamic roots come from his mother, Hanna. She and her family left Northern Turkey in the early sixties on a journey of hope to Germany. All of them except Hanna were killed or died of starvation along the way." Sweeny glanced at his notes. "According to one of Esch's former associates, Gerhard made the conversion to Islam long before coming to the U.S."

Grant laced his fingers behind his head and stared at the ceiling.

"We need to get someone inside Esch's mainframe," Sweeny said. "Any ideas?"

"As a matter of fact—" Grant reached for an orange Jolly

Rancher. "I'll have to pull a few strings to get him on board."

"Whoever it is will have his work cut out. Esch will have the latest and greatest security."

"I doubt this kid will have much trouble." Grant looked across his desk. "He cracked the Pentagon's fire wall."

"Christ," Sweeny said. "You're talking about Russell 'Hack' Thomas. I thought he was in jail."

Grant chuckled. "He is. I'll have to make a quiet deal with a certain federal judge to better utilize his talents here at the Company."

Axel Bembry nodded to the Secret Service agent as he entered the President's office.

"Madam President."

Abby looked up from the folder in her lap. "We've got to make this quick, Axel. I've got a meeting with the Pakistani ambassador in ten minutes."

"I've come to submit my resignation."

"Really?" Abby laid the folder down. "A little sudden, isn't it?"

"Not really." Bembry sat across from the President, removed a document from his attaché, and slid it across the desk. "Here is my letter of resignation. My role as NSA has been effectively neutralized since Grant Corbet became your special advisor."

Abby caught the hint of sarcasm in Bembry's voice. She picked up the letter but did not read it. "You've had hard feelings against Grant Corbet since your days as Saudi ambassador."

"As I told you earlier, Madam President, Corbet's a loose cannon."

"I disagree with your assessment," Abby said.

A wisp of a smile passed over Bembry's face. "I'm sure you do."

The President's eyes flashed. "I've checked out your allegations, Axel. A lot of problems could have been avoided had you and your predecessor listened to Mr. Corbet."

Bembry stood. "Well, that's all water under the bridge now, isn't it?"

"Yes, it is." Abby glanced at his letter. "Your resignation has been accepted, effective immediately."

Fifteen

"And?"

"The sheik's heavily guarded. Security's been increased since we got our MASD's inside the compound. We've picked up a number of references about Allah's sword gutting the infidels. Something big is obviously in the works." Jacob lit a cigarette. "Depending on the weather, I want to try for a snatch in two days. That will give me time to get the team organized. Libowitz has been running surveillance. Around three a.m. Moussawi's guards start getting sloppy."

Ira Bettleman stared out at the lights of Tel Aviv. "The risk?"

"Not in our favor," Jacob said. "It would have to be a silent op. Any shooting would alert Allah's Army reinforcements. Chances of getting our team out of the market with Moussawi in one piece would be nil."

"Entry and exit strategy?" Bettleman asked.

Jacob unrolled a map of Israel and Lebanon and spread it on the desk. "One of our choppers drops us a mile offshore, here. Two battery-powered inflatables carry the team into the harbor." The tip of Jacob's pen touched a spot. "They'll dock beneath the fishmonger stalls, located across from the market. Libowitz and one of his men will be in place to alert us if there are any unexpected militia activities. If it's a go, we make a quick in and out, snatch Moussawi, then rendezvous back at sea with the chopper."

"How many on the team?"

"Six including myself," Jacob said. "Two will stay with the inflatables, while I lead the other three in. The MASD's got us the security system codes inside Moussawi's compound."

"I don't like the idea of you going," Bettleman said.

"Time is the critical factor." Jacob stubbed out his cigarette. "I'm the most knowledgeable man we've got about Moussawi and the inner workings of his compound. Also, I'm privy to CIA intel. Terry Falco opened the files for me while we worked on a joint strategy to nab Moussawi."

"I approve your request, but don't bother informing Falco. We don't want to get bogged down in intra-agency bureaucratic squabbling over setting up a joint operation." Bettleman's gaze returned to the window. Darkness, punctuated by flickering lights, covered his beloved land of Israel. "This is risky business, but we've got to get Moussawi. God willing, he'll crack within twenty-four hours."

Jacob rolled up the map. "I hope we're not too late."

"Pray you're not. The world's supposed to change soon." The Israeli spymaster waited for Jacob Eisenberg to leave before picking up the telephone.

"Corbet."

"Hard at work, I see," said the gravelly voice of Ira Bettleman.

"There's never enough time, my friend. I'm glad you called."

"I have something."

"So do I," Grant said. "You go first."

"We have several surveillance devices inside Moussawi's compound. He's into young boys."

"A common enough practice for clerics in your neck of the woods," Grant said.

"True, but there's something else. Moussawi's a heroin addict, three doses per day."

Grant whistled. "That's good to know. Makes him vulnerable."

"The sheik told his boychick, Jamil, Allah was going to change the world soon," Bettleman said.

"He say how?"

"No. But I have a bad feeling about this, Grant. Moussawi made the statement with such cool conviction. None of the usual histrionics. I'll send a file of the bedroom scene you can download. You'll see what I mean."

"How does Nasser fit in?"

"Moussawi's travels to and from Jeddah have increased. Our people have been monitoring him. His mode of travel never varies."

"Let me guess." Grant's hand moistened around the receiver. "The Cessna Citation II that belongs to Oasis Hotel Corporation."

"The very same," Bettleman said. "In the next few days, Jacob will be paying Moussawi an early morning visit."

Grant caught the tension in Bettleman's voice. "Jacob's a tough sonofabitch, Ira. If he's successful, Moussawi will crack in a matter of days. With three hits a day, he's hooked bad."

"That's what we're hoping for. Still, I can't help worrying in my old age. I'd like to see Jacob in my chair after I retire." Bettleman paused. "You said you had something for me."

"Sweeny ran down Nasser's money man. We've got someone working on getting inside his computer."

"Timetable?"

"Hard to say," Grant said. "I know the guy Jack's got working on it is the best."

"Maybe we can tie this up before the world changes,"

Bettleman said.

"Ira?"

"Yes."

"Want to tell me how you managed to get surveillance devices inside Moussawi's compound?"

"Let's just say we had help from friendly tsetse flies."

Hack Thomas' new home was an office located in a secure area in the operations sector. Big Bertha, the name by which Hack affectionately referred to his mainframe computer, was one of the world's fastest and most sophisticated machines. It hummed softly beneath the overhead lights. A half-eaten BLT sat on the table next to the workstation. Miniature cameras behind the heating and air conditioning vents monitored the hacker's work habits.

Hack, a twenty-one-year-old MIT dropout, tossed a piece of uneaten lettuce back into the sack. He flexed his fingers and started typing. For him, this was the ultimate high. The keys, cool beneath his touch, produced a kind of magical energy in his fingers as they sped across the keyboard. Just knowing the most complex systems were subject to intrusion gave him a powerful rush of adrenaline. Still, he found it curious that he could be arrested for hacking out of the home, and then rewarded for doing the same thing when Big Brother deemed it necessary in the interest of national security.

After hitting the keyboard for several hours, Hack paused to stretch. He had invested a great deal of time and energy on his initial reconnaissance to determine the susceptibility of Esch's operating system. Learning the configuration of the network and when the other machines were on and off had been tricky. He stared at the screen, feeling his pulse quicken at the data he'd retrieved. Now he had to find out what services were active on the target system. Once he had that information, he would work on gaining access. His knuckles cracked as he massaged his hands.

"Well?"

"Ira thinks something's about to blow," Grant said. He handed his boss a CD. "Mossad got inside Moussawi's Tyre head-quarters. They filmed him in bed with his boy companion, Jamil. Turns out Moussawi's a big time heroin addict. You'll see Jamil giving the sheik a fix. Right afterwards, Moussawi tells him Allah's about to change the world."

"I'm sure he doesn't mean for the better." Zach punched a button and brought down a screen of the Middle East behind his desk. "You're still convinced Nasser and Moussawi are behind the Israeli jet going down?"

"It's logical," Grant said. "Nasser's got the green, Moussawi's got the fanatics."

"A lot of lives could be saved if we can dig up enough compelling evidence to exonerate Tartir."

"Our Tel Aviv station chief, Terry Falco, is helping Jacob Eisenberg with intel to snatch Moussawi in his Tyre compound." Grant swirled the coffee inside his Styrofoam cup. "Meanwhile, I've got Hack Thomas working on getting inside the mainframe of Nasser's money guy."

"Pretty slick of you getting the judge to loan us Thomas." Zach fished for his pipe. "How the hell did Ira manage to film Moussawi in his bedroom?"

"I asked the same question," Grant said. "He mentioned something about friendly tsetse flies."

"The crafty old son-of-a-bitch has developed a miniature aerial surveillance device," Zach said.

"Vulcan is close to perfecting MASD technology." Grant tapped his folder. "Andy Stranahan called and said they're only days away from having an operational MASD. It promises to bridge the nano gap between us and the Israelis. Jack Sweeny and I are planning to fly up for a demonstration. Can you break away?"

"I'm tied up the rest of the week with the intelligence committee, so just bring me the report. Besides, I'm afraid I might put a damper on things."

Grant saw concern form in Zach's eyes as he reached for his pipe.

"Christ, I don't know about all of this nanotechnology," Zach said. "TBOLT could very well make political assassination a way of life. If we disagree with someone, just send a miniature drone over and blow them away. If we want to eavesdrop, drop in a tsetse fly, or some other goddamned insect." The DCI stared outside. Gray skies blanketed snow-covered trees dotting the rolling Virginia landscape. "Just a matter of time before our friends perfect similar models. I can only imagine what will happen when the other side gets hold of them."

"I don't know," Grant said. "Look what the Israelis were able to learn getting a pair of MASD's inside Moussawi's compound."

"Look what unfriendly nations or terrorist groups might learn getting them inside Pentagon briefings or cabinet meetings. No one will be safe." Zach pressed tobacco into the bowl of his pipe. "The whole thing scares the hell out of me."

"Better us than the bad guys having the technology," Grant said. "At least we'll have time to develop MASD detection and de-bugging devices by the time they get them."

"Who knows? Maybe something like that would be good for the economy. TBOLT and MASD detection devices, a must-have for every man, woman, and child."

Grant drained his coffee. "Definitely ease unemployment."

"By the way, I've gotten us emergency funding for fifty TBOLT's to be delivered ASAP." Zach pointed with his pipe stem. "Another hundred will follow over the next several months."

"That's good news." Grant slipped his file back into his attaché. "I hope Jacob breaks Moussawi soon."

Zach looked up at the screen of the Middle East. "Let's hope Mossad lives up to their reputation sooner rather than later."

That evening, after Grant arrived, Abigail Stewart closed the door to the White House residence. "Explain to me how we went from a relatively peaceful world several months ago, to a world on the brink of war today."

"Our planet has evolved into a very fragile place, Madam President." Grant put his arms around her. "A single incident can trigger a catastrophic chain of events. The bad guys know this. That's why I'm convinced Tartir's being set up."

Abby laid her head on his shoulder. "Interested in another job?"

"That's a loaded question. I think I'm happy where I am. Why?"

"I had a surprise visit from Axel after our meeting this afternoon. He resigned." Diffuse light cast Abby's face into highlight and relief. "He's the first cabinet member I've lost."

"It happens to every President, sooner or later."

"He said his job as NSA had been effectively neutralized since you became one of my advisors."

"Bembry struck me as a man who enjoyed the trappings of power," Grant said. "Strange he didn't give you any warning."

"He called you a loose cannon. When I told him I disagreed with his assessment, an odd thing happened."

"What?"

"He gave me a funny smile and said, 'I'm sure you do.'" Abby squeezed Grant's hand. "The way he said it gave me the strangest feeling he knows about us."

"It's possible." Grant kept his concern out of his voice. "I don't worry about agent Caspare. She's discreet, but who knows about the rest of the White House staff. Sooner or later this will be out in the open."

"I don't think we should continue trying to keep our relationship hidden."

Grant kissed her forehead.

"We're two healthy, single adults," Abby said. "Where in the Constitution does it say a President can't have a life?"

"It comes down to a matter of perception." Grant looked away. "If Bembry does know something, he might—"

Abby put a finger to his lips. "We promised not to talk shop during our private time. Let's forget about Axel and enjoy the moment."

Grant smiled. "You're the boss."

Sixteen

Familiar gray skies filled the frame of Grant's office window the following afternoon. Oak, birch, and maple trees stretched leafless limbs over the snow and ice that covered the rolling landscape. Geese flew overhead, but he did not notice. Instead, his thoughts were on Axel Bembry. Why would the former NSA suddenly resign in the midst of a crisis? Rumors had been circulating for over a year about Bembry's political aspirations. And hadn't he seen Bembry talking with Lawrence Escope, Nasser's lobbyist, at the White House reception? Coincidence? Grant didn't think so. Years in the field had taught him to discount coincidence as a reason for the way events fashioned themselves.

The intercom buzzed, moving him back to his desk. He pressed a button. "Yes."

"Mr. Lebo is here to see you."

"Send him in."

A moment later, Leo Lebo, a field agent stationed in Israel during Grant's time as CIA Station Chief in Tel Aviv, walked in.

"Hi boss, how are you?" Lebo extended a hand. "Haven't seen much of you since your move upstairs."

"You look good, Leo. Stateside work must be agreeing with

you."

"Life here gets a little boring. Not like our days in the Middle East." Lebo shrugged. "You know how it is. You can take the agent out of the field, but you can't take the field out of the agent."

Grant looked at his friend. "I need a favor."

"Sounds serious." Lebo took a seat.

"It's not an official agency matter."

"Hey." Lebo raised a hand. "You've covered my back, and I've covered yours. I'm here to help."

"Laws will be broken. And you'll be a one-man show."

"I like one-man shows." Lebo grinned. "Besides, I remember a time or two when we bent the rules together."

"Axel Bembry resigned as National Security Advisor," Grant said. "I want to know who he talks to, when he goes to sleep, where he eats, when he gets his shoes shined... The works."

Lebo tapped the side of his nose. "In twenty-four hours, I'll have him wired so tight he won't be able to take a whiz without me knowing."

In Tyre, Lefty Libowitz watched the two Israeli inflatables dock beneath the fishmonger stalls. At two a.m. the sky was dark, overcast, and quiet. The air held a chill, smelling faintly of pollution. Sand crabs scurried across the beach as six men, dressed in matte-black, scrambled out and secured the rafts. Night goggles framed the blackened face of Jacob Eisenberg.

"Our guests have arrived." Libowitz spoke softly into his walkie-talkie. "Are their accommodations in order?"

"Hotel staff has been accommodating." A whispered reply.

Libowitz clicked on a pocket laser and aimed the red dot inches in front of Jacob's feet. A quick hand signal from the Mossad leader let him know the signal had been seen.

Jacob jabbed a team member's arm. "Go."

The man darted across the street and took up a defensive position inside the market. After receiving an all clear signal, the second member of the team raced across, followed by a third.

Jacob glanced at the other two team members. One had taken up a position with a good view down both sides of the boulevard fronting the market. The other, Zvi Morik, had connected a laptop to a cell phone and was typing in commands. A moment later, he looked up and raised a thumb.

Nodding, Jacob scanned the area around him for unwanted movement. Finding none, he hurried into the market to rendezvous with his men.

The commandos fanned out, wearing night goggles. They began making a circuitous route toward Moussawi's compound, checking streets and alleyways as they went.

Ahead on a deserted side street, Lefty Libowitz met the agent who had completed the surveillance of Moussawi's compound.

"Nothing on the east side, but there're six guards on the south entrance." The agent wiped sweat from his brow. "Three at the rear door of the compound, and three in the alley across the street."

"Not good."

"It gets worse," the agent said. "A dozen more are stationed in front of the compound. No telling how many are inside."

Libowitz clicked on his walkie-talkie. "Spectacular sunrise forecast. Half dozen vendors already gathered on both sides of the street."

Jacob alerted his men and pointed to the eastern sky. Sunrise meant they were to meet at a prearranged destination at the rear of Moussawi's compound.

Dogs barked in the distance as the team moved forward. Ten

minutes later, they were in position. Incredibly, the six Allah's Army sentries had gathered in the middle of the street, talking and smoking.

Looking like great green-eyed insects, the commandos moved in. Short bursts came from the suppressor-equipped Uzis, then all was quiet.

The Mossad team pulled the bodies off the street into the alley.

Jacob whispered into his walkie-talkie. "What's the weather like inside?"

Back at the inflatables, Zvi Morik, the agent with the laptop, typed in a command. A split computer screen materialized as the two tsetse fly MASD's scanned their areas. "Single guest asleep in downstairs bedroom, three more smoking in upstairs parlor. Security pad behind panel on doorjamb is hot. Alarm set to activate six seconds after entry."

Jacob went to the back door, picked the lock, and went inside. He opened the panel and deactivated the alarm system. A commando moved into the bedroom. His black blade arced and descended. A soft grunt, followed by an expulsion of air as the Allah's Army soldier died.

Libowitz and his agent took up positions at the door, while Jacob and the rest of the team moved upstairs. The three Allah's Army soldiers were hunched over a backgammon board. The approaching commandos still wore night goggles when one of the Allah's Army soldiers glanced up. His last thought before Jacob's Uzi coughed was how much they resembled the science fiction creatures he'd seen in a movie.

Jacob pushed open the sheik's bedroom door. The air reeked from the aftermath of men's sex, sweat, and hashish. Half smiling, Jacob removed his infra-red goggles. Moussawi and his boychick, Jamil, were asleep, locked in an obscene embrace.

The team surrounded the bed. Jacob prodded Moussawi with his Uzi. "Time to go."

Moussawi grunted and rolled over. Commandos held the sheik and Jamil down, tape covering their mouths. Needles, glinting in the semi-darkness, sank into exposed arms. The naked men's eyes glazed, followed by unconsciousness.

"The sheik has a nice rug collection," Jacob said. "Wrap them up, and let's get out of here."

Grant left Abby shortly after four a.m. When he arrived home thirty minutes later, his secure telephone sounded. "Corbet."

"You're up early, my friend," said Mossad's spymaster, Major General Ira Bettleman.

"I've been having trouble sleeping lately," Grant said.

A distant chuckle emanated from the Holy Land. "Such are the vicissitudes of our business."

Grant felt a rush of excitement. "Something's up, Ira, or you wouldn't be calling at four thirty in the morning."

"Sheik Mahmoud Moussawi and his boychick, Jamil, came to pay us a visit. They arrived early this morning."

"Jacob works fast," Grant said. "How long do you think Moussawi can hold out?"

"He's praying to Allah for strength inside his padded cell. As you Americans say, 'The monkey's on his back.' Even with Allah's help, I doubt he can last more than two days."

"What about Jamil?"

"Jacob has a team interrogating him. He's cooperating, but his knowledge is limited," Bettleman said. "We know there's a link between Allah's Army and Nasser. We'll have to wait for Moussawi to crack to learn how deep it goes."

"Our man's close to tapping Gerhard Esch's computer," Grant said. "With a little luck, we might tie it all together."

Bettleman sighed. "Who knows? With a little luck we might turn up something to help you sleep."

Access Granted.

"Hot damn!"

Hack Thomas threw Big Bertha a kiss as the two words he had been looking for blinked on the screen.

Standing, he stretched his arms and neck. A glance at the wall clock told him it was five a.m. No question, it had been a long night, but the high he felt now made it worthwhile. After washing down the last of his potato chips with an orange soda, Hack sat back down. He stared fondly at the screen and flexed his fingers. Supremely confident in his computer navigational skills, he began typing.

Thirty minutes later, he found the simplest point of entry to target the system. Next, he created multiple back doors for future attacks. Esch's system contained many sophisticated traps, but Hack worked his way through them. Of course, he thought wryly, after cracking the Pentagon, he had a wealth of experience going for him. The hacker's fingers stopped moving, his eyes fixed on the screen.

"Yes."

A rush of adrenaline coursed through Hack's body. He had just broken through Trident Holdings' fire wall. Undetected!

Not bad for a twenty-one-year-old MIT dropout.

Hack Thomas inserted a CD and clicked "download."

At Mossad headquarters in Tel Aviv, Sheik Moussawi shook violently inside his padded cell. The all-consuming pain was surpassed only by his need.

"Allah be merciful." But the ears of God were closed to his prayer. An hour passed, and any thought of mercy had been reduced to an impossible dream.

Pain ripped through his body. Moussawi rolled and jerked like a fish swimming into unknown darkness. Drawing the smallest breath was an effort in pain. Light and dark—hot and cold converged into one. He curled into a fetal position, covered in his own vomit.

"My medicine, I must have my medicine."

Jacob Eisenberg watched Moussawi on the monitor from the doctor's office down the hall. "How long before he breaks?"

"Hard to say." The doctor massaged his chin. "If the vomiting and diarrhea continue, he'll dehydrate. Then, of course, there's the possibility of seizures."

"Don't let him die on me," Jacob said. "Let me know the moment you think he's close to breaking. I want to be the first face he sees when he's ready to talk."

The warm air smelled of talc and sweat when Grant and Jack Sweeny started running slow laps around the indoor track at six a.m. Distant sounds of clanging weights and racquetballs thumping against court walls echoed inside the almost-deserted CIA gymnasium.

"Hack cracked Trident Holdings' system earlier this morning," Grant said. "Most of the good stuff is encrypted. I've got our best people working on it."

"That's something." Sweeny glanced sideways. "Have you got his line tapped?"

"As we speak, but there's more," Grant said. "Trident Holdings' computer system is connected with Alhannah's network. Hack believes that in a matter of days we should be looking at Nasser's files."

"Things are starting to pop," Sweeny said.

Grant wiped the sweat from his forehead. "Ira called earlier. Moussawi's in a padded cell, close to breaking."

"After our run, let's grab a sauna and meet in my office," Sweeny said. "I'll spring for the Krispy Kremes, and we'll go see Zach."

"You're on."

Out of the corner of his eye, Sweeny saw Grant smile. "What the hell are you grinning about?"

"You and your goddamned doughnuts."

Zach Holden dropped his half-eaten Krispy Kreme in the wastebasket after Grant and Jack Sweeny left. Then he went to the shelf where he kept his model ships and picked up *Providence*. His fingers traced lines along the smooth wood. Smiling, he remembered the hours of enjoyment he'd spent during his years with the Navy constructing her. The most victorious American ship of the Revolutionary War was a square-topsail-gaff-rigged sloop, the first of her kind commissioned into the Continental Navy.

"She was the first and she was the best," he said, echoing the words of her captain, John Paul Jones.

Zach stared at the miniature twelve guns along the sides of her decks. He could almost see John Paul Jones exhorting his men, the wind and sea billowing *Providence*'s sails as she engaged the British.

"If modern warfare were only so simple," Zach said to himself. He replaced *Providence* on the shelf and went back to work.

"We have a breaking story," the Al Jazeera anchor said. "According to Lebanese officials in Tyre, in an early morning raid Zionist agents kidnapped the spiritual leader of Allah's Army, Sheik Mahmoud Moussawi, from his Tyre residence. During the raid, ten members of Sheik Moussawi's security force were killed. Four bodies were found inside Sheik Moussawi's compound. Six dead soldiers were discovered in an alley behind the sheik's residence." Prince Nasser's dark eyes narrowed as he watched the anchor fade and an image of the bullet-riddled corpses on a dirt street fill the screen. "Despite denials of involvement by Israeli officials, the kidnapping has triggered massive demonstrations throughout the Middle East on the eve of Ramadan. Leaders of Allah's Army vow to open the floodgates of hell upon the Israeli—"

Nasser clicked off the set, then stepped out onto his balcony. He inhaled the cool mountain air, his gaze moving in the direction of Mecca, lying beyond the nexus of earth and sky.

Islam's heart and soul.

Except the heart and soul of Islam had been slowly disintegrating. Saudi Arabia's brightest students went abroad, as he had done, to become educated. Those who had returned arrived with skills necessary to build the country. But many returned harboring doubts. Doubts about the Faith mingled with memories of freedom. Nasser closed his eyes. What kind of freedom was the freedom to drink, gamble, and fornicate? An updraft of air rose over the cliff, chilling the prince.

Now Sheik Moussawi had been captured by the hated Zionists and would undoubtedly be broken. Nasser stared at the horizon. His link to Moussawi would soon become public knowledge around the world. There was nothing he could do about that. Oh, he could still call off the *jihadi,* and perhaps avoid a war. But for what purpose? He would still be hunted for his involvement in the downing of the Israeli jet.

Not for the first time in recent days, he wondered if he had gone too far, too quickly.

Certainly, he'd crossed a line from which there could be no going back. But hadn't Allah been sending signs, guiding him to his destiny? His alliance with Moussawi, the martyred Egyptian pilot, Israel's war against the Palestinians, his network of loyal *jihadi*—surely these must be signs by Allah that pointed the way. In a matter of days, the world would tremble with fear. *No,* Nasser thought, he had not gone too far. There could be no higher calling than uniting Islam, and thereby fulfilling the Will of Allah and the Prophet Mohammed.

Nasser went back inside the residence and called for his body-guard, Yousef.

"You rang, Highness?"

The prince nodded. "I've decided to send you to the United States. You'll be staying at my house in Virginia. I understand it's quite cold over there."

Just after midnight, New York time, Barry Shivers inhaled the smell of ink and hot paper as the presses of the *National Monitor* came to life. Dust blown up from the floor of the pressroom hung like plankton in columns of diffuse light as the big machines gathered speed.

Shivers took the first paper off the line and checked the front page banner headline.

"Abby's White House Love Nest Unveiled"

Beneath the headline, a profile photo of Abby, her mouth open, was next to a shot of Grant's car leaving the White House at 4:00 a.m.

"Abby heats up White House with nation's top spook, while world teeters on brink of war—"

Shivers' lips curled as he read the story's opening line. Next would come the book. He had already started on the rough draft.

The President and Her Spy. Shivers' smile broadened. The title had a nice ring.

The presses thumped out Shivers' success. He folded the paper and walked to the parking garage, whistling an old Frank Sinatra song.

Seventeen

Grant had his driver take him directly to work when he left Abby. After his morning run in the company gym, he took a quick sauna, showered and dressed. It was just after 6:30 a.m. when he stepped inside his office. Copies of the *New York Times, Washington Post, USA Today,* and *Wall Street Journal* were waiting on his desk. He filled his Washington Redskins mug, grabbed a food bar out of his desk drawer, and clicked on CNN Headline News.

"Gasoline prices have hit an all-time high," the anchor said. "Unleaded gas in most parts of the country now costs consumers more than four dollars per gallon. Meanwhile, police in metropolitan areas are bracing for another night of looting and vandalism brought about by the unseasonably cold weather. At yesterday's press conference, President Stewart called for an end to 'hysteria and speculation,' which has reached new fervor in financial markets. Unfortunately, Stewart's comments did little to calm fears as the DOW and NASDAQ plunged sharply, losing a fifth of their value before making a slight recovery. And now we take you to our national weather center for a check on local forecasts."

Grant picked up the *Wall Street Journal* and read the lead story. Homeland Security had elevated the national terrorism to red alert as Muslims around the world prepared to celebrate the Holy Month of Ramadan. He next turned to the financial section. "Christ," he muttered. The news went from bad to worse. Oil and bullion prices were soaring, while stocks and currencies plunged.

"CNN has a late-breaking story." Grant folded the paper and looked up as a picture of his car leaving the White House in the early morning hours filled the screen. "CNN has a standing policy not to report on articles that appear in national tabloids. However, due to the unusual nature of this story, management felt a journalistic responsibility to air the contents." Grant's car faded, replaced by the anchor, who tugged at his collar. "In today's edition of the *National Monitor,* Barry Shivers reported President Abigail Stewart and Deputy Director of CIA Operations Grant Corbet are romantically involved. In his article, Shivers contends such distraction undermines the President's ability to effectively lead the nation during a time of crisis. Prior to airing this story, Shivers' assertion gained credibility in a CNN exclusive interview with Axel Bembry. The former National Security Advisor and ambassador to Saudi Arabia told CNN he resigned his post as National Security Advisor because of President Stewart's increasing dependence on Corbet. According to Bembry, the President no longer sought or accepted advice from top security advisors. For more on this fast breaking story we're joined by Senator—"

"Damn, damn, damn." Grant reached for the phone and dialed Abby's private number.

The President picked up on the second ring. "I'm watching CNN now. Axel must've had you followed."

"Bembry or someone who's pulling his strings," Grant said.

"Convenient his interview was scheduled on the day the *National Monitor*'s story broke."

The telephone receiver felt cold in Grant's hand. "It stinks like hell, Abby."

Silence built over the line. "Better find Zach and get over here."

"I imagine you've all seen the morning news," President Abigail Stewart said.

Grant watched Abby focus on the center of the table, a tooth working on the corner of her lip.

"In the interest of saving time, I want to get directly to the point," Abby continued. "What Barry Shivers reported is essentially accurate. What he failed to report is that Grant and I love each other."

"Someone had me followed, and that someone wants to smear the President," Grant said. "I've got a man checking out Barry Shivers and Axel Bembry."

Secretary of State Frances Merriman managed a worried smile. "This isn't good, Madam President. The media and the opposition are going to try and Clintonize you. I think we need to come out with some pretty convincing damage control."

"The opposition on The Hill will be out with tar and feathers," Secretary of Defense Collin Jeffers said.

Abby turned to Zach. "Opinion?"

"Frankly, the two of you make a handsome couple." Zach massaged the bowl of his pipe. "I think the media frenzy is much ado about nothing. Certainly Bembry's reason for resigning can be refuted. If it were up to me, I'd call a press conference today and tell it like it is. You and Grant are single adults who happen to be in love. Who can fault you for that?"

"It's the timing of Bembry's interview, Zach," Merriman said. "Timing's everything in politics. It will be easy for some smart reporter to verify Grant relegated him to second class citizenry. Then we'll have to contend with this town's propensity for gossip. Abby is the first female President. While the West is ratcheting up for war, the press will portray her as a starry-eyed kid asleep at the wheel."

"I'm inclined to agree with Zach," Abby said. "We need to get this out of the way now. If I know anything about the American people, they will be happy for us."

"The religious right won't be satisfied by a press conference," Jeffers said. "They're rabid about this sort of thing."

"We'll just have to see about that. My personal life will remain my personal life. All they will have is speculation." Abby buzzed her secretary. "Call Lori Ramirez and get her over here ASAP."

Two hours later, Lori Ramirez, the President's press secretary, stepped up behind the microphone and faced a room full of tense reporters who covered the White House.

"Here are the ground rules, ladies and gentlemen," Ramirez said. "The President will make a short statement about the story in the *National Monitor*. Then she will answer a few questions. By a few, I mean no more than two or three."

In Tel Aviv, Sheik Moussawi sat in a padded cell, shivering, arms wrapped around his chest. He wore fresh clothes, smelling of bleach, the excrement and vomit having been cleaned away. Now he stared at nothing, his fevered mind vaguely remembering being sedated and bathed.

Why had Allah forsaken him in his time of need? Hadn't he devoted his life to defending the Faith? Now, his god had reduced him to a pathetic creature with an insatiable hunger, longing for death. Why? A spasm of pain cut through his gut like a knife. He fell off the chair and twisted into a ball.

Jacob Eisenberg entered the cell, holding a syringe filled with heroin. He knelt beside Moussawi. "It doesn't have to be this way, you know."

"My medicine—" Moussawi looked up through wild, glazed eyes. "I must have my—"

Jason tapped Moussawi's nose with the syringe. "First, tell me how Allah's going to change the world. Then you can have all the medicine you want. I'll even let Jamil administer it for you."

With an incredible effort, Moussawi turned away from the drug, faced the floor and began reciting the *Shahada*. "There is no God but Allah and Mohammed is His messenger. There is no God but Allah and—"

"Ladies and gentlemen, the President of the United States."

Abigail Stewart stepped up behind the podium. She wore little makeup, and her brown hair fell naturally to her shoulders. Her gray business suit was accented with a lapis necklace and matching earrings. For a long moment the President stared at the assembled reporters.

"Ordinarily, I would not dignify the kind of story Barry Shivers has written with a comment. However, something has happened in my life that I think the American people should know about. I am in love with a wonderful man, Grant Corbet." The President's gaze passed from one reporter to the next. "Twelve years ago, I lost my husband, Richard, in a plane crash. Since that time, I thought love was something that would be denied me. But I was wrong, so very wrong. Barry Shivers has tried," Abby held up a copy of the *National Monitor*, and tapped the headline, "to defile that love and turn it into something ugly. This, I will not allow him to do. Grant Corbet is a patriotic American, who has devoted his life to the service of his country. He is also one of my most trusted advisors. You won't read about his accomplishments in newspapers, or see him interviewed on nightly talk shows. His kind of heroism is a private matter, which makes it all the more genuine."

Abby scanned the assembly and found several reporters she would recognize. "I'll now take a few questions."

Hands immediately shot up, waving frantically.

"Jim." The President pointed to a well-known NBC correspondent.

"Thank you, Madam President. Are you and Mr. Corbet making plans to formalize your relationship?"

"If and when something like that occurs, you'll be the third to know." Laughter broke out, softening the tension. "Andrea."

"Thank you, Madam President. Could you tell us how Mr. Corbet, as the nation's preeminent spy, felt about being spied on?"

"I can't speak for Grant, but I imagine he might be thinking he's been out of the field too long." More laughter. Abby's gaze moved to the back of the room. *Might as well get this out of the way,* she thought, and pointed to the reporter for the *Christian Voice.* "Jasper."

"Thank you, Madam President. I have a two-part question. How do you respond to Mr. Bembry's assertion that you have become dependent on Grant Corbet to the exclusion of other senior security advisors? Secondly, what do you say to charges that you're providing a bad example for our young children by having an affair out of wedlock in the White House?"

The air in the room turned fragile.

"Jasper, I thought you were more professional than to engage in the kind of cheap journalism the *National Monitor* specializes in." Abby's violet eyes flashed. "The only senior security advisor whose judgment I questioned was Axel Bembry's. As for the second part of your question, what does or does not happen between me and Mr. Corbet in the privacy of my home is our business, not a subject for supposition. That's all I have to say about the matter."

"Madam President?" Hands waved.

"Thank you all for coming," Abby said. Then she turned and walked out.

"Meet me for lunch at one," Axel Bembry said. "Have you seen the news? The bitch has short-circuited us."

"I've seen it," answered Lawrence Escope. "Where do you want to meet, and what time?"

"Jean Claude's. I'll make reservations."

"See you at one."

Bembry punched in a new number. "Jacques, Axel Bembry. Lunch for two at one p.m. My usual table."

"Certainly, Mr. Bembry. Your table will be waiting."

Leo Lebo glanced at his watch: 10:30 a.m. From the looks of things, the tap he'd put on the ex-NSA's phone line had started yielding fruit. Five minutes later, Lebo left his apartment and headed for Jean Claude's.

Traffic was unusually light, and Lebo found a parking spot across the street just as the restaurant opened at 11:00 a.m. He grabbed his attaché, and folded a copy of the *Wall Street Journal* under his arm. Bad for Bembry that he'd become a creature of habit, Lebo thought. Coveted restaurant power tables tended to make one careless.

"Yes, Monsieur, can I help you?" the Maître d' asked.

"Yes." Lebo glanced at his watch. "I've just got time for a light lunch."

"Do you have a reservation?"

"No, but I'm only going to have a salad," Lebo said. "I should be out in less than half an hour."

"Of course." The Maître d' looked at his table sheet. "Right this way."

"Excuse me." Lebo gestured. "I'd like to have the corner table, over there. The view looks excellent."

The frown on the Maître d's face disappeared as a pair of crisp twenty-dollar bills found their way into his palm.

Axel Bembry glared across the table, his Caesar salad untouched. "I'm fucked, Lawrence. Where's our female version of Clinton now? The bitch will be more popular than ever. Except for a few religious right publications, the media's turning her affair with Corbet into a national celebration. Since her press conference this morning, the big question the networks and cable shows are asking is when the big day will take place. *Abby's in love. Will it be a spring wedding or summer nuptial?* Christ, we're gonna have another Camelot."

Lawrence Escope sipped his Chardonnay. "Relax, Axel. Her indiscretion is out there. The religious right and Shivers will keep hammering it. Come Sunday, preachers will start castigating her in churches across the country. Children will be asking their parents questions about the President's affair. It won't be long before her behavior will be the hot topic on talk shows. Public opinion will change."

"If it doesn't, I'm fucked. There won't be any talk show circuit, or taking the high road to grab the women's vote." Bembry stabbed at his salad. "Christ, it could all turn to shit."

"It will come, Axel. Reporters are going to start nosing around. They'll find out Corbet stepped all over your toes. There will be doubt about the President's motives." Escope lowered his voice. "Don't forget, Prince Nasser is committed to the twenty million to jumpstart your campaign. We just have to wait until the time is right to make our move."

"It had better be sooner than later." Bembry stared out into space. "Damn, where's the fucking waiter? I could use a martini."

Across the street, Leo Lebo smiled to himself as the recorder sitting on the passenger seat of his car whirred softly. "You're going to need more than a martini, bud," he said to himself.

Thirty minutes later, Lebo watched Bembry and Escope leave the restaurant. Then he placed a call to Grant Corbet.

"Good work, Leo." Grant made a quick notation. "Stay on their backs. I want to give Bembry and Escope a little more rope before taking action."

"Roger," Lebo said. "I'll be in touch."

The light on his private line blinked the moment Grant replaced the receiver. "Corbet."

"Daddy," his daughter, Jenny, said. "I saw the television reports about you and the President. I can't believe it."

A fragile silence.

"I love her, Jen." Grant massaged the bridge of his nose. "She makes me feel like getting up each day is worthwhile."

"You're never too old to be in love," Jenny said. "It's just that she's the President of the United States. You've gone from almost complete anonymity to the most talked about man in the world. It's incredible. How—when did it happen?"

The question hung a moment. "I don't know how or exactly when it happened. Probably, for me, the first time I ever met her. The heart's a funny thing, Jen. One thing led to another, and there we were, two middle-aged adults feeling first-date jitters."

"I'm happy for you, Daddy." A soft laugh. "I must say when you take aim, you shoot for the stars."

"Thanks, sweetheart. I'm glad you called. After this mess is cleared up, I'm coming down to see you and the little guy."

"Don't take too long. He might grow up in the meantime."

"Nasser's riding high in the saddle," Grant said.

Zach Holden fished for his pipe. "Meaning?"

"After Hack Thomas got us inside, cryptology put their mainframes to good work and cracked Nasser's security program. Our prince controls nine hundred b in futures contracts: oil, currency and precious metals."

"Nine hundred billion?" Sweeny cocked an eyebrow. "Christ."

"Here's the file. The buy dates are bulleted." Grant handed folders to the two other men. "Esch developed a trading program, HARPIE, to purchase ten billion in futures contracts."

"That's a sizable chunk of change to drop in the market." Zach sipped his coffee. "Ten billion would raise antennae."

"He used numbered foreign accounts to avoid detection," Grant said. "Esch modeled HARPIE to stagger his positions over a two-week period."

"So, how did ten b turn into nine hundred b?" Sweeny asked.

"Esch didn't hedge his bets," Grant said. "The futures contracts he purchased had him leveraged thirty-to-one going out."

Zach grunted. "Risky business?"

"Not really." Grant looked up from the file. "Nasser knew what forces were going to drive the markets in advance. Esch shorted currency and bet the house on precious metal and oil futures a month before the Israeli jet was blown out of the sky over Alexandria."

"Coincidence?" Sweeny grinned despite himself.

Grant glanced at the lanky Texan. "Since when did you start believing in coincidence?"

"The stench around this whole Middle East thing is rising." Zach tapped his pipe, then looked at Grant. "Lay it out."

"I've suspected Nasser's involvement since I met him at the

Arab League meeting," Grant said. "The problem was I couldn't figure out what he could gain that would be worth risking his fortune and standing in the business world."

"How about money?" Sweeny said. "He's on a fast track to become the world's first trillionaire."

Grant shook his head. "No, there's more to it than money. The more I look at Nasser. the more I think he sees himself becoming a Great Khan lording over a world Islamic community dedicated to religious correctness."

"Power," Zach said through a cloud of smoke.

"Yep, the old *P* word." Grant refilled his coffee cup. "I can't shake the notion that Nasser's a man of the past operating in a modern world. He'd like nothing better than to keep Islam locked in the seventh century."

Sweeny chuckled. "It pretty much already is. A degree in Islamic philosophy won't exactly jumpstart a young man's career into the high-tech world."

"Nasser's a rich, intelligent, resourceful sonofabitch. He instructs Esch to buy ten billion worth of futures. Then he and Moussawi arrange to blow up the Israeli jet on the eve of the Wallace Peace Plan becoming reality." Grant snapped his fingers. "Boom. Three of the world's most respected diplomats and their delegations removed."

"What about the million paid to the Egyptian pilot's family?" Zach said. "It was linked to Tartir."

"Part of the plan. Nasser knew what world reaction would be if the finger pointed at Tartir."

"It would look like an act of war committed by a quasi legitimate government," Sweeny said.

Zach leaned back in his chair, eyes on the ceiling. "Looking at it now, subsequent events seem predictable enough. Israelis expel the Palestinians from ancestral homeland, infuriated Muslims take to the streets, regimes are threatened, an oil embargo is imposed, and the West prepares for war. Currency markets fall, oil and precious metals go through the roof."

"I spoke with Ira," Grant said. "Moussawi's nearly dead, but he still hasn't cracked. We still don't know how Allah's going to change the world."

Zach tapped the used pipe tobacco into an ashtray. "Developing the Spratly Islands looks more appealing by the minute."

That evening, Abby laid her head on Grant's shoulder. Shadows played in diffuse moonlight illuminating the presidential bedroom. "I'm glad it's out in the open," she whispered.

"Me too." Grant slipped his arm around her. "The press is supporting you. So are the people."

"Us, you mean." Abby felt him wince. "What's wrong?"

"An old tic I used to get in the field." Grant drew her close. "Something rotten is about to happen."

Abby raised on her elbow. "What?"

"I put a man on Bembry," Grant said. "Today he had lunch with Prince Nasser's lobbyist, Lawrence Escope."

"Lawrence makes the rounds. I'm not surprised he's talking with Axel."

"They were having more than a friendly chat." Grant rolled over to face her. "Turns out Escope's the one who had me followed, and the one who leaked the story to the *National Monitor.* Bembry's planning to use it against you to position himself for a presidential run."

"You can't be serious."

"Nasser's going to ante up twenty million to launch his campaign."

Abby sat up. "The *National Monitor* story won't help him much. Most of the papers and networks are on our side."

"They're planning to keep hitting it," Grant said. "Bembry's going to start making the talk show rounds."

"I've admitted my love for you. Where does Axel expect to go with this?"

"That's why I've got the tic, sweetheart," Grant said. "A bunch of disparate parts are floating around that haven't come together. For one, Ira Bettleman's got Sheik Moussawi on ice. He's an extreme heroin addict, but hasn't cracked. For him to hold out with that kind of monkey on his back tells me something bad is in the works."

"You mean about Allah changing the world? The national security alert is red, 'Extreme Alert.' What do you think will happen?"

"I don't know, but whatever it is, it's been planned for some time." Grant put his arms around the woman he loved. "Tomorrow's the start of Ramadan. We'll just have to wait and see."

Five thousand Allah's Army *jihadis* unrolled their prayer rugs in various time zones around the world equivalent to 7:00 a.m. EST. Their missions, meticulously planned, had been rehearsed many times. Timing, the critical factor, dictated they reach their respective destinations at exactly 8:27 a.m. EST. Three minutes later, five thousand holy warriors would simultaneously enter their respective targets.

The *jihadis* washed to purify themselves for their anticipated journey to Paradise. It would be a glorious arrival. Imagine, spending eternity with their own stable of *houris,* the beautiful maidens that dwelled in the afterlife, and dining on the finest lamb. Facing Mecca, the city that housed Islam's most sacred icon, the Kaaba stone, they knelt on their prayer rugs and intoned the Salat. The verses from the Holy Koran that Muslims recited five times a day held special meaning for these *jihadi*. Their young hearts thumped with pride in the knowledge that Allah's blessings would be bountiful. What finer day could there be than the beginning of Ramadan to become a martyr?

At 5:27 a.m., two hundred *jihadi* stood in front of hotel casinos and truck stops scattered throughout California, Nevada, Oregon, and Washington. Another one hundred were positioned in Vancouver, Edmonton, and Calgary. In Colorado, at 6:27 a.m., two hundred more were staring at the bright lights of busy coffee shops and health clubs. Further east in the U.S., Canada, and extending to Western Europe, *jihadi* watched school children. In Russia, Japan, China, Hong Kong, Taiwan, the Philippines, and Singapore, holy warriors waited in front of crowded hotels and nightclubs.

Five thousand pairs of eyes watched seconds tick by on their synchronized watches. One minute before entering their targets, silent prayers were offered to Allah.

Book Three

Destiny—a tyrant's authority for a crime
and a fool's excuse for failure.

——Ambrose Bierce

Eighteen

Abigail Stewart looked out her office window, biting her lower lip to keep it from trembling. Less than an hour ago she had addressed the grief-stricken nation. Words and phrases that offered nothing to those who had lost loved ones. In the barren limbs of the White House trees, Abby saw herself at the Olympic trials on the back of her horse, Bermuda, sailing over the final jump, and falling into the darkness. "Life has suddenly been reduced to a series of snapshots," she said. "All I see are the faces of the children killed in those horrid attacks."

Grant stared into his coffee cup, but did not drink. "It's the final blow to peace."

"Americans are watching the news, and the horror's just now beginning to sink in, Madam President," Collin Jeffers said. "Worldwide estimates range from fifteen to twenty thousand dead, with up to five times that many wounded. We need to issue a policy statement. Try to bring a modicum of calm."

"Declare a state of emergency." FBI Director Sean O'Dell ran his fingers through his hair. "Round up every Muslim and put them in jail. Riots are breaking out, mosques being burned."

"Torture and suppression of constitutional rights is what

you're really talking about. Declaring a state of emergency would put America on the path to becoming a police state." Attorney General Authur Cohen's face was flushed. "We've got more than five million Muslims living in this country, most of whom are law-abiding citizens. How can we morally consider putting them in jail or protective custody? It would be World War II Japanese internment camps all over again."

"Try telling that to the thousands of people who just lost their children. The Japanese weren't over here walking into school-rooms and blowing themselves up. These people and those who support them are not martyrs born of poverty. They're mass murderers. That's how they should be dealt with." O'Dell's voice cracked. "Right now, no one's safe. There's no way of knowing how many other maniacs are out there waiting to kill innocents."

The President turned from the window. "Zach?"

"I'm ambivalent. Arthur's right about tilting America toward becoming a police state. But Sean's also correct. There's no way of knowing how many others are out there. Before the end of the day there will be mob rule if strong action's not taken. Anyone who looks like a Muslim will become a target. They'll be safer in jail." Zach turned to the AG. "And don't forget, Abraham Lincoln suspended habeas corpus during the Civil War. There's precedent on our side."

"Grant?"

"We'll lose every shred of good will in the Muslim commu-nity, but I agree with Zach. Being in protective custody beats facing a mob." Grant looked at Abby's chalk-white face. "On a broader basis, I suggest isolating the Muslim world. Close allied embassies, get ex-pats out, send Muslim diplomats packing, freeze their assets, cut off transportation and communication."

"I agree," Frances Merriman said. "We won't have problems from our allies. Everyone's in step this time."

"Put it together. But do it quietly. We can't afford to announce our intentions." Abby paced back and forth. "And Frances, see about expediting the ruling from the International Court about our claim on the Spratly Islands."

Later that afternoon, at CIA Headquarters, Grant walked into Hack Thomas' workroom. "Well?"

"I've got it." Hack held up a CD. "This is one nasty virus. It's virtually undetectable."

"Tell me about it."

"It's actually quite simple. Let me demonstrate." Hack slipped the CD into Big Bertha's drive. After a moment, a series of commands flashed across the screen. A yes or cancel rectangle appeared in a dialogue box. "The program dialed a number in Nasser's mainframe and is now connected," Hack said. "We are ready to attack. Click 'yes' and we will wipe out the data records stored in Nasser's and Esch's hard drives when they try and initiate a trade."

"What about backup tapes?" Grant asked.

"The virus doesn't die when the system crashes. Rather, it lies dormant and will be activated when backup tapes are loaded."

"Leaving us with the only complete record of their transactions." Grant picked up the phone and dialed a number. "Have the HARPIE trades been traced and accounted for?" he asked.

Hack picked up a piece of cold pizza and took a bite.

"Good work," Grant said into the receiver. "Have the file sent up to my office."

"Good news?" Hack asked between chews.

"Indeed." Grant picked up the last piece of pizza and looked at Hack Thomas. "Time to attack."

At Mossad headquarters in Tel Aviv, Sheik Moussawi lay in

his padded cell tied in a straightjacket. The pain, a relentless force, ripped his body as he stared at nothing through glazed eyes. "Arrrrahhhh. My medicine—must have—do anything."

Jacob Eisenberg motioned to the orderly. "Untie him and wash him down. He stinks worse than a camel."

While the orderly stripped Moussawi, Jacob filled a syringe half full. Then he knelt, thumped a vein on the sheik's arm, and injected the heroin. "This should ease the pain for a little while," he said.

Moussawi's eyes slowly dilated.

"Help him up, and give him some clean clothes," Jason told the orderly. "The sheik and I are going to have a little talk."

Nasser sipped strong Arabian coffee as he watched the Al Jazeera world news report. Nearly five thousand martyrs lost. A heavy price, but disturbing only in the abstract. Such men were expendable in the long line of millions waiting to take their place. Yet there was no question his *jihadi* had performed well. Eighteen thousand dead and more than seventy-five thousand wounded. Authorities had been completely caught off guard, denying only thirty-six martyrs from making their trip to Paradise. Perhaps, at this very moment, the lucky ones who had made the transition were lying on silk sheets, being attended by their *houris*.

The West had been crippled, but not yet killed. Of course, that would soon change. World leaders had expressed their outrage and promised reprisals. *Dogs howling at the moon,* Nasser thought. Praise Allah he had sent Yousef to America to carry out plans that did not include the bumbling Moussawi. While the West could not be defeated militarily, Allah had provided him with another way. By attacking children, the infidel's greatest weakness, chaos now reigned.

"Fear has paralyzed the world economy," the analyst said.

"Global markets are crumbling. In the wake of losing up to twenty-five percent of valuation, stock and commodities trading has been suspended until further notice in New York, London, Zurich, Tokyo, Dubai, and Shanghai. As trading halted around the world, precious metal and oil futures were up limit, while currencies plummeted."

More good news, Nasser thought. He picked up a fig and consumed the delicate fruit as the camera shifted to the anchor.

"Attacks on Muslims residing in foreign countries are rampant. Mosques are being burned, while police are jailing thousands of Muslims under the guise of putting them in protective custody. Gun dealers and retailers in the United States, Canada, and Europe cannot keep up with increased demand. For reaction in the Middle East to the latest developments, we now take you to our correspondent in Riyadh."

The anchor faded into a street scene in Riyadh. "From the Philippines to Nigeria, the scene here in Saudi Arabia's capital is mirrored throughout the Muslim world," the reporter said.

Nasser's lips curled as the mob burned infidel flags and shouted, "Death to the West." Fiery-eyed mullahs waved the Koran, exhorting them on. A mannequin of Abigail Stewart wrapped in an American flag burst into flames. The frenzied mob gathered around, hurling stones and obscenities.

The camera shifted to another part of the city, where a huge new crowd had gathered. "Down with terror. Down with terror," they chanted.

"As you can see, a growing number of counter demonstrations are taking place," the correspondent said. "Random Al Jazeera polls reflect a majority of Muslims, while sympathetic to the suicide bombers' cause, reject their methods."

"Fools," Nasser said.

He clicked off the set, walked to his balcony, and stared toward Mecca. A giant red sun hung on the horizon. Nasser took a breath and watched distant dust devils dance in the wind.

Destiny at hand, it was the finest sunset he had ever seen.

There would, of course, be those on both sides opposed to his vision of Allah's commandments. Nasser had anticipated this. But rather than feeling anger toward these people, he pitied them. Their way wasn't *the* way, and there was nothing he could do about that. They would be dealt with harshly. After all, Allah, in His infinite wisdom, had not created a perfect world. Many of His subjects had grown fat and corrupt. That too would change when he, with Allah's blessing, assumed control of Mecca and Medina. Then and only then could he reform Islam.

The desert wind whispered of things to come. *Praise be to Allah,* he thought, *Sunni and Sh'ia united by my* fatwa.

"Is it hard to take a life?"

Grant noted the ghostly countenance about Abby. The horror of the day would have a lasting effect. In what ways, he could not say, but her eerie calmness troubled him. "It depends," he said.

"I think I would rather enjoy putting a gun to Nasser's head and pulling the trigger." Abby pushed her uneaten sandwich away. "Dear God, what has he turned our world into? How could he get all those people to do such things? Killing innocent school children is beyond abomination."

"You asked me if it was hard to take a life. It isn't, if the person taking the life has justified the action in his or her own mind. When the burden of guilt is lifted, killing becomes easy." Grant reached across the table and took Abby's hand. "Nasser told me at the Arab League meeting that we didn't understand that problems in the Middle East weren't about oil; they were about religion. Islam is the tool men like Nasser use to take away the guilt of killing."

"What kind of religion is that?" Abby breathed in, her lips forming an "o" as she exhaled. "Nasser's men are nothing more than cold-blooded killers. He wanted to show the world he can strike anywhere, anytime, with impunity."

"The disturbing thing is the operational security," Grant said. "Keeping the lid on five thousand men is unprecedented."

"What does that tell you?"

"That they're living and working among us. They're disciplined and well-trained. They blend into their environment, waiting to be called to die."

"If something like this happens again, the world economy will collapse." The skin on Abby's face seemed to shrink. "Meanwhile, I've declared a State of Emergency and taken America a step closer to becoming a police state."

"Moussawi's broken."

Ira Bettleman looked up. "Anything useful?"

"Nothing much. As we suspected, Nasser provided the money, Moussawi the men." Jacob Eisenberg's voice carried fatigue. "One interesting thing is that the attacks were planned months before our jet went down in Egypt."

"Thoughts?"

"The alliance between Allah's Army and Nasser will continue when Moussawi's security chief takes over. The Saudis probably won't take anything Moussawi said seriously. Nasser's a royal. He'll deny anything we drop in the king's lap. Further complicating matters, the only clips showing on Al Jazeera are reports of burning mosques and Muslims being arrested around the world."

Bettleman rolled his neck until it cracked. "The fact they planned the attack in Egypt months before it took place validates Grant Corbet's original theory. Tartir's the wrong man."

"Then the world might go to war for the wrong reason," Jacob said.

"Not really." Bettleman lit a cigarette. "We're at war against terror. There're no territorial boundaries, only a bunch of crazies led by men like Nasser, Moussawi, and Tartir."

"They're well-organized and getting better. Moussawi told me their suicide bombers operated in five-men cells. They held regular jobs and fit in with the locals wherever they were stationed." Jacob picked up the pack and extracted a cigarette. "Think we ought to give this to the Saudis through the back door?"

"We can kiss any kind of communication with the Saudis good-bye, covert or otherwise," Bettleman said. "The Muslim world is about to be shut down."

"What do you want to do with Moussawi and Jamil?"

The Israeli spymaster continued to work on his hangnail. "Take the boychick to the Lebanese border. I'm sure he won't have a difficult time finding a new patron."

"And Moussawi?"

"See that he has enough heroin to take with him to the after-life."

Lindsey Caspare watched Frances Merriman approach the President's office the next morning. The last twenty-four hours had taken their toll on her. Usually elegant and confident, the Secretary of State looked haggard.

The Secret Service agent nodded. "Madam Secretary, JUMPER is waiting for you."

Abigail Stewart stood behind her desk, staring at nothing, when her Secretary of State came in. Tension held her rigid as thoughts about the thousands of people killed during her watch filled her mind. *Why, God, did this have to be my baptismal into the world of man?*

"Good morning, Madam President."

"Not really, Frances." President Stewart went to her desk and sat down. "What have you got?"

"The International Court held an emergency session and ruled in our favor," Merriman said. "We can start the Spratly project."

"Provisos?"

"We must notify the other countries that have claims on the islands through the usual diplomatic channels. They will have an opportunity for a hearing before the Court. But, given the current situation, that will take time."

"How long before the Court will announce its decision?"

"They postponed the announcement for a week, allowing us time to complete the diplomatic work."

Abby motioned to her Secretary of State. "Please sit down, Frances. How do you think the other claimants will react?"

Merriman kept her face bland, calm, but it hurt to see how the President's face had caved with grief. "The Muslim countries Brunei, Indonesia and Malaysia are out of the loop," Merriman said. "The Philippines will back us. Vietnam will squawk, but nothing will come of it. The big unknown is China."

"Are we ready to move?"

"Collin tells me we're prepared for any eventuality," Merriman said. "The American Petroleum team arrived in Okinawa. They'll ship out tomorrow after getting their ships refitted."

"Do it," Abby said. "And one other thing, Frances."

"Yes, Madam President?"

"Pray the Chinese don't attack our ships."

The next morning in Beijing, the director of state security, Lui Chen Hang, walked into the intelligence minister's office. "Thank you for seeing me on such short notice, Minister. I've received a communiqué from Okinawa that merits your attention."

Wang Zi nodded. "What is it?"

"Seven American Petroleum transport ships are docked in Okinawa. They're outfitted with drilling equipment."

"What's unusual about that?" Wang asked. "The Americans have joint ventures throughout the region."

"The number of ships suggests a major development is being planned," Lui said. "They are preparing to sail, and our agent's source reports equipment for platform and deepwater drilling is on the ship's manifest."

"I see." Wang stared at his leather-bound ink blotter, a touch of the old in today's too-fast world. "What are your conclusions?"

"The only undeveloped region in Asia is the Spratly Islands."

"Impossible, they have no claim to the territory." Wang's eyes turned to slits. "Even the Americans aren't arrogant enough to think China won't intervene if they attempt to develop the Spratly Islands."

"Two Class A destroyers assigned to the Kitty Hawk Battle Group are scheduled to depart at the same time as the American Petroleum ships. Perhaps—" Lui hesitated, "a military escort?"

"I want the latest information on all naval operations in and around the South China Sea." Wang glanced at a map behind his desk. "Let me know what course the Americans set, and if they are accompanied by a destroyer escort."

Nineteen

Grant filled a large Styrofoam cup with coffee and went to his desk. The usual copies of the *Wall Street Journal, New York Times, Washington Post, USA Today* and the *National Monitor* waited. His eyes narrowed as he unfolded the *National Monitor*.

18,000 Dead—75,000 Wounded
Abby plays house during worst terrorist attack in history
By Barry Shivers

As America and the rest of the civilized world count their dead, the question that must be answered is, *Who's minding the store?* It could be argued President Abigail Stewart was resting in the back room, entertaining CIA Deputy Director of Operations Grant Corbet.

Ms. Stewart appears to have forgotten that above all, presidents are elected to protect the people from enemies. Enemies that include hostile governments, terrorists, and—

"Christ!" Grant gnashed his teeth. "Goddamn bastard!" He sat for a long moment staring at the front-page photos of Abby and himself.

The telephone rang. "Corbet." His voice was pitched wrong. He needed to get control before picking up a phone.

"You okay?" Zach Holden asked.

"Sorry, Zach. Just caught Shivers' yellow journalism."

"Understood. Thought you'd like to know Bembry's about to be interviewed on the *Today Show,*" Zach said.

"Timed to coincide with Shivers' article, no doubt." Grant swallowed rising bile. "The situation's going from bad to worse."

"Try not to worry," Zach said. "Things have a way of evening themselves out."

"Maybe the rat will dig himself into a hole."

Grant replaced the receiver and clicked on the television.

"Our special guest today is Axel Bembry, the former national security advisor and ambassador to Saudi Arabia." The camera focused on Bembry. "Welcome, Mr. Ambassador."

"Thank you for having me, Tim."

"Let's get right to the point, Mr. Ambassador. Thousands of innocent people have been killed, many of them children. Shock and fear have paralyzed the United States along with the rest of the civilized world. Muslims, Jews, and Christians are being killed in the streets of America. What got us to this point? With all our technology are we, and on a larger scale, the world community, powerless to protect citizens against these barbaric attacks?"

"Sadly, Tim, terror is not new on the world stage. Nine-eleven ushered in that horrible reality on our own turf." Bembry faced the camera, his expression one of well-practiced concern. "We've known about the danger terror posed for years before 9-11. The Israeli-Palestinian conflict is a perfect example. Thousands of innocent men, women, and children senselessly killed on both sides."

"Yes, yes." The host waved an impatient hand. "What our viewers would like to know is what, if anything, can we do to prevent future attacks?"

"Quite frankly, our leaders must listen and lead. To date, our intelligence has been woefully inadequate about how to deal with the Middle East." Bembry coughed softly behind his hand. "As you know, Tim, until I resigned as National Security Advisor, I was on the front line of this issue."

"Are you saying that you resigned because President Stewart has been receiving faulty intelligence about the Middle East?"

"I'm saying there is a lot of information and disinformation out there. Presidents are routinely briefed by a number of agencies and individuals. The sum of the gathered intelligence should be analyzed to form the basis of policy. I'm on record as saying President Stewart's become overly dependent on the opinions expressed by Grant Corbet."

"Can you be a bit more specific?" the host asked. "We know the President has a personal relationship with CIA Deputy Director of Operations Grant Corbet. She stands by her assertion that he's one of her most trusted confidants."

"Corbet and I crossed paths while I was ambassador to Saudi Arabia. For security reasons, I cannot discuss the details of our connection." Bembry steepled his fingers. "Let's just say I found him reckless."

"It has been brought to this reporter's attention that you are considering a run for the presidency. Assuming that President Stewart seeks reelection, won't your candidacy have a negative impact on the party?"

"The idea of me making a run for the presidency has been floating around long before I resigned as NSA," Bembry said. "I never seriously considered challenging President Stewart. Until now. These horrific events have forced me to reconsider my position."

"We're almost out of time, Mr. Ambassador. Quickly, tell the American people what you can offer as an alternative to President Stewart."

Bembry stared into the camera. "A strong hand in foreign

affairs, tempered by experience."

Nasser watched Axel Bembry's interview conclude from his fortress home near Jeddah. The former NSA's talk show circuit had begun. His position as a viable alternative to Abigail Stewart would be further enhanced by Barry Shivers' scathing editorials. The prince reached for a date, put it into his mouth and chewed. Questions about the competence of America's Abby would become the talk of the day, cracking the foundation of her once-solid presidency. Nasser chewed, savoring the date's sweetness. Then, with Allah's blessing and a little help from Yousef, her presidency would come crashing down. Faith in the American Way reduced to a tattered dream.

The prince switched channels to World News Headlines. More good news. Muslims were being attacked and beaten by angry mobs around the world. Burning mosques lit up the night sky, the faithful arrested because they were Muslim, illegal search and seizures. A world in chaos! Prized western concepts about human rights and the rule of law were now byproducts of a bygone era.

Nasser went to his computer room and sent a message to Gerhard Esch, instructing him to start liquidating his HARPIE futures contracts. Next he sent an e-mail to his bodyguard, Yousef.

"Welcome to 'News Watch,' Madam Secretary," the host said.

"Before we begin the interview, I would like to address a specific point." Frances Merriman stared into the camera. "The recent oil embargo and the most horrific terrorist attack in history have pushed the world to the brink of war. As a result, President

Stewart and other Western leaders have declared a State of Emergency. This week, the United States and our allies officially severed diplomatic relations with Muslim countries. Embassy staffs and ex-patriots working in those regions have been recalled.

"Diplomatic initiatives have failed. Islamic countries remain united in their refusal to turn over those responsible for downing an Israeli jet over Alexandria, Egypt. Oil-producing countries threaten to destroy their fields if the United States and our allies launch a military strike. The dilemma the free world faces is obvious. We cannot risk losing or severely damaging seventy percent of the world's known reserves, nor can we endure a lengthy embargo. Either way spells global economic ruin." Merriman adjusted her lapel microphone.

"We now have a third option. Taiwan, in a gesture to maintain world peace, recently conveyed its claim to the Spratly Islands to the United States. That claim was validated by the International Court yesterday. The United States now intends to fully develop the oil reserves beneath those islands. Seven American Petroleum transport ships carrying men and equipment left Okinawa today for the Spratly Islands. This action should not be seen as an act of aggression toward our friends in the region. Rather, it is an economic venture to free countries around the world from dependence on Middle East oil."

"How did the People's Republic of China react to this news?" the host asked.

"China also has claimed the Spratly Islands," Merriman said. "Premier Jen was obviously upset when he discussed this matter with President Stewart."

"Madam Secretary, can you tell the American people if the United States is at risk of going to war with China?"

"The situation is tense," Merriman said. "Our hope is that China will recognize this venture as a much larger issue than a territorial dispute. The economic well-being of the planet might well depend on oil found under the Spratly Islands. Our strategic oil reserves are dropping at an alarming rate. We need oil, and we need it now. The United States has the expertise, equipment, and technology to bring it up quickly."

"Fools!" People's Republic of China Premier Jen Jemin shouted. He clicked off the tape of Frances Merriman's interview and looked at his intelligence minister, Wang Zi. "I told President Stewart we would not idly watch clouds pass through the sky while they develop and steal China's resources."

"It appears they are convinced otherwise," Wang said. "The Americans and British are moving three battle groups into the South China Sea."

Jen blinked. "Three?"

"Our latest intelligence shows the Kitty Hawk Battle Group is moving south in the Sea of Japan." Wang passed the premier and other politburo members a folder. "The British Royal Navy's Illustrious BG has left Australia, ostensibly to conduct naval exercises in the South China Sea. The Stennis BG is right now passing through the Strait of Malacca."

"We cannot defend against such a force," the minister of defense said.

"Then what should our response be?" Jen asked.

"We must make a forceful response." Wang felt tension crystallize in the great room. He glanced at the portraits of Mao Zedong and Chou en-Lai. The former leaders stared back from their portraits. "The West risks war with China because they are afraid to invade the Middle East."

"They fear, as we all do, that the oil fields will be destroyed," the minister of defense said.

"With good reason. The well that Prince Zyyad blew up was quite convincing." Wang lit a cigarette. "Complicating matters are the recent terrorists attacks."

"China stands as one with the West regarding the terrorists attacks," Jen said. "Have they forgotten that more than three thousand people were lost in Beijing, Shanghai, and Hong Kong? We agreed to help them isolate the Muslim world."

"I understand, Premier Jen. The motivation for their action is what I referred to." Wang studied the ash on his cigarette. "The Americans are playing a game of poker. They know we cannot let them occupy Chinese territory. What they are betting on is that we will fold our hand because we are incapable of defeating them militarily."

"Poker, betting, what are you suggesting?" Jen waved an exasperated hand. "The American and British navies are expected to arrive in the South China Sea in four or five days."

"We bluff." Wang looked at the other men around the table. Pudgy old men gone soft with China's new prosperity. "I suggest we immediately deploy our navy and blockade the Spratly Islands. We let the Americans and British know if they try to breach the blockade, nuclear warheads will be launched against Taiwan, Japan, and American West Coast cities."

"Madness, we would be annihilated in a nuclear exchange," the minister of defense said. "The Americans have more than seven thousand strategic nuclear weapons capable of hitting China. We have twenty capable of hitting them."

"True, it is madness." Wang slowly ground out his cigarette with nicotine-stained fingers. "But that's precisely why our bluff will work."

"This is a dangerous game you propose, Minister Wang," Jen said. "How can you be sure it will work?"

"Nothing under heaven is certain." Wang's hands adopted an attitude of prayer. "My suggestion is based solely on the supposition that the American president cannot justify risking millions of American, Japanese, and Taiwanese lives in a quest for oil."

Gerhard Esch stopped at Starbucks, ordered a triple espresso, and went to his office. The analysts' desks were eerily quiet when he arrived, despite the havoc that had paralyzed world financial markets. Esch picked up a copy of the *Wall Street Journal*. nodded to his assistant, then went directly to his computer. After checking his e-mails, he decoded the message from Nasser, instructing him to liquidate his positions. Esch sipped his espresso, but it did not calm the excitement churning his stomach. The timing was perfect to get out without attracting attention. World markets were in shambles, no buyers—everyone selling. Esch entered a series of commands and brought up his HARPIE program.

Insha' Allah, in two days, he would be a billionaire.

Jack Sweeny walked into Grant's office with coffee and assorted Krispy Kremes.

"Hey, Jack."

Sweeny handed Grant a Styrofoam cup and sat down. "Sorry about the horse manure being dumped on you and President Stewart. Too bad we can't make that Shivers character and Bembry disappear."

"Give them enough rope and they'll hang themselves," Grant said. "I put a man on Bembry. He's uncovered a money trail between Nasser, Escope, Bembry, and Shivers."

"Good for you. The stony lonesome is the next best thing to putting them in the ground." Sweeny bit into a doughnut. "Islamic countries should pretty much be shut down by tomorrow."

Grant watched confectionary powder stick to the Texan's mouth. "Impressive. Not a peep about it in the press. How did you manage in such short order?"

"For once, everyone took security seriously, so it wasn't all that difficult," Sweeny said. "We contacted our friends, and brought all the telecommunication and ISP companies together. They changed their software to detect outgoing calls and e-mails from Muslim countries. Voice and data transmissions go out over Wide Area Networking Class 5 switches. Now the communication links will be shut down from the Islamic countries to the rest of the world. Repatriating millions of Muslims scattered around the globe is what will take time."

"Say someone sends an e-mail from Iran to DC," Grant said. "Where does it go?"

"Who knows? Somewhere out in cyberspace." Sweeny wiped his mouth. "The WANs simply reroute the message to nowhere."

"Amazing," Grant said.

"Transportation in and out of Islamic countries will be shut down at noon tomorrow. Assets and bank accounts are being frozen as we speak." Sweeny finished his doughnut. "A curtain is being drawn over twenty percent of the world's population. Imagine, more than a billion people sealed off, all because a couple of clowns wanted to play god."

"Nasser will soon be a much poorer god," Grant said. "Hack Thomas dropped a nasty little virus into Gerhard Esch's computer system. It will wipe out his hard drive when he tries to unload his contracts."

"A trillion dollars down the drain?"

"Not really." Grant's eyes crinkled. "Esch's HARPIE program has been downloaded into our system. Once his system is down, we can initiate the trades."

"Wouldn't that be illegal?" Sweeny asked.

"I'm not a lawyer, but I don't think so. If we don't make the trades, the money will wind up in a bunch of foreign banks when the contracts expire." Grant chewed on a thumbnail, his worries about Abby lightened for a moment. "It would be a waste, entrusting such an amount to gnomes."

Sweeny nodded thoughtfully, then picked up another doughnut. "Yep. A total waste. I'm sure President Stewart can think up a trillion good ideas on how to best utilize it."

Twenty

It was late morning when Grant, Zach Holden, and Jack Sweeny were ushered into the Situation Room located in the basement of the White House.

Several minutes passed before the President arrived. She nodded to the assembly, then sat at the head of the table. The lights dimmed and the big screen lit up with Xinhua news agency's live broadcast.

A somber Chinese Premier Jen Jemin appeared. "In response to unprovoked aggression by the United States and other rebel governments, the People's Republic of China has been forced to take the following action. Effective immediately, shipping lanes around the Spratly Islands are closed. As previously communicated through diplomatic channels, the PROC will not allow drilling or exploration of any kind to take place in or around the Spratly Islands.

"To insure compliance, I've ordered the navy of the People's Republic of China to take up positions in the area. Our navy will turn back any ship entering the restricted zone, and engage any vessel that refuses to change course." Jen held up a finger. "The PROC has taken this action to protect our territorial waters. We do not wish for war. But let there be no misunderstanding about our resolve. Any action taken by any country that intrudes upon or threatens our blockade will be considered hostile military action. To protect our interests, China will immediately respond to such a threat with the full range of its military capability. I urge other peace-loving nations around the world to heed this warning."

The air in the Situation Room crystallized as the screen went blank.

Abby's back ached as she stared at the dark screen. An image of her riding her horse over the last jump, then disappearing into the abyss, briefly appeared before her eyes.

Secretary of Defense Collin Jeffers wiped his forehead. "Christ, Jen just threatened to attack us with nuclear weapons."

Abby glanced at Grant. "What do the satellite photos show?"

The big screen came back to life.

"There's increased activity around Guangzhou and Zhanjiang, the major naval bases for the PROC's South China Sea fleet." The red beam from Grant's laser pointer touched on the two sites. "From the looks of things, they're serious about blockading the Spratly Islands."

"What kind of firepower will we be facing?" Abby asked.

Grant brought up several photos and thumbnail descriptions of Chinese Navy assets. "PLAN, an acronym for People's Liberation Army Navy, has been aggressively modernizing its navy for the past ten years. This includes new-generation conventional and nuclear-powered attack and ballistic missile submarines, acquisition of Russian-built Kilo-class diesel submarines, and the acquisition of two Russian-built Sovremenny guided-missile destroyers." The laser pointer touched the photo of the destroyer. "These units are likely to be equipped with an advanced SAN-7 air-defense system, the KA-28 Helix Helicopter, and SSN-22 cruise-missile technology. The HQ-61 and HQ-7 systems are based on the French Crotale land-based surface-to-air missile system. They do not provide surface units with effective area-defense capability. This deficiency leaves Chinese surface units extremely vulnerable to air attack."

"The three battle groups we have moving toward the Spratly Islands could quickly decimate China's entire navy," Jeffers said. "That's why the threat to use nuclear weapons boggles the mind. China would be wiped out in such an exchange."

"I think Jen's being smart like a fox," Abby said. "He knows we wouldn't risk a nuclear attack on the West Coast, not to mention Taiwan, South Korea, and Japan. We would be endangering millions of people." The President's gaze moved back to the screen. "What about our Air Force, Collin."

"Four RC-135's are operating out of Kadena, Okinawa, giving us round-the-clock reconnaissance over the South China Sea. Military bases throughout the region are on full alert."

"Zach, what does the Agency recommend if the Chinese blockade the Spratly Islands and fire on our ships?"

"Return overwhelming firepower and destroy their navy," Zach said. "Then neutralize China's nuclear capacity by taking out their missile silos."

Abby turned to Grant. "Can the Chinese threat be negated by destroying their silos?"

"Not unless we initiated a first strike," Grant said. "Even then it would only be iffy. There might be silo sites we're not aware of."

"Any suggestions about where we go from here?"

"His use of 'rebel governments' in the plural suggests Jen's threatening Japan and Taiwan, perhaps even South Korea," Frances Merriman said. "We've got a full-blown situation on our hands. Will he, or won't he?"

"Jen has put himself in a position where it will be hard to

back down," Grant said. "But he's also positioned where he will be much more amenable to a negotiated settlement."

"Sorry, Grant, I'm not following your line of thought," Jeffers said.

"What I'm saying is that the crisis can be defined by a single word. Face! It's the most important asset an individual can have in China. The same is true for the way the government conducts itself." Grant tapped his forefingers against his lower lip. "If Jen backs down now, he'll lose face, and the government will lose face. For a man like Jen, that would be the ultimate humiliation. It would spell the end of his premiership."

"Seems like that would make him less likely to negotiate a settlement, especially one where we came out on top," Merriman said.

"The Chinese are masters at finding a middle ground, a way out without losing face." Grant looked around the table. "Jen's in a desperate situation. He knows China would be devastated in a nuclear confrontation. That's why he has to negotiate, even if we come out on top. The trick will be making it appear that he hasn't backed down or compromised China's strategic interests."

The President folded her hands. "Okay, ladies and gentlemen, we've got four or five days to resolve this. Meanwhile, I want to see the political, economic, and military options on my desk by this afternoon." Abby turned to her Secretary of State. "Frances, without showing any sign of weakness, find a way to get me additional negotiating time."

Gerhard Esch's eyes widened as his computer screen went black. He tried rebooting his computer. Nothing! His stomach churned in fear as he buzzed the network administrator. "Check out our system. My computer just died, and I'm in the middle of something important."

"I'm already on it," the technician said. "The traders' and office staff computers are also down. From the look of it, our entire system has crashed."

"How can that be?"

"We probably picked up a bug from incoming e-mail. It shouldn't take long to get us back up and running."

Esch felt the bile settle. "Get back to me the moment you know something."

"Weyeee."

"Mr. President, Grant Corbet here. Sorry to disturb you at such a late hour."

"Nonsense, old friend," Ping-yi Cong said. "These are difficult times. If you had not called me, I would have called you."

"You've seen Jen's response to our initiative in the Spratly Islands?"

"Yes. As a precaution, I've placed Taiwan's military on full alert."

"I need to know what your people on the ground have come up with," Grant said. "How far will Jen go?"

"Jen is in a precarious position," Cong said. "People are starving due to crop failure. They suffer further from blackouts caused by the unnatural weather. All the while, China's thirst for oil grows daily."

"Their domestic production's flat, but energy consumption grew last year by fifteen percent." Grant swallowed a sour taste in his mouth. "That's an amount equal to the total power consumption in Brazil."

"They are adding a middle-sized country every two years in terms of energy consumption." A brief pause. "There are other rumors."

"Well?" Grant said.

"It is whispered Minister of State Security Wang Zi is the guiding hand behind Jen Jemin's threat to use nuclear weapons."

"Wang's a hardliner," Grant said. "You think he persuaded Jen to paint himself into a corner?"

"Wang believes the United States will give up developing the Spratly Islands before risking nuclear attack on its West Coast. Obviously, he convinced Jen as to the merits of his strategy."

"It's all come down to a matter of face," Grant said. "Jen's been maneuvered into risking nuclear war."

A measured silence from Taiwan. "I advise against running, my friend. Look for a silver lining. It is always there."

After concluding his conversation with Grant, Cong went to his study. The glow from the fireplace cast him in orange highlight as he sat and stared at his *wei-qi* board. He picked up a white stone, rubbed it between thumb and forefinger, then placed it on a lined juncture. The intricate pattern of black and white stones had taken shape. He was in the end game, a place where the battle would be won or lost. His life's work and the future of Taiwan hung precariously. Would it be freedom or obliteration for his island home when he placed the final stone?

Cong's brandy glass rose, amber liquid winking in firelight. He had expected Jen Jemin to threaten the use of nuclear weapons. The question now was, how would America respond? Cong had no doubt that Premier Jen was bluffing. True, China had the capability to destroy Taiwan, much of Japan, and inflict damage on U.S. West Coast cities. But, at what cost to China? A nuclear exchange would kill hundreds of millions of Chinese, reducing the Asian giant to a backwater wasteland.

Taiwan's president focused his gaze on the *wei-qi* board. "Will America's Abby have the nerve to call Jen Jemin's bluff?"

Cong's brandy snifter silently rose to his lips, but the black and white stones gave no answers.

Zach Holden's gaze was fixed on a map of Southeast Asia on the screen behind his desk when Grant and Jack Sweeny walked in. "Well?"

"Esch tried unloading Nasser's contracts this morning," Grant said. "Hack's virus intervened by crashing his operating system. It will take him several days to get new hardware and software in place."

Zach began filling his pipe. "What are you suggesting?"

Grant and Sweeny exchanged a look.

"Counting Esch's contracts, Nasser controls almost a trillion dollars worth of contracts," Grant said. "We want to initiate the trades and collect the jellybeans."

"Have you run this by Justice?"

"No time," Grant said. "Our window closes tomorrow. By the time the bureaucrats get through debating, the contracts will expire."

Zach fired his pipe. "What happens to the money, in that case?"

"It'll be deposited in numbered accounts," Sweeny said. "A lot of foreign bankers will be smiling."

"The futures contracts have been paid for," Grant said. "We're seizing Arab assets. Why shouldn't we be the ones who collect? That kind of money can buy a helluva lot of markers."

"What about Esch?" Zach asked.

"We've kept Sean O'Dell in the loop," Grant said. "Esch will be having visitors in gray suits before the day's end."

"It's a breach of protocol, but it'll be a lot better if we decide what to do with the money than a group of foreign bankers. You'll need to discuss it with the President. I'm sure she'll appreciate relieving Nasser of his money." Zach's eyes twinkled. "This kind of thing makes the job fun. Let's go for it."

"Consider it done." Grant scratched the side of his cheek. "I spoke with Cong a little while ago."

"And?"

"His people think the state security minister, Wang Zi, is behind Jen's threat to use nuclear weapons," Grant said. "Cong also thinks Jen's bluffing."

"It doesn't matter what I, you or Cong think. Millions of lives will be lost if Jen's not bluffing. Still, we have to act on what we know." Zach looked at his pipe cupped in his big hands. "I happen to agree with your assessment about Jen looking for a way out—a way to save face."

Grant watched tension grow in his boss's face. "I have something in mind."

"I'm glad somebody does," Zach said. "Tell me about it."

Gerhard Esch walked up to the lead computer technician for Trident Holdings. He held up his watch and tapped the dial. "Three and a half hours have passed. You said we'd be up and running in no time. What the hell's going on?"

"Someone planted a virus in our system, Mr. Esch," the technician said. "Somehow it issued commands that caused the operating system to crash."

Esch glared at the technician. "I thought you were supposed to protect us from things like that."

"We are, but I've never seen anything like this. All the files and application programs have been corrupted."

"I don't give a fuck what you have to do." Esch's fists closed and opened by his sides. "Get us back up and running. Do something. Clean up the system and use the backup tape for God's sake."

"We did that, Mr. Esch." The technician looked away. "The

virus didn't get swept away. It attacked again, and we lost the backup data."

"How could this happen?" Fear moved through Esch like a coiling snake. "We're supposed to have the best security in the industry."

"Whoever planted the virus had direct access to our system." Esch paled. "Someone inside Trident Holdings?"

"I don't think so," the technician said. "None of our people have the capability to tamper with our security system. Some hacker with a high-speed mainframe must have done it."

A man wearing a gray overcoat walked up behind Esch and tapped him on the shoulder. "Mr. Esch?"

"Yes?" Esch turned and froze. Behind the man a team of men and women wearing blue ski jackets with "FBI" in yellow were lining up the traders, issuing instructions. "What's the meaning of this?" Esch demanded. "Who are you?"

"Special Agent Frank Talbot. I have a warrant for your arrest." Talbot's hand closed around Esch's arm. "You'll have to come with me."

Esch tried to pull away. "I'm not going anywhere without speaking to my attorney."

"Sorry, chum, Miranda Rights no longer apply." Talbot took out a pair of handcuffs. "In case you've forgotten, we're in a State of Emergency."

Yousef deplaned from the commuter flight at Reagan International Airport, keeping a safe distance behind Barry Shivers. He had gotten to know a great deal about the reporter, having spent time watching him and listening to his telephone conversations since arriving in the States. Prince Nasser's contacts had proven invaluable. Prince Nasser's contacts had made it simple for him to get anything he needed in America. Passports, poison, and wiretaps had required only money.

Earlier, Yousef had learned that Shivers planned to meet Axel Bembry at an upscale Mediterranean restaurant in Georgetown. The two men intended to spend a pleasant evening discussing media strategy on how best to undermine Abigail Stewart's presidency. Nasser's bodyguard smiled at that.

Crowds jostled as a mechanical voice announced arrivals and departures. When Yousef saw Shivers turn toward the baggage claim area, he continued on to the Budget Car Rental. After presenting his Italian driver's license, he paid for a car with his Visa card.

Yousef checked into a Holiday Inn twenty minutes later, where he got driving directions to the restaurant from the desk clerk. He went directly to his room, unpacked his carry-on and shaving bag, then lay down and took a nap.

Two hours later, after a shower and shave, he wiped the steam off the mirror and frowned at his reflection. A handsome, olive-skinned Yam tribesman stared back. The thin mustache, his only remnant of the beard worn so proudly in Saudi Arabia before he had been sent to the States, had not been easy getting used to.

In the bedroom, Yousef donned a black Armani suit, white shirt, burgundy tie, and Gucci shoes. He opened the aspirin bottle in his shaving kit and removed two tablets. For a long moment, he stared at the tiny pills that appeared to be ordinary aspirin. The broker had explained to him the similarity ended there. While aspirin relieved fever, headache, and stiff joints, one tablet of Compound 1080 could kill up to one hundred people. Colorless and tasteless, dissolved easily in water, it had no known antidote. Once exposed, victims felt no symptoms as they began to die slowly. An hour or two after initial exposure, they experienced vomiting, involuntary hyper-extension of the limbs, convulsions, and collapse. Death soon followed.

Yousef wrapped the tablets in a Kleenex. Yes, he thought, it was a fitting way for infidels to die. He wrapped a scarf around his neck, put on an overcoat, then went to his car and drove to Georgetown.

Leo Lebo turned the heater up in the SUV. He was parked across the street from the restaurant where Axel Bembry had made an 8:00 reservation. A glance at the dashboard clock told him it was 7:10 p.m. The infrared mini-cam ran noiselessly behind darkened windows. Lebo clicked on an easy-listening station and settled back. It promised to be another long night. He occupied himself watching the well-heeled crowd pull up to the valet service. The ladies wore lots of fur. Lebo chuckled softly. A helluva place for animal rights activists to gather. At 7:30 he noticed the tall, Mediterranean-looking man approach. Curious, that he had walked to the restaurant, bypassing the valet. The man stopped, took a quick look around, and removed his gloves before entering.

The restaurant simmered with hushed conversation as Yousef stepped inside. Waiters glided between tables to sounds of ice clinking softly against glass. Aromas of perfume, spice, charred meat and seafood mingled nicely.

"Yes sir?" the Maître d' asked.

"Michael Orlando. I have an 8:00 reservation for one." Yousef took off his overcoat and folded it over his arm. "Call me in the bar when my table is ready."

The Maître d' glanced at his book. "Of course, Mr. Orlando. Would you like to check your coat?"

"Thank you, please."

At the bar, Yousef ordered a gin and tonic. No sense calling attention by ordering something nonalcoholic, he thought.

Sipping his drink, he idly passed time by eavesdropping on nearby conversations.

Twenty minutes later, Yousef felt his pulse pick up a notch when Bembry and Shivers walked in.

Yousef watched them check their coats and be led to their table. Water glasses were filled, followed by the appearance of a waiter, who nodded, then returned minutes later with martinis.

"Excuse me, Mr. Orlando, your table is ready."

Yousef dropped a ten-dollar bill on the bar, and followed the Maître d'. He knew Allah had smiled on him when he slipped into a booth near Bembry's table.

A waiter appeared. "Good evening, Mr. Orlando. Let me tell you about tonight's specials."

While the waiter talked, Yousef watched Bembry and Shivers get up and walk toward the restroom.

Another blessing from Allah.

"Take your time, Mr. Orlando. I'll check back with you in a few minutes."

Yousef nodded. As the waiter left, he palmed the two 1080 tablets in his pocket and walked toward the restroom, depositing them in the martinis as he passed Bembry's table.

In the restroom, Bembry and Shivers were drying their hands. Yousef saw Bembry glance at him in the mirror.

"So, how come Lawrence no-showed?" Shivers asked.

"It's his anniversary." Bembry dropped the hand towel into the hamper. "Don't worry about it; I've got your envelope."

Back at his table, Yousef watched the waiter bring a second martini to Bembry and Shivers. The two men lifted their glasses and sipped. Idiots! They were already dead, but didn't know it. Yousef felt familiar excitement prick his back. In another hour, they would experience the first symptoms. It could be worse, he thought. At least the condemned had been given enough time to enjoy a last meal.

The waiter appeared. "Are you ready to order, Mr. Orlando?"

"Yes. I believe I'll have the Veal Oscar with asparagus, and a bottle of Pellegrino, no ice."

Yousef ate slowly, washing down the remnants of his crème brulée with coffee. He covered his mouth and belched softly. All in all, a fine meal! He signaled for the check, and a coffee refill. A glance at his watch told him an hour had passed since the 1080 martinis had been consumed. Bembry and Shivers were enjoying brandy, while working their way through dessert.

The waiter set the bill on the corner of the table. "I hope everything was to your satisfaction, Mr. Orlando."

"Very nice, thank you." Yousef inserted his Visa card into the folder.

After paying the bill and leaving a generous tip, Yousef went to retrieve his coat. From the corner of his eye, he saw Bembry double over. Vomit sprayed across his table, sloshing onto the floor.

The shocked expression on Shivers' face dissolved into agony. "Arrrrahhhh!" He pitched forward and heaved, his just-finished dinner and drinks landing in the middle of the table.

Women screamed as waiters and busboys rushed over.

"You fool." Bembry croaked the words out just before the convulsions hit. "The food—the food—you—served poisoned—"

The Maître d' stood frozen, his face ashen as Bembry and Shivers lay in their vomit, shaking like they were being electro-cuted. Screaming customers cleared their tables and rushed toward the front door.

Yousef put on his scarf and overcoat. Before stepping outside, he cast a final look at Bembry and Shivers, noting that their skin appeared as if it were being stretched off their bones.

Kitchen fire, the first thought that entered Leo Lebo's mind when he saw the restaurant customers streaming out in near panic. But there were no signs of smoke. And wasn't that the lone Mediterranean-looking man walking calmly away? Grabbing his overcoat, he got out of the SUV and raced across the street.

Twenty-one

"You didn't discuss this with Justice?"

"There isn't time," Grant said. "We need to exercise the contracts by tomorrow or they'll expire. If we don't act, foreign bankers will wind up with the loot."

"A trillion dollars?" Abby toyed with her food. "Sounds like you've orchestrated the world's largest robbery."

"Not really. Sweeny ran it by our legal department. We got a preliminary green light. There's actually no governing authority to redistribute the funds for what Nasser did. We're in a State of Emergency. Muslim assets are being seized, as are our assets in Muslim countries. The legal claimant to the money, at least on paper, is Nasser, the world's most wanted terrorist."

"Let's do this the right way. The USA Patriot Act gives the President the right to seize assets from enemies of the United States. Nasser certainly qualifies. I'll have an executive order for you in the morning." Abby pushed her plate away. "God help me, the only thing I want for that man is eternal suffering."

"The noose is tightening. With a little luck, Nasser's neck will end up in it." Grant sipped his wine. "There's a grand irony in taking his money. No telling what he would've cooked up had he gotten his hands on it."

"Axel was right. You're a loose cannon." Abby reached across the table and took Grant's hand. "But I'm glad you're on our side. It would be a shame for so much money to vanish inside dusty bank vaults."

"Money moves pieces on the global chessboard," Grant said. "Especially when there's a lot of it to go around."

"But it won't bring back the loved ones of all those people lost. Nasser's changed the world into a place of fear and hatred. Parents are afraid to take their children to school. People are being shot in the streets. Citizens are being arrested and deported." Abby looked away. "I feel like I'm slipping through a crack into oblivion."

"No, the money won't bring back loved ones." Grant squeezed Abby's hand. "But there's a good chance it can prevent others from dying needlessly."

Abby fixed her eyes on him. "What's on your mind, Mr. Corbet?"

"I ran an idea by Zach earlier," Grant said. "Here it is…"

Back in his room, Yousef connected the laptop to his hotel phone and logged online. The red digital readout on the clock approached 1:00 a.m. Several hours had passed since his last message to Nasser about the evening's events. He opened his e-mail and stared at the most recent Mail Undelivered notice. An icy finger slid down his spine. None of his e-mails had gotten though. Why? Surely, his prince would have notified him about an address change.

Yousef disconnected the computer from the telephone and dialed Lufthansa Airlines.

"Thank you for calling Lufthansa," the reservationists said. "How can I help you?"

"I'd like to book a first class ticket on the 6:00 a.m. flight to Frankfurt, connecting to Dubai."

"I'm sorry, sir. All flights to Dubai have been canceled."

"Canceled?" Yousef frowned. "Do you have a connection to Riyadh?"

"Due to the State of Emergency, air service is no longer being provided to Muslim countries."

"When did this happen?" Yousef asked. "I've seen no mention of this in the newspapers."

"It went into effect today. The public announcement will be made later this morning. We have a connecting flight to Tel Aviv."

"I'll call back." Yousef hung up, then direct dialed one of Nasser's hotels in Riyadh. The phone rang twenty times before he slammed the receiver down. He made a dozen phone calls to different businesses in the Middle East with similar results. Communications to the Middle East had been severed.

Yousef sat on the bed and thought it through. He would have to continue using his Italian passport, as Muslims were being detained and repatriated all over the world. His best chance of getting back to Saudi Arabia would be crossing into Lebanon through Israel. Once he reached Beirut, he could catch a plane to Jeddah. It would be dangerous trying to get by Israeli sentries, but a chance he'd willingly take. The Jews had no reason to keep him. After all, he wasn't wanted by the Mossad. *Yes,* he thought, far easier for the Israelis to let the Lebanese deal with another refugee.

Yousef removed his Visa card from his wallet, then called Lufthansa and booked a flight to Frankfurt, connecting to Tel Aviv.

Over the South China Sea, one of the eight translators aboard the RC-135, flying out of Kadena on Okinawa, blinked. For the past several hours, he had been monitoring transmissions between the Chang-Feng, one of the Sovremenny-class destroyers, and Chinese fleet command center at Zhanjiang.

"Six of our F/A-18 Super Hornets assigned to Kitty Hawk just passed over the Chang-Feng," he said to the pilot in charge. "The information's going directly to Beijing."

"Links are open with Kitty Hawk command center and the operations desk at Fort Meade," the pilot said.

"Beijing just ordered their air force to scramble," the translator said.

The radio crackled. "This is Admiral Hawes from the Kitty Hawk Command Center. Have they been ordered to engage?"

"At present, their orders are not to fire unless fired upon."

Hawes wiped his mouth. "That's enough fun for one day," he said. "We've made our point. I'm ordering our boys back before things go to hell. We're still two days away from reaching the blockade."

"Excuse me, Madam President. Your press secretary says it's urgent," Lindsey Caspare said over the speaker phone.

"Thank you, Lindsey." Abby stared at the ceiling, familiar dread crawling through her insides.

Grant propped up on his elbow as she lifted the receiver.

"It's three a.m., Lori?"

"I'm sorry to disturb you, Madam President," Lori Ramirez said. "Axel Bembry and Barry Shivers were found dead in a Georgetown restaurant earlier this evening. The press is all over it."

"Dead?" Abby sat up. "How?"

"We're not sure," Ramirez said. "A waiter heard Axel imply the food had been poisoned before he died."

"When will we know the cause of death?"

"The FBI has taken possession of the bodies. They've got a forensic team working on the autopsies. Preliminary results should be in later this morning."

"Keep me posted, Lori. I'll be down in an hour." Abby replaced the receiver and looked at Grant. "Better turn on CNN. Axel Bembry and Barry Shivers died in a Georgetown restaurant last night."

In his mountain home near Jeddah, Prince Nasser stood on his balcony, his gaze fixed on a hawk circling in search of food. Like the bird of prey, he had been reduced to the role of a lone predator. Access to the outside world cut off; the hard drive on his mainframe wiped clean by a virus; his business empire seized by infidels; his HARPIE contracts worthless.

His power and most of his wealth—gone! Vanished like swirling sand in desert wind. *Bested by infidels.* The thought brought bitter bile to his mouth. Hatred welled as an image of Grant Corbet conjured. He had little doubt that Corbet had played a major role in stealing his power. Nasser grabbed a nearby bowl of fruit and smashed it against the wall. He watched porcelain pieces, dates and figs scatter across the tiles.

A trillion dollars had disappeared, and he was powerless to do anything about it. Now there would be no army to enforce his *fatwa* uniting Islam; no control of Mecca and Medina. Success had been within his reach, only to be snatched away. Why? Had his God forsaken him? Hadn't Allah whispered in his ear beneath the desert's starry skies? Hadn't He sent signs?

Nasser sat, his hand moving to the Koran, the familiar leather cover soft beneath his fingers. Had it all been nothing more than a jest—a jest of God? No! That was impossible. God's ways were beyond the scope of mortals. Allah would not forsake him now.

Riding the wind, the hawk suddenly dove. Nasser watched the

bird plummet, a black speck on infinite blue sky. The predator's prey, a desert rat froze when death's shadow covered it. A rush of movement, followed by an explosion of dust.

The prince did not see one of the predator's claws nick the rat's hindquarter as it rushed to the safety of a nearby hole.

Screeching, the hawk turned skyward, its talons empty.

Premier Jen Jemin sipped his favorite tea, but did not taste it. "What is the current situation?"

"The enemy is closing in," Admiral Han said. "The two American battle groups and the British BG are a day and a half away."

Wang Zi rested his chin on steepled forefingers. "It appears they plan to converge on our blockade in unison."

"We will be surrounded, and hopelessly outnumbered. Any one of the three groups are capable of destroying our navy, along with our land-based missiles." Jen threw his hands up. "Apparently, my warning about China's willingness to use force fell on deaf ears."

"Already they test our resolve." Admiral Han wiped the sweat line from his upper lip. "Six F/A-18 Super Hornets assigned to Kitty Hawk buzzed one of our Sovremenny destroyers."

"Our response?" Jen asked.

"The American planes returned to their base after units of PROC Air Force scrambled," Wang said.

"I hardly think the Americans returned to the Kitty Hawk out of fear, Minister Wang." Jen's eyes narrowed. "The dragon of China has become snared in a trap of our own making."

"It has always been American policy to draw a crisis out," Wang said. "China will have no face if we kowtow before the barbarians prematurely."

"I'm fully aware of what China will and will not have,

Minister." Jen's fist came down on the table. "I'm also aware what will become of China in the event of a nuclear exchange."

Aaron "Rake" Friedman, the publisher of the *National Monitor*, stared out his office into early morning darkness. Steam billowed from the sidewalk grates below. "I told Barry a story like this could bite him in the ass."

"Yeah, too bad about Barry," Sam Jolsen said. "We've got time to get the story out in the morning edition. What do you think about slanting the piece to run as a joint White House-CIA plot to eliminate enemies? You know, Nixonize the story, only incorporate the element of murder."

"That's what I always liked about you, Sam. Fair and balanced news reporting." Friedman glanced at his editor-in-chief. "Run with it."

"What have you got, Leo?" Grant asked.

"I've got our boy pinpointed," Lebo said. "Let's hook up the camera, and I'll give you a bird's-eye view."

Moments later, the two men focused on Grant's television.

"Here he comes," Lebo said. "It's colder than a witch's tit, but he opts to walk from somewhere up the street to the restaurant, rather than use the valet service."

"Could be a bad guy without a beard," Grant said. "He's got the coloring."

"All that's left is a mustache." Lebo zoomed in on Yousef's face. "He made a reservation under the name of Michael Orlando."

"How did you finger him?"

Lebo fast forwarded. "Here he is coming out of the restaurant, moments before the other customers stampeded. Looks a little too calm, don't you think?"

"Pretty thin, Leo," Grant said. "That doesn't mark him as an assassin. This isn't like the old days in the field. We can't afford guesswork."

"No guesswork here. This guy made a mistake and left a trail. He didn't figure on someone like me being on Bembry's back." Lebo clicked off the television. "Orlando paid for his meal with a Visa card. I got the cashier to give me the number off the ticket. Once I got back here, I had the Visa security people get me a list of recent charges."

"And?"

"He purchased his shuttle ticket from New York on the same card. Guess who else was on the flight."

"Shivers."

"Right." Lebo removed a piece of paper from his case. "Shortly after he landed, Orlando checked into an airport Holiday Inn."

"Same card?"

"Yep." Lebo handed Grant the paper. "Our boy likes to travel. Hours after doing Bembry and Shivers, he books a flight to Tel Aviv, connecting through Frankfurt."

"He's definitely Nasser's goon." Grant's gut roiled with anger. "I'd give odds Nasser had him knock off Bembry and Shivers to discredit Abby's presidency."

"He's a few hours out of Frankfurt. Want to have our guys act as a welcoming committee?"

"No." Grant shook his head. "His best chance of getting home is through Israel into Lebanon. Let the son-of-a-bitch enjoy his flight, but have someone shadow him. I'll let Ira Bettleman know he's coming. I'm sure his people will have questions."

"Will do." Lebo sucked his front tooth. "I'd hate to be in that miserable fucker's shoes when he lands."

Twenty-two

Yousef felt a cold finger of fear trace a line down his back when he stepped off the Lufthansa plane into Ben-Gurion International Airport. Armed security guards placed every ten yards along the corridor scanned travelers, looking for anything suspicious.

People streamed along the corridor toward departure gates. Taking a breath, Yousef stepped into the jostling crowds and made his way to immigration. Due to heightened security, the lines were long, as passports were checked and rechecked.

Yousef presented his Italian passport to the customs agent an hour later.

"Are you visiting Israel for business or pleasure?"

"Business," Yousef said.

The agent stared at the passport photo. "Where will you be staying?"

Yousef felt his palms dampen as he glanced at the security guards beyond the booth. "The King David."

The customs man nodded to a pair of men, then looked at Yousef. "Have a nice stay in Israel, Mr. Orlando."

The two Mossad agents stepped forward.

"You will come with us," the taller of the two men said.

"But—" The sour odor of fear rose from Yousef's armpits.

Outside the customs booth, Jacob Eisenberg leaned against a column and watched his agents approach with Yousef. "Welcome to Israel, Mr. Orlando."

"What is the meaning of this?" Yousef said. "I am an Italian businessman. I have a passport, luggage."

Jacob lit a cigarette. "Don't worry about your passport and luggage. The King David's overbooked. We've arranged new accommodations for you."

"The Americans and British are now less than a day away." Admiral Han pointed to a map of the South China Sea on the large screen. "The Kitty Hawk BG approaches from the northeast, while the Stennis and Invincible BG's move in from the southwest and southeast. F/A 18 Super Hornets continue their sorties, buzzing like bees."

"We are about to be surrounded by the largest naval force ever assembled." Premier Jen looked at Wang Zi. "It appears you underestimated their resolve."

The minister of state security sipped tea. "I do not think they will breach our blockade, given our threat to use nuclear weapons. The Americans will look for other avenues of accommodation."

"If I may be so bold, Minister Wang?" Admiral Han stepped away from the screen. "What do you suggest as a response if our blockade is breached? The Americans have the capability to destroy China's navy, and most if not all of our land-based missile sites."

"They can also destroy our air force," General Gi said. "Most of our air fleet is based on 1950s and '60s technology. Except for a dozen Russian Su-27 advanced tactical fighters, we are hopelessly outmatched against their advanced technology."

"Only two paths are open to us if it becomes obvious they plan to run our blockade." Wang studied the bottom of his teacup. "We can either retreat or attack."

"Neither path is acceptable," Jen said. "Retreat and we are reduced to dogs howling at the moon. Attack and we face certain defeat."

"I do not believe we will have to choose either path, if we remain firm in our resolve," Wang said. "The Americans will not put their West Coast cities at risk."

Admiral Han shook his head. "A very dangerous game you play, Minister Wang."

"We live in dangerous times, Admiral. People are starving as many parts of China face famine. Blackouts are routine. And the weather continues to deteriorate. Our need for oil to fuel future economic growth is at an all-time high." Wang's gaze passed from one man to the other. "Imagine what would happen to China's position in the world, especially in the Far East, if we allowed foreign powers to seize our land and wealth at will?"

Han bit his lip and looked away.

"There are other forces in play," Wang said. "Our agents inform me that the Japanese and South Korean governments are exerting enormous pressure on Washington not to test our resolve."

"What do you hear from the renegade province of Taiwan?" Jen asked.

"They have been predictably quiet." Wang lit a cigarette. "After all, it was that imbecile, Ping-yi Cong, who assigned Taiwan's claim to the Spratly Islands over to America."

Jen Jemin stood and walked to the window. Snow covered the rock garden he used to contemplate problems. His gaze followed gold outlines of carp swimming in the pond beneath the arched bridge. "For now, China will maintain full military readiness. Perhaps the clouds will part and the true color of the sky will reveal itself before the new day arrives."

White House Enemies Murdered

National Monitor reporter Barry Shivers and former National Security Advisor Axel Bembry died mysteriously last night in a posh Georgetown restaurant. No suspects have been named, but it is well known both men were at odds with President Abigail Stewart.

Shivers was *persona non grata* at White House news conferences for exposing President Stewart's love affair with CIA super spook Grant Corbet. Bembry, on the other hand, resigned as NSA to challenge Stewart for the presidency at next year's convention.

A waiter on the scene heard Bembry say his food had been poisoned just before he died. There has been no comment from the White House concerning the—

Abby wadded the *National Monitor* into a ball. She tossed it into the trash and called Grant. "I can't believe how far these sleaze merchants will go to sell a paper. They all but accused us of having Bembry and Shivers killed."

"You beat me to the phone," Grant said. "We nailed the perpetrator. He works for Nasser. I'm sure killing Bembry and Shivers was aimed at discrediting your presidency."

"It's succeeding, Grant. My press secretary's under siege. Even the legitimate press is playing up the fact that these two were enemies of the White House. We've got to stop this before it goes any further. The public's mood is too volatile to have something like this dumped on it."

"The rats have nowhere to hide now," Grant said. "I'll have a report for you to give Lori within the hour. Leo Lebo has incontrovertible evidence Lawrence Escope paid Shivers to run the *National Monitor* stories. He also traced twenty million in deposits earmarked to finance Bembry's presidential run."

"That gets us partially off the hook. What about Nasser's assassin?"

Grant glanced at his watch. "I should be hearing from Ira Bettleman soon. Mossad welcomed him to Israel a little over an hour ago."

Grant picked up his private line fifteen minutes later. "Corbet."

"You can tell the FBI pathologist that Nasser's man used Compound 1080 to kill Bembry and Shivers," Ira Bettleman said. "We found an aspirin bottle full of tablets in his shaving bag. He dropped one in their martinis while they were in the restroom."

"Compound 1080?"

"It was originally developed to protect livestock from predators," Bettleman said. "There's no known antidote. It's colorless, tasteless, and dissolves easily in water. Plop, plop, fizz, fizz, you're dead."

"Anything else?"

"His name is Yousef, a Yam tribesman, and Nasser's bodyguard. Other than proudly admitting the killings, he's not talking."

"Paradise beckons," Grant said.

Bettleman grunted. "Jacob's got our best people working on him. I doubt he can hold out much longer."

"How about a video?" Grant asked. "I'd like to match it up with the one we have of him coming out of the restaurant."

"Check your computer. You can download it and see Jacob greeting Yousef at Ben-Gurion International Airport." A brief silence came over the line. "Our people on the other side tell us isolation has created chaos. Battle lines are being drawn between Nasser-style traditionalists, who want to go back to the seventh century, and the more contemporary thinkers, who prefer the modern civilized world."

"Let's hope it's the latter who wind up controlling the military," Grant said.

"*Insha'Allah.*" The Israeli spymaster blew through his mouth. "I see the South China Sea situation has reached the boiling point. You think there will be a confrontation?"

"It could go either way," Grant said. "Right now, it comes down to a matter of face."

"A big word in Asia, my friend."

An hour and a half later, Lindsey Caspare ushered Grant into the Oval Office. Abby motioned him to the couch, where she was watching CNN on a monitor built into the coffee table. "The press is relentless about Axel and Barry Shivers' murder. They're actually implying you and I had something to do with it. Whatever happened to reporting the facts?"

"The media deals in sensationalism and endless chatter nowadays." Grant kissed Abby on the cheek, noting the darkness under her eyes. "There's not a helluva lot of good news floating around, so they resort to muckraking."

"The opposition is reveling in the dirt."

"Then maybe you should have Lori hold a press briefing and lay a little of this on them. There should be plenty of red faces afterwards." Grant clicked open his attaché and removed a package. "This ought to occupy the headlines for a few days."

After viewing the video and reading the report, Abby looked up at Grant, her eyes brighter. "You came through, Mr. Corbet. One of the reasons I love you so much."

Grant glanced at his watch. "Lawrence Escope should be under wraps in a few minutes. Sean O'Dell planned to pick him up personally."

"Then the entire nasty bunch has been accounted for." Abby's mouth twisted. "Except for Nasser."

"We'll get him," Grant said. "It may take time, but we'll get him."

Abby buzzed her secretary. "Get Lori Ramirez down here ASAP." She looked at Grant. "Bring me up to date on the latest satellite information. The Chinese ambassador will be here in an hour."

FBI Director Sean O'Dell and two special agents stepped off the elevator and into Lawrence Escope's office complex.

The room smelled of fine leather and tobacco. Silk rugs from Iran were scattered over the polished hardwood floor. A Picasso and Chagall adorned the paneled walls.

"Nice digs," one of the agents said.

"Can I help you?" the receptionist asked.

O'Dell removed his gloves, then pulled out his identification folder. "FBI. Please let Mr. Escope know we are here."

The receptionist's eyes flitted nervously as she pressed the buzzer.

Moments later, the former Nevada-senator-turned-lobbyist walked out, attired in a gray Armani suit. "Yes, gentlemen, what can I do for you?"

"We'd like to talk to you about your relationship with Prince Abdul bin Suleiman Nasser," O'Dell said. "It's extremely cold outside. I suggest you bring an overcoat."

"Are we sure about this?" Abby asked.

"The overheads look good. We've run simulations tracking changes in deployment going back a year." Grant scanned the file again. "Our satellite data checks with what the Russian birds have come up with."

"But we're still not certain, are we?"

"Nothing's a hundred percent," Grant said. "There's a lot of activity around the sites, suggesting China will make a preemptive strike rather than see their missiles destroyed. The trick will be hitting them all, and quickly, before it comes to that."

"Dear God, I've stepped onto a playing field larger than I ever imagined." Abby stood, her arms wrapped around her breasts. "The consequences are unimaginable if we're wrong."

"At this point, the only thing I know for sure is, you mustn't dwell on how the world got to this point."

"How can I not dwell on it?" Abby turned away. "All I see are the faces of those who have died."

Abby's secretary buzzed. "Madam President, the Chinese Ambassador is here."

"Would you do the honors?" Abby said, glancing at Grant.

He nodded and walked out. By the time he returned to the West Wing with the Ambassador, Lindsey Caspare and four other Secret Services agents were positioned outside the Oval Office.

Caspare opened the door and followed them inside.

"Good day, Mr. Ambassador. Please have a seat." Abby gestured to one of the chairs across from her.

"Thank you, Madam President."

The ambassador sat. Grant took the chair on his right.

"I understand you have an urgent message from your government," Abby said.

"Time is short, Madam President. On behalf of my government, I urge you to rescind orders to breach our blockade." The ambassador shifted in his chair, summoning his words. "The consequences—"

Abby overrode him. "Our claim to the Spratly Islands has been given legal authority by the International Court. We intend to develop their natural resources."

"I remind you, Mr. Ambassador," Grant said, "your navy is

committing a criminal act by blockading international shipping lanes."

The ambassador's neutral expression hardened. "We wish to have a peaceful solution to the crisis. However, you are leaving us little room to negotiate."

"Have your navy withdraw," Grant said. "China and the other countries who claim sovereignty over the Spratly Islands can present their cases to the International Court of Justice."

The ambassador turned to Abby. "Does Mr. Corbet speak for the United States?"

"I speak for the United States, Mr. Ambassador," Abby said calmly. "But in this case, Mr. Corbet speaks for me."

"You leave us little to work with, Madam President."

"A decision of your government's making. Premier Jen has threatened the United States and your Asian neighbors with the use of nuclear weapons." Abby felt her pulse thumping as she stared at the ambassador. "We sincerely hope China will seek a peaceful solution to resolve the current crisis."

The ambassador frowned. "My government will not allow our land and natural resources to be stolen by outside forces."

"We're claiming what we have legal title to," Abby said. "I regret your government's decision. Do you have anything further to say on this matter, Mr. Ambassador?"

"No, Madam President."

"Very well, sir. I won't detain you further."

Grant stood and walked the ambassador out, returning a minute later.

"Timeline?" Abby asked.

"A matter of hours."

"I pray this works."

"Yes."

"Highness, Sheik Mustafa al-Sudra wishes an audience," the servant said. "He asked that I convey it concerns a matter of the gravest importance."

"Bring tea and fruits." Nasser's hand moved to the Koran. "I shall receive him out here, on the balcony."

Moments later, Nasser watched Sheik Mustafa al-Sudra walk out on the balcony. The tribal council leader's face was craggy and lined, as if scored by desert winds.

"My dear al-Sudra, an unexpected surprise."

The two men exchanged ritual kisses on their cheeks.

"Many years have passed since we last spoke, Prince Abdul bin Suleiman Nasser." Arthritic fingers clutched Nasser's arms. "The likeness to your father, peace be upon him, is remarkable."

"You must be tired after your journey." Nasser took the sheik's arm. "Come, make yourself comfortable. I have freshly brewed tea and fruit."

The two men waited in silence while a servant poured tea.

Once they were alone, al-Sudra looked at Nasser. "The lands of the Prophet, peace be upon Him, are being swept by the whirl-wind."

Nasser lifted his teacup and sipped.

Al-Sudra's black eyes flashed in the moonlight. "People cry for a new leader. one who can unite Islam."

"Our people are fractured," Nasser said. "Tribes fight tribes. I fear what you seek is hopeless."

"I have met with the tribal elders," al-Sudra said. "The Bedouin will rise up and become as one to cleanse our sacred lands of infidel influence."

Nasser stared in the direction of Mecca. "Have you decided upon such a leader?"

"You are that man, Prince Abdul bin Suleiman Nasser." Al-Sudra laid a hand on Nasser's arm. "You are that man."

Suppressing an urge to smile, Nasser sipped his tea.

Twenty-three

"The seven American Petroleum ships are less than six hours away from the northeast boundary of our blockade," Admiral Han said. "Three U.S. frigates are escorting them."

Jen Jemin popped an antacid tablet. "Have the Chang-Feng order them to turn back. Tell them they will be fired upon if our blockade is breached."

"F/A 18 Super Hornets are giving air support." Han tugged at his uniform collar. "What if the Americans refuse to turn back?"

"Continue sending the warning." Jen glared across the table at Wang Zi. "We are a minnow attacking a whale. Fortunately for you, there are still several hours to see if your plan works."

"The Chang-Feng has ordered the American Petroleum ships to turn back," one of the translators aboard the RC-135 said. "Their orders are to fire on our ships if they attempt to breach the blockade."

"Shit," Frances Merriman whispered.

Abigail Stewart turned to her secretary of defense. "Recommendations, Collin?"

"The Chinese cannot possibly stand against the force we've assembled, Madam President. America has a long-standing pledge to protect vital shipping lanes. Lanes the Chinese are now blockading." Jeffers gritted his teeth. "I say we stand firm."

"Admiral Hawes, your assessment?"

The radio link to the Kitty Hawk Command Center crackled. "I suggest we position the three frigates escorting the American Petroleum ships in the lead, Madam President. If the Chinese fire, they will be firing on the United States Navy in open waters."

"And our response should be?"

"Immediate, overwhelming force. Destroy the Chinese Navy and all of their known land-based missile sites."

"Are the sites targeted?"

"Yes, Madam President. It won't be pretty if they fire on our ships."

Abby bit her lip. "All right, Admiral, order our frigates to the front."

At midnight, in Riyadh, Crown Prince Faisal stared into his empty brandy snifter. "The lands of the Prophet are disintegrating into civil war," he said without looking up. "With no link to the outside, we live in a great vacuum. Now there's no way of knowing when or if the infidels plan to attack."

"Madness rules," Foreign Minister Prince Zyyad said. "Rumors and innuendo drive the fear. Our most trusted officers are wavering."

"The mobs are growing." Faisal's eyes were focused on nothing. "I fear the Royal House will be toppled from within."

"Mobs are spawned from camel dung." Zyyad refilled their glasses. "Mullahs we have supported for years are whipping the filthy animals into a rage."

Faisal took a long drink. "Filthy animals or not, their numbers have swollen into the millions. They cry out for a new leader. The army cannot move against the entire country."

"Dispatching death squads around the globe, killing thousands—" Zyyad gnashed his teeth. "What could that imbecile Moussawi have been thinking?"

"The answer to that question remains with Allah and the Mossad."

Faisal clicked on the Al Jazeera news network. "From Tripoli to Riyadh, massive riots have erupted throughout the Muslim world," the anchor said. "In Baghdad, the recently elected government, Hassan Donat, has been toppled by followers loyal to Grand Ayatollah Ali Haseen. Meanwhile, in Indonesia—"

"Sh'ia." Zyyad's voice cut through the air like a lash. "Allah protect us from such fanatics."

"Protect us from fanatics, my dear cousin? What do you think we've been producing for years in our schools?" Faisal laughed wistfully. "Open the window, Zyyad. Listen carefully and you will hear."

Zyyad, concerned by the eerie calmness on the face of Saudi Arabia's future king, drained his brandy and went to the window. He waited for Faisal to turn off the set before raising the glass. In the distance, rising like a great storm, came, *"Allah-u Akbarrr, Allah-u Akbarrr."*

"What do you propose we do, cousin? We've no friends, our money is worthless, our assets abroad seized, food, medicine, and other essentials cut off." Faisal gestured at the open window, the ten-carat diamond on his ring finger catching the overhead light. "The people await our answers."

In Beijing, Premier Jen wiped at the sweat on his forehead.

"The Americans shot down one of our Su-27's?"

"Yes, sir," PROC Air Force General Gi said. "Our pilot locked onto one of the F/A 18 Super Hornets patrolling the area and warned them to immediately leave Chinese airspace."

"And?"

General Gi looked away from the premier's intense stare. "The American pilot took evasive action and retaliated."

"So they shoot us from the sky as easily as a frog catching a mosquito." Jen leaned on his desk, knuckles down. "A deer does not provoke a tiger. There must be another way."

"The three frigates escorting the American Petroleum vessels have been positioned in front," Admiral Han said.

"The foul Americans are clever. If we attack, we attack the United States Navy. Then we will have given them their excuse to retaliate with overwhelming force." Jen looked up. "What is the current position of the American and British battle groups, Admiral?"

"At present, the Kitty Hawk BG is holding one hundred miles northwest of our fleet. The Stennis and the Illustrious groups are respectively holding seventy-five miles to the southwest and southeast of the blockade. We've sent repeated warnings for them to stand down, but—" Admiral Han offered truth calmly. "Their battleships, destroyers, submarines, and frigates continue to advance."

"Fighter jets darken our skies like insect swarms," General Gi said. "Military bases around the world are on full alert."

Jen pointed at Wang Zi. "You still doubt America's resolve in this matter?"

"I do, Premier Jen. We have given the Americans and the rest of the world ample warning about our intentions." Wang's hand trembled. "I'm not convinced Abigail Stewart will breach our blockade. Japan and South Korea continue to apply pressure. The risk to human life is too great."

"The rest of the world is aligned against us in this matter, in case you've forgotten," Jen said. "Yet, we cannot allow our resources and land to be confiscated at will."

"If the West attacked the mainland, we would have the army behind us," General Gi said. "But in the air and on the water we are no match."

"Yes, yes, I know, General." Jen paced. "Still, Minister Wang has a point."

"If we appear weak, we open the door to all manner of predators," Wang said. "China will have no face anywhere in the world."

"Admiral Han."

"Yes, Premier Jen."

"Order our destroyers to fire on any ship that attempts to cross the blockade."

"They could be monitoring our communications and launch a preemptive strike," General Gi said.

"I'm counting on that not happening, General." Jen clenched his hands, feeling the terror of the situation settle over him. "Do not send the order until their vessels are in sight."

Admiral Han coughed softly. "And if they retaliate?"

"We will have to deal with that possibility when the time comes."

"Attention Kitty Hawk Command Center, visual contact has been made between the Chinese Navy and our three frigates," the interpreter aboard the RC-135 said. "Beijing just issued orders for the Chang-Feng to engage our ships if they attempt to pass through the blockade."

"Yes sir, I understand," Commander Ng said. He hung up the

handset and turned to his communications officer. "Tell the Americans to turn back now or we will initiate an attack."

The junior officer's composure cracked. "Yes, sir."

"Do it now," Ng said.

"Attention Kitty Hawk Command Center, turn back immediately or we will open fire. I repeat, turn your vessels back or we will open fire. This is your last warning."

"Madam President?" Admiral Hawes asked from his Kitty Hawk Command Center.

"Send a message to the Chang-Feng that we intend to escort the American Petroleum ships to the Spratly Islands." Abby stared at the back of her hands. "If they attack American ships in international waters, the United States will consider it an act of war, and respond appropriately."

Hawes' voice lowered a decibel. "Yes, Madam President."

"Admiral Han, the Kitty Hawk signaled back that they intend to escort the American Petroleum ships to the Spratly Islands." Commander Ng's palm was slick on the handset. "Any attack on our part will be considered an act of war."

"Commander Ng, fire a warning shot two hundred meters off the bow of the lead frigate," Admiral Han said.

"Yes sir." Ng turned to his second-in-command. "Give the order."

The junior officer blanched and took the handset. "Fire a round two hundred meters off the bow of the lead frigate."

A moment later, the computer on one of the Chang-Feng's big guns locked in just in front of the American ship and fired.

Admiral Hawes clicked on the handset aboard the Kitty Hawk Command Center. "Madam President, the Chang-Feng just fired a cannon round off the bow of our lead frigate."

"The miss was intentional, sir," the interpreter aboard the RC-135 said. "Beijing gave the order to fire a warning shot only."

"Did you hear that, Madam President? Beijing ordered a warning shot."

"Roger, Admiral." Abby looked around the table. "I think Premier Jen's sending a signal he's looking for an honorable way out. Any thoughts?"

"He'd be a damned fool to fire on our ships," Collin Jeffers said. "China would wind up a backwater country."

"Jen's trapped. On one hand, he's counting on the President not risking a nuclear attack on our West Coast and Asian allies. On the other, he can't risk destroying China." Frances Merriman rubbed her mother's brooch, comforting under her touch. "I'm in agreement with Grant's earlier assessment. Jen doesn't want to be perceived as weak. He's looking for a way out that will allow him to save face."

"Shall we proceed through the blockade, Madam President?" Admiral Hawes asked.

"Negative, Admiral. For now keep our ships on the perimeter of the blockade." Abby exchanged a glance with Grant. "I've got a phone call to make."

"The American and British ships have stopped moving toward the blockade," Admiral Han said. "They are holding around the perimeter."

Wang Zi sipped jasmine tea. "I did not think the American

president had the stomach to risk nuclear war."

"All indications suggested they were ready to engage," Admiral Han said. "Apparently they've been ordered to stand down."

"I would not bask in confidence, gentlemen." Premier Jen chewed two more antacid tablets. "Abigail Stewart is a formidable opponent. She will not walk away like a whipped dog."

Just then, Jen's aide knocked and entered the chamber.

Jen glared at the aide. "I told you I was not to be disturbed under any circumstances."

The aide approached, and whispered into Jen's ear. "You have a telephone call, sir. I don't think you want to miss it."

Twenty-four

Grant looked out the plane window as Air Force One prepared to land at Beijing Capital International Airport. The gray skies were thick with pollution and falling snow. "Reminds me of home," he said.

"It's been so long since I've seen the sun, I sometimes think it died." Abby gripped Grant's hand. "I feel like I'm running on a treadmill, going nowhere."

"It will end soon. Sometime during the next few hours we'll know where we stand." Grant moved closer. "Besides, I think you're going to pull this off."

"Really think so?"

Grant nodded. "I do. Anything's possible."

"*Possible*, a nice, fuzzy word," Abby said. She turned to the window, her usually bright eyes clouded. "I hope the weather isn't a precursor of things to come."

"Madam President, air traffic has been canceled in and out of the airport," the pilot said over the intercom. "Looks like a lot of soldiers on the tarmac are carrying guns. Do you want me to abort the landing?"

"Damn! Jen's sealed the airport." Grant looked outside. "I

didn't expect this kind of welcoming committee."

"I imagine I would have done the same thing if he were coming to Washington." Abby picked up the receiver and buzzed the pilot. "Negative, Captain. Proceed with the landing."

"Roger, Madam President."

Minutes later, Air Force One touched down light as a cloud.

While the presidential plane taxied to the gate, a team of security specialists studied the surrounding area through monitors connected to Air Force One's bank of cameras.

One of the security specialists looked at Lindsey Caspare after the plane bumped against the exit ramp. "JUMPER'S clear to go."

Caspare's team of Secret Service agents quickly deplaned and took up positions along the corridor. Abby and Grant followed, another team of agents close behind.

At the end of the tunnel, a somber Premier Jen and an aide waited. Heavily armed security forces were positioned along both sides of the empty concourse. "Welcome to China, Madam President," Jen said through his interpreter. "I regret we could not have given you a more formal welcome, but given the gravity of the circumstances…"

Abby accepted the extended hand. "Apologies are not necessary, Mr. Premier. This is my advisor, Grant Corbet."

"Welcome to China, Mr. Corbet, your reputation precedes you," the interpreter said.

Grant felt the fifty-nine-year-old leader of China take his measure through thick glasses as they shook hands. "Thank you for meeting us, Premier Jen, under these difficult conditions."

Jen returned a tight-lipped smile.

"Premier Jen understands time is of the essence. He's arranged to use the Air China lounge for your discussions." The interpreter gestured down the hall. "Please follow me."

Scents of incense and freshly brewed tea wafted pleasantly inside the dimly lit lounge. Ming vases lined the walls, and Chinese silk rugs were scattered over the hardwood floors. Tea and assorted Chinese delicacies had been set on a round rosewood table at the far end of the lounge.

Halfway across the room, Abby touched Jen on the shoulder. "Mr. Premier," she said in perfect Mandarin, "due to the delicate nature of our talks, I suggest we keep the conversation between the two of us."

"Your Chinese is excellent, Madam President. I wondered why an interpreter did not accompany you." Jen bowed, then looked at his interpreter. "See that Mr. Corbet and the security staff enjoy our finest Chinese cuisine."

Jen sat across from Abby. Behind the premier was a huge painting of a red and black Earth Dragon, one of China's most revered symbols.

Abby studied the painting. China's indomitable guardian was positioned, jaws agape, talons bared, behind the Celestial Throne of Heaven. After a long moment, her gaze moved back to Jen. "You've chosen a fitting place to hold our discussion, Mr. Premier."

Jen filled their teacups. "Tea before conversation will help clarify matters."

Lifting her cup, Abby paused to inhale the fragrance. "Jasmine, I believe."

"Yes, my own special blend."

"The possibility of war between our two countries is very real." Abby sipped, then set her cup down. "It is my hope this direct dialogue between us will quickly put an end to our differences before it is too late."

"Your country and your allies are preparing to attack China," Jen said. "Three battle groups are in the South China Sea, the skies are dark with warplanes, you and your allies' military bases around the world are on full alert. You have ordered your navy to attack if we do not remove the blockade."

Abby stared at Jen. Thick glasses distorted his eyes, preventing her from looking inside them. "Those orders were issued after you announced China's willingness to use nuclear weapons against the United States and your neighbors if we attempted to develop the Spratly Islands. My government takes such threats seriously."

"We wanted the world to know China will not allow its land and natural resources to be taken by outsiders." Jen's features hardened. "I'm sure Mr. Corbet has shown you satellite photos of increased activity around our land-based missile sites. If those sites were attacked and destroyed, China's borders would be vulnerable to invaders. We will not allow that to happen."

"So you would initiate rather than defend against such an attack." Abby's lips pressed together. "A dangerous strategy, Mr. Premier. *Wei Ju Lui Laun*, as dangerous as piling eggs one on top of another."

"You are familiar with our ancient sayings, as well." Jen spread his hands. "Still, that does not change the simple, but dangerous, reality of the situation."

"The reality is the International Court of Justice gave a ruling that validated the United States' claim to the Spratly Islands."

"Madam President, we both know that an invasion of the Middle East would jeopardize seventy percent of the world's known oil reserves," Jen said. "The International Court's ruling was one of expediency, giving you the right to steal China's natural resources."

"The United States does not wish to steal China's or anyone else's resources." Abby's violet eyes caught the dim light. "Nor do we want war with China. Nor do I think China wants a nuclear war."

"Conflict can be avoided if you withdraw your forces from the South China Sea, and" —Jen held up a finger— "give up any plans of drilling on the Spratly Islands."

"This I cannot do," Abby said. "The Spratly oil reserves are vital to world stability. It offers an alternative to Middle Eastern oil."

"The oil belongs to China." Jen's lowered his voice. "It appears our talk has failed to bear fruit. We continue to reach a familiar impasse."

"You are wrong, Premier Jen. Most of the world is experiencing abnormal weather conditions, crop failures, plunging stock markets, and malcontent populations." Abby stared at Jen. "I believe a golden thread can be found even under these most adverse conditions, if one looks long enough." ·

Jen sighed. "Yes, we find ourselves in a position where remote possibilities must be examined. What do you propose?"

"I have a plan that can get us each what we want without the horrors of nuclear war. Under the agreement, China and the United States and Great Britain will recall their forces. Our respective countries will gain enormous political respect by lifting the threat of nuclear war from the planet."

"What about the Spratly Islands?"

"The United States will relinquish its claim to the Spratly Islands, and by joint agreement with China and Great Britain turn the area into an International Economic Zone. Think of it. We will give the world an alternative to Middle East oil. Such a move will solidify China's position as Asia's preeminent leader." Abby watched Jen's features soften as he leaned back and listened. "Speed is essential in developing the Spratly oil reserves. The United States has the technology to do it quickly."

Abby watched Jen take off his heavy glasses and wipe them with a spotless handkerchief. The premier of the world's most populous country appeared curiously vulnerable before replacing them and returning his gaze to her.

"And if I reject your proposal?"

"Then you will have to live with the consequences."

A faint smile crossed Jen's face. "Consequences I do not wish to shoulder."

"Nor I, Mr. Premier."

"In truth, I think your words have merit," Jen said. "Face could be saved on both sides. Do you have details?"

Abby took a file from her attaché and slid it across the table. "There are copies in Chinese and English. I'd like for us to have a final draft completed within the next twenty-four hours. Then we can arrange for a joint statement to be made by you, the British Prime Minister, and me."

"I agree in principle," Jen said. "You and I can negotiate the final details and avoid endless bureaucratic squabbling."

"Excellent. When would you like to start?"

Jen rubbed his hands together. "In China, we seal a bargain with a fine meal. My personal chef is quite gifted. I would be honored if America's Abby joined me for dinner."

"I'd be delighted, sir."

"I wonder." Jen stood, and tucked the file under his arm. "Would you have breached the blockade had we not reached agreement in principle? Or were you, as Americans say, bluffing?"

"The game ended before I had to show my cards." Abby glanced at the Earth Dragon behind Jen's chair. "Now we have a new deck that's just been reshuffled."

"You're a formidable poker player, Madam President."

"As are you, Premier Jen. As are you."

The steward delivered the champagne and caviar to the lounge area outside Air Force One's presidential suite, then quickly disappeared.

"I thought a little bubbly and caviar were in order." Grant winked at Abby. "It's not every day a President negotiates a way out of war, turns a foe into a friend, and gives the world hope for a brighter tomorrow."

Abby didn't smile. "I couldn't have done it without you. Using part of your ill-gotten gain from Nasser to ease China's trade deficit cinched the deal. Jen nearly did a cartwheel."

"Insuring that he spends it back in the good ol' U.S. of A. means a lot of jobs," Grant said. "Any idea on how you're going to spread around the remaining eight hundred billion?"

"Help the families who lost loved ones, reimburse our corporations for loss of assets in the Middle East, wipe out part of the deficit, rebuild the school system, fund alternative energy development. The list goes on."

"That will ease the pain for a lot of folks," Grant said. "Your alternative energy initiative will be another boon for the job market."

Abby picked up a cracker and nibbled. "If only—"

Grant studied her face, catching the pain. "If only what?"

"If only the images would go away." Abby dropped the cracker in her plate, tears sliding down her cheeks. "The dead children's faces have become part of me."

"No one could've done more than you, Madam President." Grant wrapped Abby in his arms and kissed away the tears. "Sometimes terrible things happen for the better good."

"At night, I hear Nasser laughing."

"It's terrible, but don't let that piece of human garbage ruin your moment, sweetheart. We'll get him. You know that."

"Maybe." Abby pulled back. "But the images of the dead will remain."

Grant put his hands on her shoulders and peered into her eyes. "The world's a better place because of you, Abby."

"I love you, Grant." Abby wiped her eyes with a tissue. "Couldn't have made it without you."

"You've made a better person out of me," Grant said. "I've learned how to love again."

"So have I."

"Look outside."

Abby brushed her hair back. "The sun's shining."

"Even the weather's on your side." Grant lifted the champagne bottle out of the ice bucket, popped the cork, and filled two long-stemmed glasses. "Here's to smooth sailing all the way home."

"You're right, damn it. I'm not going to let Nasser ruin the moment." Abby moved close to him. "Like I said before, I couldn't have done it without my loose cannon." She dipped a finger into her glass and touched it against Grant's lips. "We make quite a team."

"I was thinking the same thing." Grant inhaled the lilac scent in her hair. "Abby? Abby… Will you?"

Abby saw the unasked question in his eyes. "Yes," she said. "Yes, Grant, I will."

Twenty-five

"President Abigail Stewart has just laid the first wreath at the 'Solidarity Memorial,' commemorating those who died during the horrific terrorist attacks three months ago." The camera zoomed in on Abby, whose head was bowed in prayer. She was flanked by her cabinet, Supreme Court justices, and members of the House and Senate. "By the President's side is her husband-to-be, Grant Corbet," the CNN reporter whispered. "Next to Mr. Corbet are his daughter, Jenny, her husband, Leyton Childress, and their son, Harlin. Once today's ceremony is concluded, the couple and their guests will fly to Camp David, where they will be married. According to press secretary Lori Ramirez, the world's most highly anticipated nuptial will be a relatively small affair, limited to family and a few close friends."

The camera changed to an overhead image. "Jim, it appears the memorial service is over," the anchor said. "President Stewart and Grant Corbet are walking toward their limousine, stopping to shake hands with dignitaries along the way. We will now switch to our fashion editor, Lisa Evans, for an inside look at what America's first lady President plans to wear at her wedding this afternoon."

Several hours later, Grant and Jenny walked out onto Aspen's deck. The rolling hills of Camp David were covered in a pristine blanket of snow. Beneath an incredibly blue sky, sunlight glinted off icicles clinging to bare tree branches. The crisp air smelled faintly of burning logs and wet bark.

"She's wonderful, Daddy," Jenny said. "This past week, spending time with you and the President, has been awesome."

Grant watched a pair of squirrels scamper along the deck railing. "She led the world out of a nightmare."

"With help from a certain gray-eyed grandfather I know." Jenny poked him in the side. "I'm happy for you, Dad."

Grant hugged his daughter. "I love you, sweetheart."

Just before noon, Grant touched the speed dial on his cell phone.

Vulcan Industries vice president Andrew Stranahan picked up on the first ring. "Stranahan."

"Andy, are we good to go?"

"Affirmative," Stranahan said. "The satellite link to the big screen is operational. All you need to do is tune in to Channel 3 when your cell phone vibrates. Two predators are keeping watch. You should be getting an invitation to the party in about two hours, if behavioral patterns remain the same."

The sun balanced on the horizon like a giant tangerine ball when Prince Nasser returned to his fortress home near Jeddah on his stallion, Al Mukalla. Smells of human and animal sweat swirled around him as he rode into the stable area.

Nasser's eyes glowed in the semi-darkness. He had once again connected with his God. Incredible that, only days ago, he'd almost believed Allah had forsaken him. God's voice had stopped whispering to him on dark desert nights. His quest to unite Islam had seemed a hopeless cause, lost in desert sands. He believed he'd lost everything, perhaps even his soul. Paradise denied.

Until tonight!

The mighty stallion snorted beneath Nasser's loins. How wrong he'd been to question the ways of God. Sheik Mustafa al-Sudra, tribal elders, and a huge gathering of the faithful, obviously sent by Allah, had been waiting for him on the outskirts of his estate.

"Nasser, Nasser, Nasser." The roar of the crowd still rang in his ears.

Like a conquering prince, he'd ridden through the throng on Al Mukalla, his white djellaba billowing in the breeze.

"How was your ride, Excellency?" the trainer asked.

"Al Mukalla flew like the wind." The prince dismounted, passed the reins, and nuzzled the great beast's dilated nostrils. "See he's properly cooled."

"Of course, Excellency." The trainer stroked the stallion's neck. "We heard a great crowd waited for you."

"Bedouin tribal leaders gathered with their clans." Nasser stared into the distance. "True Arabs look for direction in these troubled times."

The trainer bowed deferentially as he watched Nasser walk away. The prince's shoulders were straight, his stride purposeful, befitting one born of the Prophet's blood.

Nasser seated himself at the table on his balcony and called for tea and fruits. He had bathed, and now wore a black *bisht* over a stark-white *dishdasha*. His hair and beard were meticulously groomed.

Gurgling sounds from the manmade pond moved Nasser's gaze to his garden. Palm fronds rustled in the evening breeze, the air smelling of bougainvillea and desert flowers. A great pleasure enveloped him as his prized oasis once again became a place of peace and quiet contemplation. True, he'd lost his business empire, but he had gained Islam in the process. A small price for such a prize.

A servant arrived with a silver tray of assorted fruits and tea. "Is there anything else you require, Highness?"

"That will be all." Nasser's hand moved to the leather-bound Koran on the table. He opened the book and silently read.

For it is written that a son of Arabia would awaken a fearsome Eagle. The wrath of the Eagle would be felt throughout the lands of Allah and lo, while some of the people trembled in despair still more rejoiced; for the wrath of the Eagle cleansed the lands of Allah; and there was peace.

Nasser breathed deeply, closed the Holy Book, and stood. He faced Mecca, arms extended by his sides.

Andy Stranahan made an adjustment on the control panel for the Predator's camera. It zoomed in on Nasser's face.

"He looks pretty upbeat," the technician next to him said.

"Wait till it plays out." Stranahan chuckled. "This will be a damn sight better than going to the movies."

The last of the guests had arrived when Grant's cell phone vibrated. He collected Frances Merriman and Collin Jeffers and led them over to where Abby was talking to Zach Holden and Ira Bettleman.

"Andy Stranahan just gave me the heads-up." Grant took Abby aside. "Sure you want to see this?"

The President nodded. "You're forgetting I'm the one who wanted to put a gun to his head."

Grant motioned to the others and took Abby's arm. He led the group to the media room and clicked Channel 3 on the big screen.

Nasser appeared.

Abby gripped Grant's arm.

"He looks pumped about something," Merriman said.

Grant punched in a number on his cell phone.

"See what I see?" Stranahan said after a moment.

"Sure do, Andy. The audience is assembled."

At Vulcan Industries headquarters in Reston, Virginia, Andrew Stranahan pressed a button on the control panel. The TBOLT launched itself off the back of the Predator, hovered momentarily, then silently glided toward Nasser's balcony.

"Looks like a miniature B-2," Bettleman said.

Grant motioned to the split image on the television screen. "The Predator camera provides the imaging on the left, TBOLT's on the right."

The group's eyes were riveted on the screen as they watched the TBOLT land on the table in front of Nasser.

"Hello," the mechanical voice said in Arabic.

Nasser stared at the red flashing nosecone.

"Good-bye," the mechanical voice said.

The Predator's side of the television screen blossomed orange. Flame and debris shot into the air like an erupting volcano.

Grant put his arm around Abby as they watched Nasser's home and dreams crash like a felled eagle slipping through Allah's hands down the Sarawat mountain into oblivion.

-END-

Check out these other fine titles by Durban House
at your local bookstore or online bookseller.

EXCEPTIONAL BOOKS

BY

EXCEPTIONAL WRITERS

FICTION

A COMMON GLORY
Robert Middlemiss
A DREAM ACROSS TIME
Annie Rogers
AFTER LIFE LIFE
Don Goldman
an-eye-for-an-eye.com
Dennis Powell
A MEETING OF MINDS
Elizabeth Turner Calloway
BASHA
John Hamilton Lewis
BLUEWATER DOWN
Rick O'Reilly
BY ROYAL DESIGN
Norbert Reich
THE BEIRUT CONSPIRACY
John R. Childress
CRISIS PENDING
Stephen Cornell

CRY HAVOC
John Hamilton Lewis
DEADLY ILLUSIONS
Chester D. Campbell
DANGER WITHIN
Mark Danielson
DEADLY ILLUMINATION
Serena Stier
DEATH OF A HEALER
Paul Henry Young
DESIGNED TO KILL
Chester D. Campbell
EXTREME CUISINE
Kit Sloane
THE GARDEN OF EVIL
Chris Holmes
HANDS OF VENGEANCE
Richard Sand
HORIZON'S END
Andrew Lazarus
HOUR OF THE WOLVES
Stephane Daimlen-Völs
THE INNOCENT NEVER KNEW
Mark W. Danielson
JOHNNIE RAY & MISS KILGALLEN
Bonnie Hearn Hill & Larry Hill
KIRA'S DIARY
Edward T. Gushee
THE LAST COWBOYS
Robert E. Hollmann
THE LATERAL LINE
Robert Middlemiss
LETHAL CURE
Kurt Popke
THE LUKARILLA AFFAIR
Jerry Banks

THE MEDUSA STRAIN
Chris Holmes
MR. IRRELEVANT
Jerry Marshall
MURDER ON THE TRAP
J. Preston Smith
NO ORDINARY TERROR
J. Brooks Van Dyke
OPAL EYE DEVIL
John Hamilton Lewis
PRIVATE JUSTICE
Richard Sand
PHARAOH'S FRIEND
Nancy Yawitz Linkous
ROADHOUSE BLUES
Baron Birtcher
RUBY TUESDAY
Baron Birtcher
SAMSARA
John Hamilton Lewis
SECRET OF THE SCROLL
Chester D. Campbell
SECRETS ARE ANONYMOUS
Fredrick L. Cullen
THE SEESAW SYNDROME
Michael Madden
THE SERIAL KILLER'S DIET BOOK
Kevin Mark Postupack
THE STREET OF FOUR WINDS
Andrew Lazarus
TAINTED ANGELS
Greg Crane
TERMINAL CARE
Arvin Chawla
TUNNEL RUNNER
Richard Sand

WHAT GOES AROUND
Don Goldman

NONFICTION

BEHIND THE MOUNTAIN
Nick Williams
FISH HEADS, RICE, RICE WINE & WAR: A VIETNAM PARADOX
Lt. Col. Thomas G. Smith, Ret.
I ACCUSE: JIMMY CARTER AND THE RISE OF MILITANT ISLAM
Philip Pilevsky
MIDDLE ESSENCE: WOMEN OF WONDER YEARS
Landy Reed
MOTHERS SPEAK: FOR LOVE OF FAMILY
Rosalie Gaziano
THE PASSION OF AYN RAND'S CRITICS
James S. Valliant

PROTOCOL (25th ANNIVERSARY EDITION)
Richard Sand, Mary Jane McCaffree, Pauline Innis
SEX, LIES & PI's
Ali Wirsche & Marnie Milot
SPORES, PLAGUES, AND HISTORY: THE STORY OF ANTHRAX
Chris Holmes
WHAT MAKES A MARRIAGE WORK
Malcolm D. Mahr
WHITE WITCH DOCTOR
John A. Hunt

SPRING, 2005

FICTION

A COMMON GLORY
Robert Middlemiss

What happens when a Southern news reporter falls in love with a WWII jazz loving English pilot and wants to take him home to her segregationist parents? It is in the crucible of war that pilot and reporter draw close across their vulnerabilities and fears. War, segregation, and the fear of death in lonely skies confront them as they clutch at the first exquisite promptings of a passionate love.

BLUEWATER DOWN
Rick O'Reilly

Retired L.A. police lieutenant Jack Douglas wanted only one thing after years on the bomb squad—the peace and serenity of sailing his yacht, Tally Ho. But Lisa enters his carefully planned world, and even as he falls in love with her she draws him into a violent matrix of murderers and terrorists bent on their destruction.

BY ROYAL DESIGN
Norbert Reich

Hitler's Third Reich was to last a thousand years but it collapsed in twelve. In Berlin, in the belly of the dying Reich, seeds were sown for a new regime, one based on aristocratic ruling classes whose time had come. Berlin's Charitee Hospital brought several children into the world that night in 1944, setting into motion forces that would ultimately bring two venerable Germanic families, the Hohenzollerns and the Habsburgs to power.

THE COROT DECEPTION
J. Brooks Van Dyke

London artists are getting murdered. The killer leaves behind an odd signature. And when Richard Watson, an artist, discovers the corpse of his gallery owner, he investigates, pitting himself and his twin sister, Dr. Emma Watson against the ruthless killer. Steeped in the principles of criminal detection they learned from Sherlock Holmes, the twins search for clues in the Edwardian art world and posh estates of 1910 London.

CRY HAVOC
John Hamilton Lewis

The worst winter in over a hundred years grips the United States and most of the western world. America's first lady president, Abigail Stewart, must deal with harsh realities as crop failures, power blackouts, shortages of gasoline and heating oil push the nation toward panic. But the extreme weather conditions are only a precursor of problems to come as Prince Nasser, a wealthy Saudi prince, and a cleric plot to destroy western economies.

DEADLY ILLUSIONS
Chester D. Campbell

A young woman, Molly Saint, hires Greg and Jill McKenzie to check her husband's background, then disappears. It starts them on a tangled trail of deceit, with Jill soon turning up a close family connection. The deeper the McKenzie's dig, the more deadly illusions they face. Nothing appears to be what it seemed at first as the fear for Molly's life grows.

EXTREME CUISINE
Kit Sloane

Film editor Margot O'Banion and director Max Skull find a recipe for disaster behind the kitchen doors of a trendy

Hollywood restaurant. Readers of discriminating taste are cordially invited to witness the preparation and presentation of fine fare as deadly drama. As Max points out, dinner at these places "provides an evening of theater and you get to eat it!" Betrayal, revenge, and perhaps something even more unsavory, are on the menu tonight.

THE GARDEN OF EVIL
Chris Holmes

A brilliant but bitter sociopath has attacked the city's food supply; five people are dead, twenty-six remain ill from the assault. Family physician, Gil Martin and his wife Tara, the county's Public Health Officer, discover the terrorist has found a way to incorporate the poison directly into the raw vegetables themselves. How is that possible? As the Martins get close to cracking the case, the terrorist focuses all his venom on getting them and their family. It's now a personal conflict—a mano-a-mano—between him and them.

KIRA'S DIARY
Edward T. Gushee

Beautiful, talented violinist, seventeen-year-old Kira Klein was destined to be assigned to Barracks 24. From the first day she is imprisoned in the Auschwitz brothel, Kira becomes the unwilling mistress of Raulf Becker, an SS lieutenant whose responsibility is overseeing the annihilation of the Jewish prisoners. Through the stench of death and despair emerges a rich love story, richly told with utter sensitivity, warmth and even humor.

THE LUKARILLA AFFAIR
Jerry Banks

Right from the start it was a legal slugfest. Three prominent men, a state senator, a corporate president, and the manager of a Los Angeles professional football team are charged with rape and sodomy by three minimum wage employees of a catering firm, Ginny, Peg and Tina. A court-room gripper by Jerry Banks who had over forty years in the trade, and who tells it like it happens—fast and quick.

MURDER ON THE TRAP
J. Preston Smith

Life has been pretty good to Bon Sandifer. After his tour in Vietnam he marries his childhood sweetheart, is a successful private investigator, and rides his Harley=Davidson motorcycle. Then the murders begin on Curly Trap Road. His wife Shelly dies first. A fellow biker is crushed under a Caddie. And his brother is killed riding a Harley. When Sandifer remarries and finds happiness with his deaf biker bride, the murderous web tightens and he grapples with skeptical detectives and old Vietnam memories.

PHARAOH'S FRIEND
Nancy Yawitz Linkous

When Egyptian myth permeates the present, beliefs are tested and lives are changed. My Worth vacations in Egypt to soothe the pain over her daughter's death. She dreams of a cat whose duty is to transport souls to the afterlife. And then a real cat, four hundred and twenty pounds of strength and sinew, appears at an archeological dig. Those that cross its path are drawn into intrigue and murder that is all too real.

SPRING, 2005

NONFICTION

**I ACCUSE: JIMMY CARTER AND THE RISE OF MILI-
TANT ISLAM**
Philip Pilevsky
    Philip Pilevsky makes a compelling argument that
President Jimmy Carter's failure to support the Shah of Iran
led to the 1979 revolution led by Ayatollah Ruhollah
Komeini. That revolution legitimized and provided a base
of operations for militant Islamists across the Middle East.
By allowing the Khomeini revolution to succeed, Carter
traded an aging, accommodating shah for a militant theo-
crat who attacked the American Embassy and held the staff
workers hostage. In the twenty-four years since the
Khomenini revolution, radical Islamists, indoctrinated in
Iran have grown ever bolder in attacking the West and more
sophisticated in their tactics of destruction.

MOTHERS SPEAK: FOR LOVE OF FAMILY
Rosalie Fuscaldo Gaziano
    In a world of turbulent change, the need to connect, to
love and be loved is greater and more poignant than ever.
Women cry out for simple, direct answers to the question,
"How can I make family life work in these challenging
times?" This book offers hope to all who are struggling to
balance the demands of work and family and to cope with
ambiguity, isolation, or abandonment. The author gives
strong evidence that the family unit is still the best way to
connect and bear enduring fruit.

THE PASSION OF AYN RAND'S CRITICS
James S. Valliant
    For years, best-selling novelist and controversial philoso-

pher Ayn Rand has been the victim of posthumous portrayals of her life and character taken from the pages of the biographies by Nathaniel Branden and Barbara Branden. Now, for the first time, Rand's own never-before-seen-journal entries on the Brandens, and the first in-depth analysis of the Brandens' works, reveal the profoundly inaccurate and unjust depiction of their former mentor.

SEX, LIES & PI's
Ali Wirsche & Marnie Milot

The ultimate guide to find out if your lover, husband, or wife is having an affair. Follow Ali and Marnie, two seasoned private investigators, as they spy on brazen cheaters and find out what sweet revenge awaits. Learn 110 ways to be your own detective. Laced with startling stories, *Sex, Lies & PI's* is riveting and often hilarious.

WHAT MAKES A MARRIAGE WORK
Malcolm D. Mahr

Your hear the phrase "marry and settle down," which implies life becomes more serene and peaceful after marriage. This simply isn't so. Living together is one long series of experiments in accommodation. *What Makes A Marriage Work?* is a hilarious yet perceptive collection of fifty insights reflecting one couple's searching, experimenting, screaming, pouting, nagging, whining, moping, blaming, and other dysfunctional behaviors that helped them successfully navigate the turbulent sea of matrimony for over fifty years. (Featuring 34 *New Yorker* cartoons of wit and wisdom.)